SHARP Change

BLACK MEADOWS PACK

NEW YORK TIMES and USA TODAY
BESTSELLING AUTHOR

MILLY TAIDEN

Published By

Latin Goddess Press

Winter Springs, FL 32708

http://millytaiden.com

Sharp Change

Edited by: Tina Winograd

Cover: Willsin Rowe

Formatting by Lia Davis at Glowing Moon Desgins

SHARP CHANGE

Sophia Reece is a genius geneticist who's isolated the link between shifters and their animals. Unfortunately, she's also a very shy and clumsy woman. That's never more evident than when she has a not so little accident with her lion and wolf samples and ends up becoming her own guinea pig. Watch out, those needles are sharp. Damn, shit just got real.

Alpha wolf Chase knows Sophia is his mate. And if she weren't so shy and always running from him, he'd have made his move with her. He can't stop thinking about her sexy human body and how badly he wants to dip his tongue into all her curves. But when shy Sophia suddenly flashes golden eyes and smells of heat, he's not sure what's going on, but is more than ready to get her naked ASAP.

Sophia isn't prepared for her first mating heat or the fact her feelings for Chase refuse to remain under wraps. When someone wants her research, she'll find out what she's really made of. Who says smart girls can't be alphas too? Things are a lot more complicated than being perfectly mated. The race is on to stop the bad guys from getting their hands on her work and staying alive. Sophia's about to learn that being in love doesn't stop someone from coming face to face with death.

— For my curvy readers

You deserve a man that will love you with all he's
got.

PROLOGUE

Sophia sat next to the hospital bed, holding her unconscious sister's hand. Hours had passed since the attack and still Julia was unconscious.

It was a damn bite on the arm. But it *was* from some monster creature. She'd say a wolf, but wolves could not grow that large. They were not the size of horses. Not that she'd been around real-life horses. But they didn't seem that big on TV.

God, maybe moving here had been a bad idea. Maybe she should've gone to the West Coast or Tahiti. The weather was always nice, but it was so damn expensive.

She'd read that the town of Black Meadows was one of the safest towns in the Midwest. Almost no crime or accidents. That's why she chose this place to live after fleeing the big city.

A research scientist like her didn't make a lot of money. Julia, lying silently in the bed, didn't have much technical skill, but she was good in an office. Her sister could type and answer phones, file, and be the social butterfly. Which was exactly the opposite of her.

Sophia was a lab tech for a reason. Usually, they worked alone and mostly unsupervised. If someone stood over her shoulder, watching her work, she wouldn't be able to do it.

Her hands would get shaky, palms sweaty. Beads of perspiration popped out on her forehead. Her stomach would churn at the thought of being yelled at for doing the slightest thing wrong. Then she'd throw up all over the lab specimen.

Luckily, the professor let her retake that test after a couple weeks. Seemed the acid from her upchucked lunch of fries and a Coke devoured the test tissue and they had to wait until another donor was found.

Anger gurgled up inside her. She hated being so insecure, so shy and antisocial. She wanted to be like Julia, the center of attention, the life of the party. Then again...

In her childhood, she tried to be the center of attention at a party by doing a magic trick she'd practice for hours. Right when it came time for the sleight of hand to pull off the trick, her fingers fumbled the glass and it shattered on the floor.

Everyone laughed, but not for the right reason. She ran to her room and hid in her closet until Julia found her when it was time to go to bed.

From that moment on, she remained in the background, watching others do their thing.

Even now, tears filled her eyes from thinking about that event. Dammit. Sophia wanted to curse herself for being so weak, such a coward. What she wouldn't do to be strong and assertive.

Julia's hand twitched. Sophia jumped to her feet from the chair.

Leaning over the bed, she pushed hair from her sister's forehead.

"Julia," Sophia whispered, "are you awake?" A groan croaked from her sister's throat. "Come on, Julia. Open your eyes for me."

Julia's lids fluttered then lifted. Her pupils were larger than normal, but she focused on Sophia's face.

"Hey, how're you doing, sweetie?" Sophia cooed.

Julia rolled her eyes. "I'm not a baby, Soph."

Sophia stuck her tongue out, throwback to their childhood.

"Yes, you are a baby. My baby sister," Sophia said with a smile and leaned back, away from Julia's face. Her sister looked around and the slight smile she had turned to fear.

"My God, Sophia. Why are we in a hospital?" Her voice became shriller with each word. "Am I hurt?" She sat up, running her hands over her torso and legs. "Am I dying?" Julia was slightly prone to dramatics and over-exaggeration. The product of being the center of attention all the time.

Sophia grabbed her wrists before the IV needle pulled out. "No, Jules, you're not dying." She didn't think, anyway. "You don't remember what happened?" With gentle pressure, Soph eased her sister back to lying on the pillow.

"I remember we were hiking in the woods in the park, looking for the stream…" Her voice trailed off with lack of memory, it seemed.

Sophia rubbed her thumb over the back of her sister's hand. Decision time.

So, should Sophia tell her she was bitten by a furry monster with four legs or tell her something made-up?

Monster, made-up? Made-up, monster? Shit. She'd do anything and everything to protect the only family she had left, that included little white lies — very little and white.

"Julia, this big ole tree limb came out of nowhere a hit you on the head." Okay, maybe not so little, nor so white, or even believable. Her sister narrowed her eyes.

"Soph, you always sucked at lying." Julia crossed her arms and winced at the pain in her bicep. "Ow." Noticing the bandage wrapped around her arm, she said, "Hit on the head, huh?"

Sophia winced. "And the arm?"

"Just tell me. My entire upper arm is covered." Julia started to get excited, and not in a good way.

"Calm down, Jules," Sophia said. "It's not as bad as it looks." *It's worse.* And one of the scariest moments of Sophia's life.

Being somewhat new to the area, she and Julia went for a walk through the park at twilight. A wooden sign saying "Creek" pointed to a trail. Due to the late hour, Sophia wanted to head back home, but Julia wanted to see the sight.

Soph wasn't leaving her sister alone, so she went along. After leaving the park far behind, Soph began to worry about their safety. But the town was among the safest.

Just as she relaxed her guard, a howl split the air. Hair on her nape not only stood, it tried to pull itself out and run. Sophia thought that was a great idea and grabbed her sister's wrist.

"Run!" Sophia yelled when Julia didn't move. Being heavy set, Sophia wasn't the fastest turtle in the race, but her adrenaline pushed her faster than ever before.

After several yards, Julia was ripped from her hand. Sophia turned to see her baby sister punching and kicking a dark, furry creature attached to her upper arm.

All logic and emotion fled Sophia. Survival instincts kicked in, taking over her body.

Sophia launched at the monster, grasping fists full of fur and pulling it away from Julia. Kicking and screaming, Sophia went totally batshit crazy on the animal.

She didn't know why or how Julia was released, but the creature backed away after spitting out her sister's arm.

Things got blurry from that moment. She remembered dragging Julia into the park and screaming for help. The ride in the ambulance, blood everywhere on Julia and herself. Then arriving at the ER where they took Julia down a hall but they wouldn't let her follow.

Now, hours later, all that seemed like a bad dream, except for the bandage.

Sophia let out another sigh. Her sister was right, she couldn't lie for shit. And seldom tried. Time to 'fess up.

"Julia, you were—"

The door opened and the female doctor walked in with two of the most gorgeous men she had ever seen. The first guy took her breath. And by the gasp Julia made, he had the same effect on her.

A surge of jealousy and anger zipped through Sophia until she saw Julia was staring at the other guy.

Sophia's eyes snapped back to the first guy. He was staring at her, a grimace on his lips. Her face flushed hot and she stepped away from the bed, turning her eyes to the floor.

Her heart beat so hard, it almost hurt. She tried to slow her breathing to stop the panting.

"Ah," the doctor said, "you're awake. That's good." As the three newcomers gathered around the bed, she squeezed herself more toward the corner, but let her eyes look through her lashes to watch what was going on.

The second man leaned over Julia's head and inhaled deeply. To Sophia's surprise, Julia raised her nose and did the same.

What the hell was that about?

"Julia, Sophia," the doctor said, "this is Chase and River. They are —" Sophia looked up at the pause. *They are* what? "They are at the head of the shifter community in Black Meadows."

Shifter community? What was she talking about?

A loud crack echoed in the room and Julia screamed. Another pop and Julia stopped breathing, or was it herself who'd stopped? She wanted to ask what was happening, but couldn't get her brain to work.

The doctor jumped toward the bed.

"No. Chase, don't let her shift. Her DNA isn't taking the change well."

Her DNA? What?

River wrapped his hands around Julia's face, but with another crack, she jerked away from him. Chase yanked down the sheet.

To her horror, Julia's legs were twisted and covered with…thick hair? When was the last time her sister had shaved? By the looks, never.

"She's too far along to stop her now. It could kill her," Chase said. He turned to her. "Is this her first shift?"

Sophia gawked like a fish out of water. Shift? Did he mean shave?

The doctor said, "Yes, she was bitten a few hours ago."

Were these people crazy? Was she crazy?

Julia continued to scream, tears pouring from her eyes. River kept telling her to "let it happen, don't fight it." He tried to soothe Julia to no avail.

Shrieks from her sister freaked Sophia to the point of meltdown. She wasn't even sure what was happening to her sister. There was nothing she could do. She felt helpless. A horrible feeling.

Sophia made a promise to herself at that moment. She would do whatever it took to figure out how to cure her sister so this never happened again.

ONE

Six months later

Holy hell! She'd done it.

Sophia stared at the computer screen and couldn't believe her eyes. The number and letter sequences in front of her drove her excitement. A slow sliver of fear raced up her spine when she thought of what could happen if the information got into the wrong hands, but it wasn't enough to stop her from smiling ear to ear.

She'd finally singled out the particular chromosome in the DNA strand that made shapeshifters shift. This little baby was the hottest ticket in Shifterville. It's what bonded with the rest of a human's DNA to create the furry beast that lived inside these weird people.

If it were a person, she'd kiss it, hug it, probably spank it for being bad and making it so hard for her to find. She grinned; she couldn't help herself. Julia would be able to have a choice in life now after being attacked by a rogue werewolf.

The one positive outcome was that her sister had met River, the beta of his pack and Julia's current husband. Talk about love at first bark. His animal had taken one look at her sister in the hospital bed and had literally rolled over for her to pet his tummy. It was sweet and kind of creepy, considering how damn big he was in his wolf form.

River was a nice guy, too, but nothing beat freedom of choice in Sophia's mind. He loved her sister and treated her better than any other human she'd been with, not to mention the man was absolutely gorgeous. Then there was his brother, the pack alpha.

Thoughts of Chase, the alpha of the Black Meadows pack, made her heart torpedo in her chest and rockets shoot off in her stomach. The better-than-a-sundae, delicious-looking man with golden-brown skin and enough muscles to share with his friends, turned her into a puddle of goo.

The man had so much sex appeal, her girl parts were ready to lift a white flag in surrender just by looking at him. Even thinking of him made her tongue wag. Seeing him was like having your favorite dessert and knowing you couldn't eat it.

There was no way she'd ever be able to talk to him or even approach him. She'd die if she said something stupid in front of him. In fact, she'd probably forget how to talk if she was that close to him.

She was very aware of her physical appearance whenever he came around her. She was short, fat, and shy, and now that she'd hit thirty-two, she also felt old.

She had long ago given up on the idea of finding Mr. Right and had started focusing on Mr. Right Now. Unfortunately, that hadn't worked out so well either. She ended up dating boring, geeky guys, and sex tended to be nothing to write home about.

Shit, sex tended to be nothing she'd want to try again with any of those guys, having been responsible for her own orgasms for as long as she could remember. Heat crawled across her skin when she thought of the last guy she'd been with, Jake the Asshole Schnake, before she'd moved to Black Meadows. He was the reason she'd ended up looking for a new job.

The asshole had stolen her research and tried to pass it off as his own. Luckily, she always backed up her work on a flash drive and had months of data to prove the work was hers.

On her own, Sophia never would've taken action against Jake the Asshole Schnake. She was too shy to cause that much attention to be focused on her. So Julia took the jerk to court and got a settlement. It included money, but not much. Enough to get out of town to make a new start somewhere else.

But most importantly, Jake the Asshole Schnake was blacklisted with labs across the country. Not her fault he couldn't play by the rules.

Sophia never wanted to see that conniving prick ever again.

She blinked and squinted tired eyes, then rubbed cold fingers under her rimless glasses, drawing in a deep breath. A burst of energy rushed through her blood when she thought of what she'd just accomplished. Exhilaration made up for the lack of sleep. She'd been burning the candle at both ends working and doing her own private research.

She swatted away the guilt that tapped her shoulder over using the lab resources for her own experiment. Too much depended on the results of her first test to worry about being found out. And if she was—oh well, they did encourage "groundbreaking" and "outside the box" research.

Her sister Julia would have kittens if she knew. Or should she say puppies, now that Julia was a wolf shifter? The woman had been a straight pain before, but now that she had a dramatic animal inside, she'd taken theatrics to a whole new level. Her tears could appear and disappear faster than Superman at the scene of a crime.

Black Meadows was by no means a small town, but with only the research facility and a car plant, it was easy to see people as either scientists or engineers. Then there were the blue-collar plant workers and the small-business owners.

Looking through the microscope at the samples of the particularly special FB chromosome, Sophia had to smile. Yes, she had called the chromosome Furry Beast. It was her special way of keeping herself from losing her mind after working on this for what felt like forever.

Finally, she'd pulled a sample of DNA from

both sets of shifters and created pure chromosome strands of a cat and a wolf. A slow smile slid across her face. She could swear she heard birds chirping and a Hallelujah Chorus above her head while she stared through the small eyepiece of her microscope.

"Goddamn, I fucking rock!" Laughter and excitement unlike any she'd ever experienced, not including meeting man-candy Chase, popped and fizzled through her until she was bouncing on her stool, grinning like a fool.

Now that she thought of man-candy Chase, her brain did the usual X-rated stripping of those rock-hard limbs. Mmm, man-candy Chase…he was her biggest temptation. If she had an affliction, it was called Furry Beast Alpha, or FBA for short.

Side effects included, but were not limited to, making a woman stop, stare, and drool on the spot; panties somehow finding themselves off and thrown his way; and finally, if said subject were to smile, blacking out from sudden excitement.

She was still unable to figure out how one minute he could be smiling at her, and the next she would be sitting in a chair counting fuzzy bunnies running across her field of vision.

Thank goodness, she still hadn't gone as far

as the panty throwing, but she was tempted...God, she was tempted. Every time she got near him, her hands itched to tear off the little slip of lace, wave her arm in the air, and yell, "Pick me, pick me!"

She giggled and bounced in her seat, causing her short hair to tickle the nape of her neck. Looking to celebrate, she turned on the radio at her desk to some dance mix. She stood and stretched, lifting her white T-shirt in the process and showing her softly rounded belly. All alone in the lab, she didn't care if she showed some skin.

Her full breasts strained against the cotton while her stonewashed jeans clung lovingly to her generous hips. When she bent over to stretch her back, the move made her jeans ride low, and cold air caressed her lower back enough to show off the one thing she had ever done to be wild—a tattoo of a pink and purple fairy on her upper right cheek. Thankfully, there was no one around to see that.

She started singing along completely off-key to some song that talked about being sexy and knowing it. Snorting to herself, she knew even singing it was a lie. There were no feelings of sexiness anywhere in her—they only happened when FBA was around.

She pulled out two syringes, filled one with

werecat and the other with werewolf chromosomes, and laid them on the small collection tube tray. She sang louder as she moved. It wasn't like anyone was around to hear her sad attempt at singing.

She needed to find her special vials so she wouldn't confuse these specimens with any of her other samples. She put away the older mixed strands she wasn't actively using in the cold storage only she had access to, now that she'd changed the passcodes to her biometrics. When she began working at the lab, there was little security. That changed as soon as she made her first breakthrough in shifter DNA.

Because she was the head of the genetics department, she was allowed her own work space. It also meant she got a big lab to use for her research.

Other than equipment and coded papers, the place was kept immaculate. Large and small machines were strategically placed to make the movement of samples from one to the other quick and efficient, along with multiple computers and printers.

The lab was also really cold. Goose bumps broke out on her caramel skin as she thought of the heater sitting by her desk. Outside, the weather was beautiful, but an iceberg lived inside the building.

She knew complaining would do nothing, since the best way to keep instruments from growing bacteria was to keep them cold. She would have to go to her office, which was located next door, to write her notes before she left, so at least there, she'd be warm. Glancing at her watch, she realized the hour.

Oh, shit! She was going to be late for her meeting with the lab's facility director.

Holding her precious tray of sharps, she hurried toward the other metal table to get to her special-colored vials.

In her haste, and her hips being well-rounded, she hit the corner of the table.

What came next, she would later tell herself was due to her own stupidity at trying rush around when she was not as coordinated as she liked to think.

Bouncing off the edge and falling forward in a sickening loss of balance, she saw the floor rush up to meet her face. Instinctively, she let go of the tray with one hand to try to catch her fall.

Everything around her narrowed to just the sound of her breathing. Distantly, she heard the metal tray smack the floor, and she landed on top of it, keeping the vials from falling and shattering on the concrete.

Thank God.

She winced and picked herself up off the floor.

The damn underwire in her bra pinched her breast; it always seemed to break through the casing at the worst time. She wouldn't have bothered with them if they didn't make her breasts look so lingerie-catalog good.

"Ouch, dammit!" Looking down at the tray, she saw that the sharps were not there. Panic seized her, and sharp blades of terror stabbed her gut while she scanned the ground. The pinching sensation in her chest drew her attention to where the two long sharps dangled from the area between her breasts.

Icy fear numbed her brain and lodged in her throat, making it impossible for her to breathe. Frantic, she pulled the two long needles out carefully and examined the amount in each.

There was a minute amount missing from each.

A panicked scream wrenched out of her. Her first thought was to take a blood sample and check for any alterations in her DNA. After a second of logical thought and some frenzied breathing, she decided a few days of waiting were best.

No notable change would show up straight away if there was a delayed reaction. If there had been any life-altering changes to her DNA, she would see it in a few days.

Tears of frustration filled her eyes. Had she destroyed all her hard work with a stupid accident? She'd have to wait until Monday when she returned to the lab to run tests, unless there were any strange occurrences sooner.

Her stomach churned at the thought of her foolishness, but there was not much she could do other than wait and see. She stood, carefully grabbed the two vials with shaky hands, and stored her previously untainted samples.

She secured her storage freezer with her fingerprint and voice, which turned on the double-locked safe. There was no way in hell she was going to take any chances with what was in there. It was a good thing the freezer was made of the thickest metal available and resembled a bank vault.

She headed for her office. Her previous happiness turned into a desolate sense of impending doom when she thought of the notes she would have to write to detail the calamity from that afternoon.

Sophia popped the tiny flash drive from

her laptop's USB port and stuck it in her pocket. She locked up her computer, then grabbed her purse and headed out the door.

* * *

Shit. Shit. Shit. She was late. Her stomach churned at the thought of being yelled at for her ineptitude.

But Ms. Winchester, the facility director, wasn't that way. She was a nice older woman who had an easy way about her.

In the past, the sweet old lady had been so busy, she'd never been able to meet with Sophia at her office. Their meetings always ended up taking place outside the research facility at some restaurant where they would eat and catch up.

Victoria, or Tori as she preferred to be called, was sitting at a table. She smiled softly at Sophia, motioning for her to take a seat.

Tori Winchester looked amazing for her age. She was short, slim, and so petite, she made Sophia feel like an Amazon at five-foot-three. Her short silver bob hugged the curve of her neck and was coiffed to total perfection.

She wore a forest-green suit that screamed wealth. Tori's emerald eyes were filled with life. The older woman was alert and sharp as a tack, which had allowed them to have some incredibly intellectual discussions in the past.

"Good afternoon, Sophia. How are you doing?" Tori asked.

Sophia was about to beg for forgiveness for being late, but that wretched feeling in her stomach was gone. Technically, she'd put in so many hours of overtime, being five minutes late wasn't a big deal.

What surprised her most was that her gut fear was gone.

"I'm great, Tori. Thanks for asking," Sophia replied.

Tori laughed. "Something good must've happened."

Sophia gave her boss a questioning look.

"I've never seen you so joyful," Tori answered. "What is making your life so happy?"

Sophia chewed on her bottom lip. She was so bad at lying, but if the head of the facility found out she'd been doing unauthorized work...

Tori slapped her hand on the table. "Did you finally extract what you needed from the shifter DNA?"

Sophia sat stunned. No one should've

known what she'd been doing.

One side of Tori's mouth curved up. "Are you asking how I know about that?" Sophia nodded. Her boss patted her hand. "It's my job to know, child. Do you think I haven't noticed the hours you're putting in? Have you slept in the past six months?"

She fumbled for words. "I, uh…" Normally, she'd be under the table in embarrassment, hoping the earth would open and swallow her whole.

Instead she said, "I did find a way to separate chromosomes from genes. All I need to do is create a serum and…" Sophia froze. Did the woman know all of what she had been researching? Did she know the end game?

"And what, dear? Serum for both feline and the wolves?"

A waitress saved her from answering. "What can I get you all to drink?"

She opened her mouth to order her normal sweet tea, but something else came out. "I'd like a glass of milk."

Tori raised a brow and ordered her usual unsweet tea. "We'd like to place our order." Tori looked at her. "Do you know what you want?"

They frequented this restaurant since it

was close to the office and never had a line at the door to get a table. Sophia liked this place for the salsa chicken. Fresh veggies for the salsa made her mouth water.

She said, "I'd like a steak." The server wrote down the order and asked how she wanted it cooked. "Still mooing, please." At that, the waitress glanced at her, but kept writing. After taking Tori's order, the waitress went to put in their orders and get their drinks.

"Sophia, what has gotten into you?" the sweet woman asked. "You've never ordered steak before."

She shrugged. She wasn't sure what was going on. But she couldn't tell her boss that. "Well, I thought a change would be nice." She thought no such thing. Could she have brain damage from working too much with little sleep?

Tori unwound her silverware and put the napkin in her lap. "Now, what were you saying? Something about creating a serum for what?"

Dammit. She'd hoped the too-smart woman would've forgotten. No such luck.

"I could go a few different ways, but my goal is to let my sister be able to stop the shift if she wanted to."

"Fabulous, dear. I knew you would figure it out."

"You're not mad about me doing my own thing?" she asked.

Tori's brows lowered. "Why should I be? You have all current jobs under control with the lab techs and nothing dire is waiting." Her boss leaned in as if to share a secret. "Besides, what you're doing is groundbreaking and simply amazing. I want you to succeed."

Sophia sat back, surprised. "You do?"

"Of course, young lady. We women have to stick together if things in this sad world of ours is to get better. We have to take control and make change happen."

Sophia was shocked by the enthusiasm coming from her boss. The wonderful woman never got riled about anything.

Tori's eyes scanned the room quickly. "You are securing your work, right? Locking it up somewhere?"

Sophia nodded, her eyes darting around, trying to see what Tori was looking for. "I'm putting it in the cold storage every night."

"What about your laptop and notes?" Tori asked.

"I keep them locked in the lab's cabinet,"

Sophia said.

Tori gave her a nod. "Including tonight's notes? If you made the breakthrough, tonight's are the most important."

"I haven't written the analysis yet, but the data is backed up on my flash."

Tori scowled. Shit, Sophia knew why, and should've kept her big mouth shut.

"You know, Sophia, it's against policy to take any type of data out of the building." Sophia cringed, ready for a tongue lashing. "But in this case, I think it's a good idea."

Again, Sophia was surprised. "You do?"

Her boss laughed. "Don't be so shocked, dear. Do you think I'm some old curmudgeon who doesn't live in the real world?"

"No!" Sophia replied. "I've never thought that."

Tori patted her hand again. "Good. Because I'm not. I think we should take extra precautions with your work. Having a backup is smart. Keep it somewhere but the lab."

"I take it home with me where I have a hidden spot for it," she said.

"Excellent," Tori said. "Now, let's celebrate your remarkable achievement."

Their waitress returned with a tall glass of milk and tea. Sophia stared at the white drink then drank it down in one tip of the cup.

"Would you like another?" the server asked, somewhat astounded.

"Yes, please." What the hell was up?

TWO

Chase took a swig of crisp, cold beer while scrutinizing the crowded bar. The Back Door was packed on Friday nights, and Julia was behind the bar, serving drinks with a smile. Chase's brother watched from a seat next to him.

Looking at the pitiable adoration pasted on his brother's face, Chase wanted to smack him upside the head to bring him back to the land of the non-pussy-whipped. What the hell happened to his strong, no-nonsense beta? The one that always told Chase "not me, I never want a mate."

He'd turned into an overgrown puppy is

what. After River met Julia, he'd given a new definition to the phrase love-struck fool. Chase snorted, gulped down more of the draft, and scanned the entirety of the bar for any idiots who might want to start trouble.

His gaze bypassed the women who stared and struggled to catch his attention. Pack and human females had a tendency to fling themselves, and articles of clothing, at him. He knifed cold fingers through his black hair, unconcerned if he messed up the strands and ended up looking like a wild animal.

He didn't really care most of the time how his hair hung, but women seemed to love the shaggy, untamed look. It wasn't done on purpose—his hair just grew so much that it became an annoyance to get it cut every two weeks. There were more important things to do than make a trip to a barber to make him look tame.

Julia smiled at one of her waitstaff as she filled glasses. Her long dark hair was in a ponytail and gave her the appearance of a teenager among adults.

Unlike most shifters, she wasn't a stick figure. After she'd been turned, she'd lost some weight, her body gaining the rapid ability to metabolize fat. Shifters were slimmer, since each shift made it easier to burn a large number of calories.

Julia was a little rounder and softer than most, which explained his brother's love for groping her whenever he thought nobody was looking. Julia had a flair for the dramatic, which made it sometimes painful to be around her when she was in one of her tearful moods.

He observed his sibling's mate and immediately thought of Sophia. Julia's older sister was petite, remarkably smart, and so hot, the air crackled with fire, the temperature going from warm to blistering whenever she was around.

With a body that wouldn't quit, she made him want to get on his knees and beg. She resembled a 1950's pin-up model, all sexy curves. He pictured himself blowing raspberries in the valley of her luscious breasts. Her hips—dear Lord, they were a thing of beauty; all rounded, they showed off her nipped waist to perfection.

Caramel skin, thanks to their Latin heritage, glowed when she smiled, as though the sun recently kissed the silky flesh. Her full lips begged him for a kiss every time he got a glimpse of them. It was hell holding back.

Those sexy, sleepy, gray eyes gave her the just- rolled-out-of-bed look and made his cock jerk whenever she turned them his way. Chase was not normally a fan of short hair, but her brown curls had him itching to run his fingers through the silky mass.

Her scent drove him to distraction; she always smelled of peaches and cream. Whenever he was around her, he marveled at her fragrance. If he licked her, would the flavor be as sweet as the scent?

Unfortunately, she wasn't interested.

Her disinterest was like a slap in the face. He struggled against the impulse to get near her, and wrestled his lust for dominance in order to stay away.

When he first tried getting close to her, she'd blush and make a beeline to somewhere else. Anywhere else. His wolf growled at him each time, telling him to follow. But Chase wasn't about to push himself onto a female who didn't want him.

Turning toward his brother, he realized River had been saying something while he'd been mentally stripping Sophia and doing all kinds of dirty, probably illegal-in-some-states things to her.

The barrage of sexual thoughts overran his brain like a virus on a hard drive. Whenever her name popped into his head, he got so hard, he felt the denim tighten around his cock into a painful, unyielding fist.

"So?" River's brows lifted as he waited for a response.

"So, what?" He winced at his brother's disgustingly happy smirk. God, just shoot him now. He was going to have to put up with this for how long?

"You weren't even listening to me, were you? I said Sunday, Julia and I are having a barbecue, and we want you to come over. It's not a party, so there's no need to freak out thinking you're going to be dodging panties. It's just the four of us."

River's strong features resembled his own — dark hair cut to the nape of his neck and brown eyes they got from their mother, and the fierce, angular planes of their faces from their father.

His brother was a little shorter than Chase's six-foot-three. Both were muscular and got a lot of female attention. Of course, now his brother was oblivious to any woman but his wife.

"The four of us?" Chase put his empty beer bottle down.

Julia came over, put down a napkin, and plunked down a fresh bottle. She leaned over the counter and gave her husband a quick kiss. Great, so he was going to have to watch them play footsie while Sophia pretended he didn't exist.

"Did you ask him?" She smiled at River, then turned to Chase.

"I just did, sweetheart. He still hasn't said if he's coming." He grabbed her hand and lifted it to his lips. She stared at him, the heat in their eyes clearly visible for anyone to see.

Julia gave Chase a small frown. "Well? Can you come? I really want you there, Chase." She gave her husband a small, pleasure-filled smile. "We've got something we need to tell you guys, but we only want to do it once, so you have to be there." She grinned and her eyes sparkled when she spoke.

He'd never seen River as happy as he was since meeting his mate. It made Chase feel uncomfortable to be a voyeur to their love-fest.

"Ah, shit, come on, Julia. Do you honestly think I'd ever say no to you? I'd never hear the end of it from Don Juan over here." He curled his lip in his trademark smile and winked at his sister-in-law.

Julia was family now, and he'd do anything in his power to make the females in his family happy. Even if that meant torturing himself to be near the woman of his every dirty fantasy.

She laughed, grabbed Chase's face, and kissed him loudly on the cheek, which shocked a blush out of him. Fuck, now she was trying to turn him into a domestic animal.

No way, he was alpha. Hear him roar.

"Great!" she said. "Just make sure you come, or I'll have to hunt you down and make a wolf rug out of you." Without waiting for a reply, she went back to serving drinks, her happiness radiating warmth all around.

"So, are you going to be okay with Sophia joining us?"

Chase's gaze landed on his brother and his shrewd stare. He didn't want to know what River meant by his probing, but he could only think that his sibling had noticed Sophia's obvious dislike of him.

For fuck's sake, the woman acted like he had rabies. Whenever he walked in, she walked out.

"Yeah, why wouldn't I?"

"Hmm. Her shyness toward you drives you nuts."

Chase snorted. "Whatever. She's never around long enough for me to get to that stage."

His brother sighed. "Don't take it personally, bro. She's that way with most people. Shyness is hard to overcome."

"So you say." Chase swallowed half his beer. "I'll be fine. Don't worry about me."

River slapped him on the shoulder. "That sounds more like the brother I know. I'll call you Sunday. Don't forget." River gave him the look that he'd given him before his wedding, the one that said *if you try to get out of this, I'll bitch and moan so much, you'll visualize killing me multiple times.*

Fan-fucking-tastic.

* * *

Ratface tossed his cell phone onto the table. The *smack* as it hit the wood echoed in the windowless room. It was fucking cold in there; being underground, it was like being in a freakin' cave.

He hated the cold. If he wanted to be frozen all the goddamn time, he'd be in fucking Alaska or some shit.

The four others at the table snapped awake

with his entrance. What a pathetic group of misfits. He was amazed they'd gotten as far in life as they had. Only good thing about it was that it made them dispensable. If one died, then another could easily replace them.

All except him, of course.

"Our person in the field just called," Ratface said. "Seems our target ate dinner at a restaurant tonight and discussed things they shouldn't have wanted sensitive ears to hear."

"All right, boss," Goon said. "What did they say?" A high-pitched squeal giggled through the hyena.

Ratface sighed and looked at the shifter. "I was gonna tell you until you interrupted, shit head." He looked around the table. "We got confirmation. The goods are at her home and the lab in something called cold storage." He mumbled to himself about more damn cold shit.

"We gonna go get it now, boss?" Goon asked. The others nodded, giggling and licking their lips.

"No, we are not," he said. "We have to come up with a plan. Now shut up before I shut you up." The group around the table fell quiet.

Ratface paced. Without the boss telling him what to do, he'd figure it out himself. He could do this. He was smart, too. He owed this to his boss. Of all the things that happened, this was the least he could do.

If the woman had stuff at her home and lab, then they needed to get to her home and the lab. Yeah, he was smart.

They'd have to watch her and wait for a time when she was gone. From what intel they had so far, she spent a lot of time with her sister when not in the lab.

The woman was so damn boring, working *all* the time. She didn't even take breaks to eat. Only a human could do that. And she didn't talk to anyone. Only when her boss made her leave to meet and eat did she get out.

He wasn't worried about this first task. Humans were so easy, too predictable. A whiny laugh trickled out of his throat. He couldn't wait.

THREE

Sophia woke to a loud ringing next to her bed. She groaned, turned over, and tried to ignore the cell phone on her bedside table. But the boisterous sound of Cindy Lauper's "Girls Just Wanna Have Fun" wouldn't shut up.

Why the hell had she let Julia pick her own ringtone?

She reached blindly until her hand grasped the phone and pressed the button on the side to stop the annoying sound. She put the device to her ear under the pillow, her voice muffled when she spoke. "The house better be burning down around me or you are so dead."

Her sister's tinkling laughter on the other

end made her wince. God, when did she start laughing so loudly?

"Get your ass up, you lazy bum. Did you forget our barbecue? You've got exactly two hours to get up, get ready, and get a chocolate cake at the bakery." Julia's voice turned a little rough. "Do *not* forget the chocolate cake, or I'll make you go back and get it."

"What the heck do you mean the barbecue? Isn't that on Sunday?"

"Sophia? Are you okay? You do know it's Sunday, right?" Her sister's humor faded as worry filled her voice.

Ah shit! It had taken all of two seconds to burst her sister's bulletproof happiness bubble. "Of course, I know it's Sunday," she lied with a chuckle. "I'm just messing with you. I'll see you in two hours, 'kay? Don't worry, sis. I'll be there."

She took a deep breath. Thank God Julia wasn't next to her, or she'd smell the lie in no time. Stupid shifter senses. There was no hiding the truth from any of them.

Ugh, her body was sore and sensitive, like when she was PMSing or ready to get the flu. *Keep working like a robot, you nimrod, and your mistakes are only going to increase*, she thought.

The groan that slipped through her lips

came out sounding more like a strangled frog, which begged the question, was she also getting a sore throat? She couldn't believe she'd slept through Saturday. She must have been super exhausted.

She needed coffee. Tossing the pillow to the floor, she sat up and looked around her room. Something was off, but she couldn't put her finger on what. Her nose wrinkled at a distant foul smell. Something to investigate later; right now, she needed to take a shower.

She sat on the toilet, relieving her ready-to-burst bladder. Still wondering what was different, she kept her eyes closed, stripped off her tank top and shorts, and walked into the shower. A low hiss pierced the air as warm water caressed her skin.

She looked around, wondering where the noise had come from.

There was nothing.

She took her time washing her hair and hummed while she brushed her teeth. Much more awake when she got out of the shower, she stretched and yawned.

She grabbed a fluffy blue towel and dried off, noticing how the material felt coarse on her skin. Sandpaper would probably feel softer.

Apparently, she needed to change her fabric softener.

Wrapped in her short purple robe, she walked out of the bathroom, not bothering with the foggy mirror. A noise at her front door grabbed her attention as she was about to get dressed.

"Coming," she yelled as she walked to the door.

Leaving the chain on, she opened the door to look outside. On her front lawn lay her weekend newspaper, ready to get soaked by the sprinklers that were going to turn on in a few minutes.

Growling at having to go outside and get it in her robe, she peered around and saw no one. She ran out onto her front lawn just as two of her neighbors walked out.

The man across from her, Henry—or was it Harry—had asked her out once, but she'd declined. He grabbed his paper and took a deep breath. His head snapped up, and he looked right at her.

The other man, Richard Lezz, she knew from The Back Door the few times Julia made her leave the house. He was a regular there and made her feel super uncomfortable with his slick, toothy smiles and I'm-too-sexy demeanor.

Richard, or Dick as he preferred —
although why he'd like to be known as Dick
Lezz was beyond her understanding — also
took a deep breath and turned to stare in her
direction. Then to her consternation, they both
started walking toward her.

Something weird was going on with their
faces. Dick had never looked so severe, and
Harry looked positively feral. Self-
preservation made her run into the house and
lock the door.

What the fuck?

Taking shallow breaths, she peeked
through the peephole and saw them stop in
the middle of the street. They stared at her
house for a few moments and turned back to
their own, walking back slowly and looking at
her place every few steps.

What the heck was that about? She was
tempted to make the sign of the cross and find
some holy water. As she walked back to her
room, she decided she'd have to control her
mental instability at the barbecue. No need for
Chase to know she was halfway past
deranged.

She pulled on a charcoal wrap dress and
flat sandals. Walking to the bathroom, she

looked at her hair and almost collapsed. When the heck had it grown so long? Granted, she pulled it back when it got into her face while working, but had she been ignoring it to the point it now reached her shoulders?

She knew she'd gotten a cut only two weeks ago...hadn't she? There was no debating she'd been preoccupied with her research. One thing was for sure: that long sleep seemed to have helped her get some color back.

Her skin was positively glowing with vitality, and even her eyes had a clear, gemstone sparkle to them. Hey, maybe now that she actually looked better than just a geeky geneticist, she could find a way to make her vocal chords work in front of FBA Chase.

For some reason, she didn't want to question, she felt the need to check the street before she walked out. Her two neighbors' reactions had scared the crap out of her. Plus, she didn't have any weapons to fight big, four-legged, super-fast man-animals. Hmm...manimals...now that was funny. She'd made up a new word.

Slapping her mental self into focus, she reminded herself those two neighbors were part of the shifter group. Thank God for the automatic starter button on her key ring.

Her hands made a move toward the hall table and stopped. About to grab her prescription sunglasses, she frowned, lifted a hand to her face, and realized she wasn't wearing her glasses.

Squealing, she dashed to the bathroom and stared at her eyes all over again. Holy shit! She took in her surroundings with much more accuracy, and her jaw dropped. Her usual myopic vision was gone. It had been replaced with sight so perfect, she could see right down to the few strands of hair that littered the floor.

She retrieved her smartphone and made a note of the first evident change that occurred after her accident. She grinned. That was one kind of side effect she wouldn't argue with. Perfect vision rocked.

Grabbing her black shoulder bag and keys, she made a run for the car. Surprisingly, it took her less time than she thought to get to it. She floored it when she saw Dick's front door opening.

She looked in her rearview mirror and caught him standing in the middle of the street, watching her car speed away.

She'd stop at Tryx's Bakery on her way to Julia's house; otherwise, she'd find herself with one angry wolf.

Tryx's shop was an absolute delight of yumminess. There were cakes, cookies, truffles, pastries, assorted specialties, and of course, Tryx's signature chocolate mousse cake. She only made that by request. Everything was displayed to make the customer want to try it all.

Sophia walked in and was instantly surrounded by enough sweets to give her dentist work for at least six months. Every time she walked into the shop, Sophia was sure she'd gone down the rabbit hole.

"Sophia!" Tryx grinned and came around the counter. As the only female in the alpha family, River and Chase's cousin was thrilled to have Julia keep her company. Her short, spiky hair feathered over her face with a couple of blonde, pink, and blue strands, making her look like a little pixie. She wasn't very tall for a shifter, only about two inches over Sophia's own five-foot-three frame. She was slimmer than Sophia and Julia by a good twenty pounds.

Tryx hugged her tightly and then lifted her head, narrowing her eyes.

"What?" Sophia asked at the strange expression on Tryx's face.

Tryx gave her a look as if she were stinking up the place. She hoped she'd put on enough deodorant and didn't smell funky. She'd had to stop wearing body spray to keep her sister's new, sensitive shifter senses from complaining over the strong scent.

"You smell weird." Tryx wrinkled her nose and sniffed Sophia's shoulder.

Sophia took a tentative step back to put space between herself and the other woman's frown. "Um, oh, that. You see, I got this dress dry-cleaned, and they told me they mixed it with someone's stuff by mistake, so I think you might smell the other person. I think they were a shifter, too.

"Anyhow, do you have that cake? I don't want to disappoint Julia with as busy as she's been lately."

After another sniff, Tryx's brow smoothed and she smiled at Sophia. "Of course. I would never want to see my beautiful new cousin angry. It's all ready, and I've added a bag of cookies just for you."

She strode to the counter and picked up a white bakery box and a bag. Both were closed and tied with pink and gold ribbon, the shop's signature colors.

After she handed Sophia the box, Tryx stared into her eyes for what felt like an eternity, then gave her a soft, warm smile.

Completely sure there must have been something wrong with the water, Sophia was glad to get out from under Tryx's scrutiny. Not to mention she could smell the cookies in the bag, and her mouth was starting to water. She was sure if she didn't eat one soon, she'd drool on her dress.

She turned to face the door and almost jumped out of her skin. Five men stood there scrutinizing her. She staggered back with a thread of unease. Shit, hadn't these guys ever heard of moving to the side to let a lady pass? Or at the very least not blocking the frigging door?

Tryx jumped in front of Sophia and urged her back. Sophia stared at the other woman's back as Tryx took an aggressive stance.

Growling, Tryx unleashed her claws. The male faces were tense. The men stood rigid, as though they wanted to start a fight with her or turn the woman into puppy chow. It made no sense.

The she-wolf snarled loudly and two of her big male assistants came out of the back, jumped over the glass counter and were ready to help the angry Tryx.

Sophia wasn't sure what was going on, but she was grateful when the men walked out the door, even if they did so reluctantly.

She was about to give the pixie wolf her thanks but was cut off before she even started.

"We'll walk you outside, Sophia. Can you just do me a favor? You're not stopping anywhere before you go to Julia's house, right?"

Tryx was obviously worried for her.

"No. This was my one stop. After this, it's straight to her place." She hoped her response had reassured the wolf sprite. Her stomach cramped, and her eyes darted to the cake box. The sharp needling pain reminded her she'd yet to eat, and damn it all, she was hungry.

"Is Chase going to be there?" Tryx looked hopeful.

"Um, I guess. As far as I know, I think it's just the four of us." She didn't really feel comfortable talking about Chase. The thought of him made her hot and bothered, not a good thing as far as she was concerned. That line of thinking was hopeless. Chase was known for his discerning taste.

Picky was his middle name. Sophia had seen one of his girlfriends and was sure the woman came off the cover of *For Him Magazine*. Only the sexiest feminine bodies in the planet graced that cover. Green with jealousy, Sophia had visualized doing horrible things like calling in Father Dominico and saying the girl was a hooker in need of salvation.

Tryx looked her straight in the eyes. "Promise me that even if Chase isn't there, you'll have Julia call him over. He'll know why once he gets there."

"Why? What's wrong?"

"Just promise, okay?" Tryx had gone from cute to way-out-there bizarre, but Sophia supposed it was best to just nod and get the heck out of there before somebody else acted weird.

After agreeing to Tryx's demands, Sophia was safely on the road again, munching on the distracting cookies. She wondered what the hell was wrong with everybody. Not herself—she knew she had a few screws loose. It was what made her so good at being alone too long.

* * *

Chase sat in one of the lounge chairs by his brother's pool with a cold beer in his grasp. He'd just walked out of the cool water and had to admit he was actually having a good time. Of course, Julia had yet to do one of her Oscar-worthy performances, but it was still early.

It was clear summer had arrived by the presence of the high temperatures, the smell of barbecued meat, and the uncovered pool ready for use. Every few minutes, Julia would bring out more food to the side table they had set up. What was she feeding, an army?

Granted, he and his brother could eat, but she'd made enough food for twenty. His stomach grumbled in complaint, letting him know he was easily able to eat enough food for twenty.

Julia was really excited about the news she was going to share with Sophia and him. Of course, he knew what the news was. His keen sense of smell detected the change in her the minute she'd conceived, but he'd kept his mouth shut. Women were strange about being pregnant, having babies...and weddings.

A car pulled up in the front, a door opened, and a soft voice called, "Jules, I'm here." His gut clenched. Whether he wanted to admit it or not, Sophia had arrived, and the wolf that had been lying dormant inside him lifted its head in sudden interest. She came around the side of the yard straight to the back. She was wearing a short-sleeve wrap dress that showed off her curvy body.

He frowned when he saw long, loose

brown curls hugging her shoulders. He knew the last time he'd seen her it had been cropped to her jaw line. Her glasses were also missing.

Knowing she could barely see without them, he found that strange. Julia had said Sophia didn't like contacts—they irritated her eyes since she worked such long hours. But it seemed she must be wearing them.

She carried a white box in her hands, and the minute she saw him, she stopped midstride. He watched her nostrils flare and her eyes brighten to a molten gray when she took in his wet and barely-clothed state.

He tightened his stomach muscles in a conscious effort to keep her gaze on his body. His dick hardened at her perusal of his physique, and when her tongue darted out to lick her lips, he got the impression she liked what she saw.

Interesting.

Would it be too much if he walked over, grabbed her hand, and placed it on his aching cock? Yeah, it might seem somewhat depraved and give her the wrong impression...or it might give her the right impression—that he was so hard for her, he couldn't fucking think straight.

Sophia stopped walking the minute she caught sight of Chase lying on a lounger like an erotic, half-naked sex god. His skin was wet from having been in the pool, and it glistened with a healthy bronze glow.

She took a moment to stare at the only man that made her babble and left her tongue-tied at the same time. Overwhelming, lust-filled heat invaded her body. Fascination seized hold. She watched drops of water crawl slowly down his muscular torso and cling to his nipples.

Oh good Lord, help me not attack this man and tear those shorts off that sexy ass.

Her mouth turned into the Sahara Desert, and her tongue licked at her suddenly dry lips. The wicked water droplets on Chase's chest seemed to beckon her as they traveled his six-pack abs to the waistband of his brown swimming trunks, right where a smattering of hair peeked.

Gulping to try to slow down her breathing, Sophia's breasts grew heavy and full, her nipples puckered into painful hard points that rubbed against the cotton fabric of her bra, which seemed much rougher against her skin than normal. Her pussy clenched in need, and moisture gathered between her thighs, soaking her panties.

Chase was truly a feast for hungry eyes. She longed to use her tongue and suck on each errant drop of water. To get down on her knees, rip his trunks off, grab his cock, and suck until he came in her mouth, on her breasts and belly. She wanted him to take her from behind, come inside her pussy, wanted him to fill her with his seed and claim her as his mate.

What the hell?

Where were these thoughts coming from? She'd never been an overtly sexual person, but now she was positively frantic for him to fuck her. Besides, how could he possibly want somebody like her, short and curvy, when he could have tall and drop-dead gorgeous?

Need clawed at her womb and again she pictured him giving her the rough, explosive sex she was craving. The kind of sex that made everything around her disappear while leaving only his delectable body in hers, over her and all around her, bringing her to the height of pleasure. She knew Chase would make her finally have the big O without having to use one of her battery-operated toys.

Shaking her thoughts out of her daydream, she walked to the food table and placed the cake box next to the other fruit trays and assorted cookies.

Wanting to get away from the sight of a

nearly-naked Chase, she turned to go into the house when Julia opened the screen door and walked out.

Her sister was wearing a short white denim skirt with a peach T-shirt that read "Baby Mama."

It took her a moment to realize what that meant, but then she looked up at Julia's twinkling smile and couldn't help the scream that came out of her. "Oh my gosh. Congratulations!" Grinning, she ran toward her sister and enveloped her in a hug.

Julia was hugging her, just as excited, when she took a sniff and pulled away from Sophia. Julia looked at her and frowned. Her eyes widened, and alarm and anger cloaked her features.

What was it with people and frowning at her that day?

"What?" She took a few steps back from her sister, who looked a little like she was about to turn into her she-wolf persona.

"Sophia! What did you do?" Julia yelled at her in that rough, deep, wolf-is-about-to-come-out-and-maul-your-ass voice. Julia was so angry, she was practically vibrating. This was so wrong—her own sister was about to turn her into a doggy snack.

Taking a couple more cautious steps back from her sibling, Sophia backed into a wall of muscle. A hand steadied her elbow. Chase, who had left the lounger and come up behind them, was holding her.

He turned her into his arms, and she ended up plastered to his hot, wet torso. What the… *Mmm…*

Her body decided that was exactly where it wanted to be and immediately curved into him. Her arms wound around his neck to hold him near, and at that moment, the most unbelievable thing happened. She purred.

Sophia quickly became lost in the blissful sensation of having Chase hold her. His warmth surrounded her and seeped into her pores, lighting a slow fire in her womb. She rubbed her nose into the curve of his neck and licked the harsh pulse that beat at the base of his throat.

A sensual fog closed in on her and disabled all human thought processes. Her mind turned blank and sexual need took over.

Chase had never had such a hard time keeping his skin. He'd seen Julia's anger and knew he needed to step in. He wouldn't allow her to hurt her sister or accidentally shift, which would put her baby in danger. He grabbed Sophia's arm and turned her toward him.

What he hadn't expected was for her to plaster herself to him like they were made of Velcro. It was so shocking, it took him a moment to realize she was purring. His eyes narrowed, and he lowered his head to take a deep inhale of her scent.

He smelled the peaches and cream that was pure Sophia, but he also scented wolf *and* *cat* in her. He sniffed her again, deeper, and couldn't help the growing erection at her blatant rubbing of his body with her own.

She was in heat. Which meant any logical thinking on her part went out the window. Shifter women in heat were a potential disaster. Males would tear each other apart to get to an unclaimed female in heat. And the female would encourage the destruction, wanting the strongest, the best.

Even a shy, innocent like Sophia could turn savage and not even have a clue of what she was doing. She wouldn't even remember what happened when her animal was in such a frenetic state. And two animals…

He didn't know how, but Sophia had a cat and a wolf inside her, both animals currently desperately needing to mate. She licked his neck and ran her lips over his jaw. His biggest fantasy had just come true.

Sophia was hot…for him.

Arousal spiked through his system. It spiraled like a derailed train with only one focus: to get Sophia's body closer to his. A rumble sounded in his chest.

The effect of her body fanned the flames that licked through his veins and injected an urgent need to possess and seize the woman within his grasp.

Chase's wolf challenged him for dominance. He'd wanted to claim Sophia as his mate ever since he'd gotten a whiff of her sweet scent the first time he'd seen her. The animal could smell her need and wanted to take her as his own. It took every ounce of Chase's willpower to pull the wolf back and calm him down. The caged beast was horny and wanted out of the skin. He wrapped his arms around Sophia's waist and held her closer to him.

Her scent drove him wild, every pore in his body yelled for him to take her, lick her until he stamped himself all over her, to eat her cream and suck on her swollen wet folds over and over while she screamed his name. She was so ready for him that when he licked his lips, he was sure he could taste the honey dripping down her thighs.

Julia grabbed Sophia's arm and attempted to pull her away from Chase. Sophia growled and burrowed deeper into the heated skin of his neck.

Chase's head snapped up. "Mine," he snarled loudly at Julia, baring his teeth in a clear threat.

He watched Julia take a hasty step back into her husband, who had appeared after Sophia had attached herself to him like crazy glue. Chase's gaze met with River's, and it was clear from River's expression that he was trying to make sense of what was happening. River moved Julia behind him for her own safety.

"Chase?" Julia peered over River's shoulder at him.

The anxiety in her expression cooled some of the sensual haze surrounding him and Sophia. Chase struggled to clear his head. He needed to think, to figure out how Sophia had ended up with not one, but two animals inside. Lifting his head, he looked into her lust-clouded eyes… Fuck! Sophia was gone. It was just her animals.

He needed to get her alone and show her who she belonged to. To claim her. His wolf… His cat… His woman… His mate.

MILLY TAIDEN

No, no, no. Not like this. He wanted her with her knowledge, with her human mind agreeing.

He took a deep breath. "Sophia?"

She ignored his call. The licking and kissing on his neck and jaw made it a challenge to keep his mind on getting answers. His dick had become so hard, he could have sworn it had petrified.

He pulled her arms from around his neck and held her about a foot away, trying to ignore her purring. Fuck, but that was hot. Her entire body vibrated, and the sound did something to him that pushed his control to the snapping point.

"Sweetheart, you need to listen to me. Can you hear me?" His voice had become hard, commanding, to show her he was the alpha in charge.

Her unfocused gaze peered at him from under dark lashes on a beautiful, flushed face. Her pink tongue licked her plump lower lip. He clenched all his muscles to keep from doing something only a brainless idiot would do, like fucking her in front of his brother and her sister.

There was one sure way he could get her out of her sensual haze, even if for a few minutes. The situation called for him to act. His gut burned with distaste. He called on his animal, who didn't really want to follow his instructions and upset his mate. It took him a moment of irritated ordering to finally get his wolf to growl at her.

She stopped, frowned, and cocked her head at him, her eyes a little more focused than before.

Growling again, he watched as her gaze cleared. It bothered him to have to do it this way, but he refused to mate her without her clearheaded consent. He would not have her regretting her actions later.

FOUR

"Sophia?" With tears in her eyes, Julia looked at her sister.

The woman he desired looked up at him. Chase watched as she cleared her passion-dazed eyes and kept swallowing in an attempt to get rid of a dry throat.

He was sure that the moment she saw where she was, her upper arms in his grasp, she'd pass out like the last time she was so close to him unexpectedly. She'd disliked him so much, she would've rather been out cold than have him touching her.

Guess all that had changed now.

Sophia's face drained of color when she realized where she stood next to him. Well, maybe things hadn't changed.

He read the question in her eyes: how did she get there? She was talking to Julia before the animals' heat took over her conscious mind.

She stumbled out of his hold and turned to her sister. "Why are you crying?" Sophia asked Julia.

How in the hell was he going to explain this? First off, though, he wanted answers. "I think we all need to sit down. Sophia needs something to drink."

He motioned for Julia to stroll with her to a lounge chair. If they had any hope of figuring out what had happened to her, he needed to stay away from her, or they would end up right where they were before.

The next time he wouldn't stop until he was buried so deeply inside her, they'd need a crowbar to separate them.

River stayed a few steps behind with him. The wind blew his hair into messy threads across his forehead.

River gave him a questioning look. "Did I smell what I think I smelled? Sophia has two animals inside?" Concern and astonishment colored his words. His eyes followed the women as they made their way to the drink table.

Somehow, Chase wasn't surprised. He'd need to keep better track of his mate, or the woman could get herself into a heap of trouble and not even realize it.

"What I want to know is how. We need to talk to her before the heat becomes unbearable for her again. We might only have a few minutes, and we have to find out as much information as possible."

Looking at his mate, he knew they had very little time. Her hands shook as she swallowed the icy drink her sister handed her.

"Sophia, what did you do?" Julia's outward calm was not deceiving anyone. The tension in her face was evident in the way she held the glass in a white-knuckled grip. She waited expectantly for Sophia to reply.

"What do you mean? I haven't done anything." Her head turned away, hiding her face.

Three sets of eyes watched as she gulped down the water like she'd been suffering from dehydration.

Julia dropped into her seat with a dramatic sigh. Even Julia had taken awhile to adjust when she'd first turned. Her body had fought the new physiology, not to mention the near-death experience from the rogue wolf that had attacked her.

Those had been some very tense months, when no one was sure how the change would affect her. Her first shift was much too soon and almost killed her there in the hospital.

Chase wasn't sure what kind of effect this would have on Sophia's body, but he was sure it wasn't going to be good.

"Sophia, I know you've been doing something in that lab of yours, and you're going to tell us what it is before you start the weird shit we just witnessed a moment ago." Julia's hysteria rose until she ended the sentence in a high-pitched squeak. Tears filled her eyes all over again.

Chase was unable to stop the wince that covered his face at her theatrics.

"What the hell is wrong with her?" Sophia asked, looking from Chase to River. "And what is really going on here? I mean, has everyone in this frigging town lost their mind today?"

As he thought, she didn't remember any of it. Not good. Chase questioned her in a voice that was unbending steel. "What are you working on at your lab, Sophia?" He used the don't-fuck-with-the-alpha attitude that ensured his pack members knew he meant business. Her animals would obey.

What he got from Sophia was a strong whiff of arousal at his tone.

So she liked a dominant male. His wolf rolled over in excitement, ready to burst his skin and do flips.

She blushed and tried to look away, but his eyes locked on hers as he waited for her to answer him. "I...I wanted to find a way to help Julia go back to being human or stop her from shifting."

Her sister's shocked gasp filled the humid afternoon air. "Why would you do that?" Julia demanded and jumped to her feet. Her tears had miraculously disappeared.

Chase ignored Julia's question and proceeded with his own. "And did you find a way to do it? To stop her from shifting?" His voice whipped around the quiet yard, and his hard gaze never wavered from her face.

"Yes and no. Of course, if I had a couple more weeks at the lab, I might be able to turn her into a full human again. Shit, give me a few months and I can make her Batman." The fire in her eyes revealed how proud she was of her work. She'd done what no one else ever had.

He knew they needed to keep her work under wraps. It would create chaos among shifters if they realized what she'd discovered. She'd be hunted.

The thought didn't sit well with his animal. It pushed at the skin cage once again and tried to get free. Chase bit back a snarl at the imaginary threat to his mate.

"How did you figure out how to do this?"

Her eyes flashed when questioned and her usual patience was surpassed by the aggression contained inside. A shifter with two animals was unusual. It would create a problem with the dominant one, but from what Chase had scented, Sophia appeared to have two alpha females inside that were presently getting along quite well.

She exuded the dominance and power that reigned in alphas. His wolf howled in happiness, so much passion, aggression...and *both* animals were his.

"I singled out the shifter gene from a strand of DNA and created a pure sample of FB chromosomes."

Bingo. Chase knew he'd found the answer to her change. But wait... "What's FB?"

"My tag for the chromosome that creates the animal inside all shifters.

Furry Beast." Her face turned tomato-red while she spoke.

He laughed. There was no holding it back. She had a silly sense of humor.

Eliminating the mirth from his voice, he continued with the questions. "What did you do with the pure samples?" He expected her to say she tested them on herself.

"What do you mean, what did I do? I locked them in my cold storage." She furrowed her brow.

"Did you use the sample on yourself, Sophia?" His carefully worded queries were getting them nowhere.

"What? Of course not. That's highly unethical, not to mention dangerous. I would never do that on purpose." Outraged, she jumped to her feet and glared at him, hands fisted at her sides. Her eyes turned a dark, stormy gray, and his wolf pulled at his skin, wanting out of the human skin.

She was so hot when she was angry. Her features changed a little to show first her wolf pushing, and then her cat trying to come out and rip him to shreds. He really hated the eternal erection that didn't want to go away when she was around.

Unlike Julia, who'd had a hard time with

her change because she had been recuperating from near death, it looked like Sophia would have no problem shifting.

"I didn't mean to offend you, darling, but we need you to tell us how you ended up with two animals inside."

"Two animals inside where?" Couldn't he ask a question without going around in circles?

* * *

Sophia's mind felt wooly, like it was filled with cotton, making it hard for her to think clearly.

She stared at the man she'd been fantasizing about for months. She knew what he was, and she wasn't going to lie to him. It didn't help that his total I'm-in-charge attitude made her so wet she had to squeeze her legs shut, hoping his super-sensitive nose couldn't smell her.

"Two animals inside your body." He met her gaze and held it, sending electric shivers down her spine, and conveying with his look the gravity of the situation.

How the hell could he make her so hot her panties needed wringing from just one look? The whole dominant thing he did was making her want to get on her knees in front of him and lower her head in submission.

Dear Lord, she'd never thought that kind of stuff would turn her on. Yet, here she was, ready to beg him to cuff her to the nearest tree and spank her ass until she stopped being a bad girl. Of course, just the thought of him spanking her made her want to be bad.

Dear God, how could he know already? It'd just been barely thirty-six hours since her lab accident. No need to test her blood now. She knew the truth.

Shit. Should she fess up or deny it until she had run several tests to check things out? A good scientist never went public too soon with research. She had to verify and make sure. So that called for refuting any claims.

"What the hell are you talking about? I don't have animals inside my body." The words had just left her mouth when she felt the push of fur against her skin.

She bowed her head and watched in horror as her nails grew into long talons...claws. First, thick brown fur pushed out, covering her arms, and after a moment it receded. Then, short golden fur pushed out of her arms and receded. Wide-eyed, she jerked her head up to meet Chase's hungry gaze.

"Darling, you're not just a shifter; you're a

dual shifter. How did you do it, Sophia?" This time his question was filled with admiration, which made her foolishly glow inside.

Why the hell was she happy? Not just happy—horny and happy.

"I..." She gulped. Gig was up. "I had an accident."

Chase's eyes narrowed with concern. He scanned her body, but she knew she had no visible injuries.

"What kind of accident?"

She blushed and called herself all kinds of fool for not being more vigilant while she worked. Not to mention for letting her body melt every time his eyes flickered with a heat that screamed of possession. At this rate, she'd end up worse than a stick of butter on a hot sunny day, a puddle of goop.

"I tripped. I was distracted on my way to transfer the samples from the sharps to their designated vials. The sharps ended up stuck in me. But only for a second—I probably got like one cc in me, not enough to make any kind of difference." All three listened intently as she explained.

"How much is that? Compared to the amount you'd get from a bite wound?" Julia's distress made her lower her voice.

"I'm not sure, but I would think with the amount of saliva transferred during a bite wound, it would be a lot more than that single drop." She frowned.

Shit. Was she going to grow a tail now? Want to sniff people's asses? To pee on trees to mark her territory? Would she want to pee on Chase to claim him as her own? Now, there was a visual she didn't need.

A surge of wind tossed her hair into a mess all over her head, making her tunnel shaky fingers through it to get it out of her face.

"Your body adjusted so quickly. The strands must have bonded with your DNA immediately." River sounded amazed.

It was as if she were a live science experiment, the way all three of them looked at her like she was some sort of new species. She peered around and everyone was staring at her with different expressions.

Julia was one step away from full-blown panic. Nothing strange there. River was curious. Chase's look was hot, wicked, and not appropriate for minors. Shit, she wasn't even sure it was appropriate for her. She tried not to blush at his proprietary gaze. The man would easily melt an iceberg.

"Sophia, your samples and data, where are they?" Chase was back to barking questions at her.

She knew she'd made a mistake, but the man didn't want to let up with his infuriating grilling. "They're in my lab, all right! The samples are in cold storage and my data under lock. Both are secured by my fingerprints, voice, and other security measures. Trust me, my research is locked up tighter than two dogs in the act."

Why the hell had that come out of her mouth? She noticed their raised brows at her example and got defensive. "What? Okay, bad example, but I've had horrible experiences before with my data being stolen."

Julia stood and grabbed her hand, sad eyes conveying she wanted to speak to her alone. She bit back the urge to roll her eyes at her sister's over-the-top emotional outbursts. They walked into the house in silence.

Sophia looked around the kitchen and was always impressed at the beauty of the space. The room, open, airy, and light, made her want to sit there all day. Windows surrounded the soft blue space, trimmed with off-white cabinets and appliances, and fresh flowers scented the air with delicate fragrances that wouldn't upset Julia's sensitive nose.

Sophia felt an immediate sense of peace every time she went into that space. Her sister had made her entire home a welcoming, serene escape.

Under other circumstances, Sophia would have been ecstatic to be sitting in the kitchen with her best friend. But not now. Julia gave a loud sigh as she took a seat across from Sophia.

"Sophia, I know you thought you were helping me by looking for a way to get me back to what I was before. But you needn't have bothered. I'm happy with who and what I am, and most importantly, I'm just happy. River loves me. I love him, and we're going to have a baby." Her face glowed with joy and love.

"I remember how difficult everything was for you right after the attack and I felt so powerless to help. I wanted to give you the option of changing your body to who you used to be, without having to shift into a wolf."

The hell she'd seen her sister live was not something she would wish on anyone. It was horrible to see her suffering as her body was overcome with the change.

She could still hear the screams of pain as the bones popped and the fur pushed out of her the first time while she was still recuperating from her attack.

"The wolf is a part of me now, Sophia. If she weren't there, I'd feel less than whole. I would never change back if it meant losing her." Julia grasped Sophia's hand and looked at her with unease. "What are you going to do now?"

"What do you mean?" God, what a day it had turned out to be, and it wasn't even lunchtime yet. She needed a stiff drink or better yet, a stiff cock, preferably the one playing macho alpha outside.

She hadn't been with anyone since she moved into town, and it depressed her that it had been so long ago. Fuck this! She wasn't going to let some fur and a tail turn her into a crybaby.

"Sophia, you're in heat, both your animals want to mate. You would have stripped Chase naked outside and raped him if he hadn't stopped you. Of course…I think he was more than willing to let you do whatever you wanted to him." She grinned, and a small laugh escaped her at Sophia's flabbergasted look.

"I don't remember that!" Holy crap, she'd thrown herself at Chase? Man-candy Chase? FBA Chase? The man that every night stripped for her in her mind? Who proceeded to do some really shameless, depraved, and corrupt things with his hands, tongue, and cock…in her head? Oh, hell no.

Her pulse beat erratically, and she tried to keep her brain cells functioning. Blurry images of his arms holding her tightly while his face rubbed against her neck were all she could draw up.

Her hormones went into overdrive. Everything female in her begged for him to come and stroke her, to show her how big and strong he was in the most basic of ways.

But that was so not her. She was shy and timid and…

"Of course, you don't remember it," Julia said. "When you're in heat, your body turns off everything but the most crucial need, the need to mate and procreate."

"Wait, what? A mate? As in, I want to have sex, right? But procreate? I don't know about that." She could feel herself starting to hyperventilate. Babies? Sure, she wanted kids like most women, but first she needed a man for that.

She needed a steady relationship…

Screw that. What she really needed was some amazing sex, some sheet-melting, hair-tearing, make-me-hoarse-from-screaming, multiple-orgasm sex.

And then she could see herself wanting babies.

What the hell had she done?

"Mate," Julia answered. "As in someone to claim you for his own. You want him for yourself and no one else. And procreate? Well, I hate to tell you this, but how do you think I ended up with this little bun in the oven?

"It took me longer to go through heat because of the length of time my body took to adjust to my change. Your body absorbed it so quickly, it's like you were born a shifter."

Suddenly, all kinds of strange questions started running through her brain.

"Oh…my…God." She looked at her sister in dismay. "Does this mean when I have kids, I'm going to have kittens? Puppies? Poodles? Iguanas?" A hysterical laugh escaped her. She was quickly losing what small hold she had on her mind.

"Sophia! Be serious. There are no poodles or iguanas! As for the pups, you only have them in that form if you conceive while in wolf form. Which you *won't do*."

"Damn straight, I won't. Because I'm a human!" Did she sound deranged? She could already see the headlines: *Geneticist Loses Mind from Lack of Sex*, or even better, *Woman Who*

Thinks She's a Dog Caught Chasing Mailman.

"You risk miscarriage when you shift. So, you have to spend the duration of your pregnancy in whatever shape you were in when you conceived." Julia's tone was annoying her. She spoke as if Sophia should know that stuff.

Who cared about having puppies when her whole life had just turned upside down? She could sprout fur and claws faster than it took the Flash to go around the world. Her dental bills were going to go through the roof with the new hardware, and she didn't even want to think about what she was going to spend on bikini waxing now.

"This is insane. We're discussing things that are beyond my realm of reality. I don't need a mate. I am not trying to conceive, and I most definitely am *not* in heat." Frustration made her growl the words out.

"I beg to differ."

Chase. Damn it. That voice. Deep, rough, and a little raspy, it caressed her skin like warm caramel being dripped over her favorite ice cream. She tilted her head to look into his eyes and felt the growing need clawing at her again.

"We need to talk, Sophia." He looked at his

brother and her sister. They shared some kind of understanding, because one minute they were all in the kitchen and the next he was pulling her into one of her sister's spare rooms, her sandals tapping on the wood floor. Once inside, he closed the door and flipped the lock.

She walked to the other side of the room to give herself some space. "Listen, Chase. I'm so sorry about outside. I...I'm not sure what's going on here, but I'm positive that in a few days, whatever this heat is will go away." She perked up as she spoke, completely ignoring him.

He stood in front of the closed door. Sophia gripped the dresser behind her with all her might. Goddammit, if she let go, she might jump him.

He inhaled slowly... Crap, he could probably smell her arousal.

He smiled at her in such a hot wicked way, she almost drooled. He moved his hands to the T-shirt he must have put on while she was in the kitchen with Julia. He lifted it slowly and revealed his stomach, chest, and arms.

Her eyes widened until she was sure she looked just like a Tarsier as she watched him. Her fingers itched to touch the golden skin she knew was warm and soft over the bulging muscles.

Her breath hitched when he threw the piece of clothing to the floor. He bunched his arm muscles and moved his hands toward the tie on the swimming trunks.

"Uh, Chase, what are you doing?" she squeaked. The evil imp on her shoulder told her to shut the hell up and enjoy the show. God, but the man was built in the image of her every wet dream. Every part of him dared her to touch.

"I'm about to get to know my mate a whole lot better." He grinned, the jerk. He was probably enjoying how flustered and shell-shocked she was while trying to appear indifferent to what he was doing. But how in the world could she be indifferent when all that golden skin was making her eyes water? She was going to end up blind from that sinful vision.

The rod straining the fabric was growing before her very eyes. Big…bigger…and then, hell yeah.

FIVE

"Sophia, I've wanted inside your delicious little body since I first laid eyes on you. I just didn't want to rush you into anything. But make no mistake—you are my mate." His words were earnest as he strolled lazily her way.

He took his sweet time prowling toward her, the ultimate predator. He stopped a foot away. "You're going to have to tell me now if you want this or not, Sophia. I don't want you to go mindless with heat and find yourself mated to me because you couldn't hold back your hormones."

Was she in the Twilight Zone? He wanted her as a mate? She looked at his eyes and wondered if he spoke the truth. He really wanted *her*? He actually desired her short, fat body?

"Why would you want me? You can have any woman in and out of your pack. I've seen them looking at you at the bar. They practically throw themselves at your feet. I'm nobody. I'm short, fat, and geeky." Chin lifted in defiance, she said the words that kept her from allowing her mind to want him.

He caressed her cheek with one hand while he wrapped the other around her waist, pulling her body flush against his. She gave a little moan in the back of her throat.

"I'm going to say this quickly before your mind is too cloudy to remember. First of all, you are not short, you are petite. Second, you are not fat; your body is absolute perfection. You're luscious and your curves make my mouth water. Believe me, Sophia, you're perfect.

"Third, you are not a geek. You're the most intelligent woman I've ever met, and even though your body makes me hungry to taste you, your mind fills me with pride to know you.

"You're beautiful and exactly what I want. I don't want any other woman. I only...want...you." He drilled out each word slowly and clearly to make sure she understood. There was no joking or laughter in his eyes, just honesty and lust.

"Please, baby. I need to know you're with me on this." His voice was hoarse with need. He grazed her cheek with a big, warm hand. Fire flashed through her veins, pooling at the center of her womb and making her pussy throb with its own heartbeat.

"Yes," she said, shocked with her own reply as she locked eyes with him. "Make love to me, make me yours, Chase. I don't want anyone else, either."

He swooped down and kissed her with all the desperation she thought only she had felt. A dam of need broke inside her, driving the urge to run her fingers over his skin, to touch every part of him and feel his flesh against her own. Their kiss turned harsh, demanding.

Lips locked and mated in hunger with enough fever to scorch them both. Tongues dueled and clashed in a bid for domination that neither wanted to cede. She murmured incoherently in the back of her throat. He slid his tongue along hers, then nipped at her lips, drawing ragged moans from her.

Wet trails of heat followed his small nips and kisses up the curve of her cheek to the shell of her ear. When his velvety tongue licked the outer rim, she groaned. She rubbed her sensitive breasts on his naked chest, cursing the dress and bra keeping skin-to-skin contact from them.

Her small, nimble fingers touched the hot flesh covering his large frame. She was lost in the pleasure of feeling the hard planes of his shoulders, the shifting muscles of his arms, the smooth contours of his chest, and the satin-covered steel pushing into her belly.

His hands were all over, touching, squeezing, and branding her over the thin material of the dress. He squeezed the round globes of her ass and ground his stiff cock into her pussy, and she hissed.

The dress came off with a loud rip, followed by her bra and panties. His head dropped, claiming a swollen areola. He suckled and flicked one stiff berry tip deep into the hot cavern of his mouth. His hand kneaded the other breast, switching back and forth between them to even the delicious torture.

He nibbled the taut tips then lovingly enveloped them with the flat length of his tongue. She whimpered words of encouragement while her hands moved, nails burrowing into his biceps.

Unable to keep still, her hands traveled the expanse of his chest, slowly tracing every muscle in her downward path. His breath hissed when she scored his abs.

Upon reaching the waistband of his shorts, she looked into his eyes and smiled.

Her claws came out on demand. They allowed her to rip and shred the material keeping his shaft from her touch.

"You are so fucking hot. I can't wait to eat your pussy and lick all that delicious honey calling out to me." His voice had deepened to a low groan.

"Yes, yes. Fuck, Chase." His words, his actions brought a new flood of juices dripping down her thighs.

"I'm going to fuck you until you come over and over on my mouth, my tongue, and my cock. You belong to me," he growled.

His fingers fisted in her hair tightly, pulling her head back and displaying her neck for his access. She pulled back even farther and turned her head sideways in a sign of submission that made him groan. He licked the pulse on her neck that was beating at the speed of a runaway locomotive.

He pulled away from her for a moment to peruse her naked form. Her golden flesh was flushed and coated with a light sheen of perspiration. Her full breasts were tipped with honey-beaded nipples and calling for his lips to taste them.

His vision caressed the dip of her waist, the softly rounded belly he knew would carry his young, and the curve of her generous hips. Finally, he reached the small line of trimmed curls at the apex of her sex, glistening with cream.

"So fucking beautiful." Her fragrant scent wafted up his nose, and he licked his lips at the heady way her body summoned out to his.

Her heat was strong and so delicious he could taste it. Taking a deep breath, he tried to calm the impulse to bury his dick inside her and fuck her like the animal side in him urged. He wanted her to enjoy every second of every time they came together.

She peered at him with eyes filled with desire. "Chase, I need you. I want you so bad it hurts."

"Soon, love. Fuck, stay with me, Sophia."

He kissed her neck and shoulder, nipping on the bend he'd soon bite on to claim her as his mate. Strong, calloused hands ran up her sides to the curve of her breasts, squeezing the soft globes in his palms while tweaking the tight, sensitive tips with his fingers. Her hands strayed from behind her back.

Her fingers curled around his thick, hard length, making him groan. His hips jerked in her hands, his cock seeking relief. She pumped his velvety length slowly with one hand while she ran the nails of the other over his sac.

Beads of precum slid from the slit. He pulled her hand up to his face, kissed her fingers, and dropped a short, hard kiss on her too tempting lips. He picked her up in his arms and deposited her gently in the middle of the large bed.

She lay on the soft mattress with her legs spread. He sat on his heels between her thighs and took in the sight. With a grin, he lifted one leg and kissed from knee to clit. Lowering to his belly, he brought both of her legs over his shoulders.

He looped his arms around her thighs to hold her down by her hips. Her eyes flickered, met, and locked with his. She wiggled and whimpered. He inhaled her sweet scent of warm, earthy woman and musky sensuality.

"It's okay, baby. I'm going to make it all better now."

Slowly making his way to her pussy

lips, his tongue licked her in one smooth glide from ass to cunt. Cool lips fastened on the engorged clit in a move so unexpected, she jerked and then cried out. His raspy tongue flicked mercilessly over the nub.

Her nails burrowed into the sheets and fisted in a white-knuckle grip. Not letting up, he pushed on, greedily lapping at the swollen pink petals of her nether regions. Spearing his tongue into her, he sipped at the honeyed nectar flowing from her weeping sex.

"More. Please, God. Chase, so close…" she pleaded in husky pants.

He wanted to rub his entire face on her wet folds, spread her essence on his flesh, and scent mark himself as hers. He fucked her pussy with his tongue. Hard.

He assaulted her smooth folds, and her body undulated, begging to come. He clamped his mouth on her swollen clit and grazed his teeth over the super-sensitized tissue. Her screams of pleasure pushed him to rub against the bed, humping the mattress in an attempt to soothe his straining cock.

He licked and growled, dragging out her release as long as possible. As she was coming down from her first burst of heaven, he crawled over her body to kiss her, his arms braced at either side of her head.

Sophia's hands tunneled through his hair and pulled, bringing him close for a deeper, harder kiss. She wrapped her legs around his waist and rubbed her swollen pussy on his dick.

"Fuck. You're killing me, baby," he groaned.

The heat inside her made rational thought difficult. God, but the man had a tongue that worked absolute magic. He rolled his hips and drove his cock straight into her slick pussy, half in.

All thoughts of anything but his dick inside her body went out the window. His shaft stretched her until her body held him in a tight suction hold. He grew wider and thicker inside her, as if the farther in her he went, the longer and thicker he became.

He pulsed within her, and she groaned at the delicious feeling of fullness. She watched him clench his jaw, the cords of his neck popping out as proof of the effort he made to restrain himself, fighting the urge to sink balls-deep into her before her body had a chance to adjust.

Her walls parted and stretched for him.

When he was seated all the way in, his cock jerked, and she moaned.

Sophia gazed into his intense eyes, the pupils so dilated she could barely see the brown in them. It was beyond hot—it was her biggest fantasy come true.

"Fuck me, Chase. Right now, hard, fast. However you want. Just do me." She tilted her hips to take more of him inside. "Please, please fuck me, right now."

He kissed her hard and drew his dick in and out of her body.

Hard…fast…thrust…withdraw. Her body gripped his cock tightly, the first flutters of her climax upon her.

"Mine," he growled.

"Yours," she agreed breathlessly.

Her body curved and bowed, looking for the release it needed. Turning his hips, Chase fucked her at an angle that hit the mouth of her womb. Her breath hitched, and she screamed his name as she came.

Her body convulsed in ecstasy, and her lungs fought to draw in air. He pulled out of her, and she lay spent on the bed. He flipped her on to her stomach and lifted her ass in the air, giving her a quick pat on the round globes. Holding her hips up, he shoved his still rock-hard cock into her pussy from behind.

Gripping the pillow, she groaned and propelled back into his harsh thrusts. He grunted in appreciation. Their skin, slick with perspiration, allowed for a smooth glide. His balls bumped her sensitive lips with each driving thrust. His pelvis pounded her ass, skin slapping and grinding.

"Mine." He drove her body with his. The fingers of one hand fisted into her hair, pulling her head to the side revealing the curve of her neck.

"Yes, yes. Yours, Chase. Only yours." Everything within her heightened until all she could feel was him all around her. His power, his body, his dominance washed over her and licked over her skin. She whimpered as her body's keen hunger for him grew.

Caging her body under his, he continued to fuck her forcefully until her pussy started to contract around him. He licked the curve of her shoulder, and she shuddered. He bit down, breaking skin, and held her in place.

The pain from the bite combined with the furious pounding in her cunt was too much for her body to bear, and she came, screaming.

He buried himself as deeply inside her as possible. His penis thickened, grew, and burst in a hot gush. Her pussy sucked him in and drained him of his seed. Warm semen filled her, soothing the heat overwhelming her. Teeth still clamped on her shoulder, he continued to jerk in spurts inside her.

Her legs were still shaking when they lay on their sides with him still deeply inside her. His tongue licked slow circles over her shoulder. Exhaustion claimed her while he kissed her, and she fell into a happy slumber.

SIX

Sophia was having a wonderful dream of soft kisses trailing down her chest. A hot, wet tongue was licking her nipples, making her pussy throb. A big hand spread her lips, and she smiled when she heard a groan as a thick finger fondled her wetness.

The wicked digit moved to pump into her slowly, making her squirm and try to ride it. She pouted when the finger left her and heard a chuckle as a thick, long cock breached her cunt in its place.

Desire flooded her. Her eyes opened to find gorgeous, man-candy Chase buried inside her, filling her with his trophy-worthy cock.

She smiled at the look of hunger on his face. She ran her hands over his chest to curl them around his neck and then pulled him down for a mind-numbing kiss. Aggression she wasn't aware she possessed took hold.

She wrapped her legs around his hips and caught him completely unaware when she flipped him onto his back. His stunned look made her laugh, and she sat up with him still buried deep inside. *"Mine."* The possessive instinct rushed through her, insisting she mark him as her own.

"Does my big puppy want to play?" she cooed, laughing when he growled and made a face.

"I'll show you a puppy, you naughty hellcat."

"Oooh, I'm scared. I think my big puppy needs to learn who the boss is." She rocked her hips, making him groan as she started to ride him.

Newfound assertiveness filled her. *He's yours. Fuck him!*

He lifted to his elbows so he could suck her nipples. Sophia slammed down harder with every nip he gave the small buds. Her breath hissed out in shallow bursts.

Squeezing around his shaft, she felt his

thick length rubbing inside her sensitive channel. Chase squeezed her nipple with one hand, his fingers pinching the tender tip, tightening the knot of tension growing inside her.

"Chase, oh God. I'm going to… Fuck." She broke off on a moan.

"Come for me, beautiful. I want to feel your hot little pussy tightening around me." He groaned and lifted his hips off the bed to slam into her as she slid downward.

He rubbed his thumb on her swollen clit and tweaked the other nipple roughly, urging her over the edge. Her head fell back, and she screamed.

Her pussy sucked on him, propelling him into a climax that had him gripping her hips tightly while he jerked and filled her with his semen for long, intense moments.

Boneless, she landed on his chest, closed her eyes, and tried to catch her breath.

Her body felt like a big lump of jelly and was completely satisfied. His big arms curled around her, holding her over him while he rubbed his cheek over her hair in a gesture of affection. Her heart melted at his warm embrace.

If someone had told her Chase was going

to screw her until her spark plugs burned out, she would've laughed in their face. Yet, here she was, her body still humming over the fantastic multiple orgasms the man had given her, her brain one giant Chase-loving groupie.

She didn't get a chance to think too many mushy thoughts before her stomach started rumbling...loudly.

"Sophia?" His soft call broke through her happy trance.

"Hmm?" she sighed, too content to move. "Are you planning to have any of the food I brought you, or did you have a different kind of thing in mind to put into your mouth?"

She blinked and lifted her head to look at his grinning face and twinkling eyes.

"You are such a pervert!" Heat flooded her cheeks, and she smacked him on the chest.

It was strange having a man joke around with her. Not to mention the man-candy FBA who now belonged to her. It blew her mind.

"What—why? I'm only giving you choices, darling." He grinned and left the bed to walk into the attached bathroom.

He left the door wide open as he took care

of his business. The man had no shame and was completely at ease with his nudity. It didn't help that he had such a great ass that she couldn't stop staring at it while he was facing the toilet.

Disgusted with herself, she pulled on a robe that hung on the back of the door and walked to the tray of food lying on the dresser: fruit, juice, muffins, a couple of half sandwiches, and a large piece of chocolate cake.

She picked up the piece of cake and ate it first. She'd never been much of a chocolate lover, but it called to her.

She absently ate and thought about the events of the previous night. She had actually begged Chase to fuck her? Good Lord, she'd lost every scrap of decency she ever had, and she didn't even feel bad about it.

Taking a sip of juice, she remembered how he'd kissed every inch of her body. She raised her hand to touch the teeth marks on the back of her right shoulder. He'd marked her, branded her as his, and made her his mate. A small shiver went through her.

She was so wrapped up in her thoughts that she didn't hear him approach. She jumped slightly when he wrapped his arms around her waist and lowered his head to kiss her neck.

"Not very hungry, were you?" He rubbed his lips over the back of her ear.

She looked down and saw that she'd eaten everything on the tray. Shocked with her overindulgence, she dropped the muffin in her hand and turned around in his arms.

He looked incredibly sexy with his scruffy beard and rumpled look, not to mention all that naked skin on display.

"Why are you stopping? You need to eat if you're hungry." He frowned at her.

"No, I'm good. I need a shower." She pushed out of his arms and walked into the bathroom, closing the door behind her.

She needed to get her body under control and stop imagining sex with Chase every second of her life. Talk about getting a taste of the good stuff and never wanting to stop. She was already addicted.

She leaned forward with her hands flat against the wall. Letting the water slide down her body, she tried to clear her head of all things Chase, but luck wasn't on her side.

The curtain rustled, and she knew he had joined her. A moment later she smelled soft vanilla shower gel. His hands rubbed the liquid over her back. She wanted to resist, but her body had other ideas, and she relaxed into his touch.

His hands were absolute magic. They caressed the soap onto her shoulders, down her back, and over the curve of her ass. His head bent to kiss the curve of her neck and suck on the back of her ear. Shudders racked her body at the intense sensation of his tongue on such a sensitive spot.

Slipping soapy hands between her ass cheeks, he fondled her anus, making her breath hitch as his finger slowly circled and dipped into the tight rosette. She pushed into his hands, wanting to feel more. He stopped, moved his fingers to roam her sides, and turned her around to face him.

She looked into his passion-filled eyes and knew she was beyond wet and oh-so-ready for him to sink his hot, hard cock into her. Her nipples beaded to tight points while her sex clenched.

Their lips came together urgently. She sucked and bit his lower lip, purring in the back of her throat. He roughly thrust his tongue into her mouth. The frantic movements increased the heat inside her body and made him growl.

He rubbed more soap over her chest, kneading her breasts and squeezing her nipples. She whimpered. Her hands moved to his shoulders, and she dug her nails into his thick muscles. His long fingers traveled down her belly to settle between her thighs. Dipping into her swollen folds, he found her slick and ready.

He moved her under the spray to remove the soap from her flesh and wrapped his arms around her body, bringing her flush up against him. Her legs curled around his waist and he dug his fingers into her ass cheeks as her back hit the tiled wall.

They groaned when he slid home in one quick thrust. Her pussy clenched and grabbed his shaft, tightly wrapping around him. He thrust and withdrew in and out of her body in short, quick moves. She moaned. He hit a sensitive spot inside her, rapidly bringing her to the edge of reason.

"Chase...Chase, please...fuck me harder...harder...I need—" She broke off when he locked his lips on hers, fucking her with his tongue in addition to his cock.

"You like that, baby? You like it when I fuck your tight little cunt so hard it makes you come? You're going to like it when I fuck your tight little ass, too. Oh, baby, I can't wait to lick that special little spot and bury my cock into your virgin ass."

He took her nipple into his mouth. He

rolled the tip with his tongue and nipped it.

He let one of his hands travel the crevice of her wet ass, and very slowly he pushed one soapy finger around the rim of her anal entrance. Her body tensed a little at the unexpected invasion in that position.

"Relax, sweetheart, I'd never hurt you." He rubbed her in slow circles until her body relaxed into him, pumping his finger in and out of her.

He brought his head down and roughly bit her nipple while he rammed her body hard with his cock.

He fucked her fast and wild. Her breath came in broken whimpers.

"Yes…yes…God, that feels so good. Chase. Oh my God I…I'm—" Her body tightened to an almost painful degree and everything shattered inside her.

Chase gripped her hard, growling into her neck. His teeth clamped down on her shoulder, marking her again, while his hot seed filled her, coating her insides and soothing her sex.

He held her up and shut off the water. Wrapping her in a towel, he carried her back to bed. Neither was willing to go anywhere until her heat passed.

* * *

Ratface and his group snuck through the bushes into the scientist's backyard. She'd been gone for a couple days. They found her car at the sister's home and had been watching to see if she left.

None of his guys saw hide nor hair of the target outside the house, but she wasn't anywhere else in town. She had to be there.

Ratface waved his man forward to the back door. Goon pulled his lock pick tools from his pocket. Squeaky giggles rolled off the hyena and Rat slapped him upside the head.

"Shut it or I'll shut it for you."

Goon cringed and leaned out of his reach. "Sorry, boss." A few seconds later, the door swung open.

The group swiftly moved in.

"Search everything," Ratface said. "We're looking for scientific stuff."

One of his men asked, "How will we know if it's scientific?"

Ratface shook his head. How could he fly like an eagle when he was stuck with the dogs?

He said, "If you can't tell what it is and it

has a bunch of numbers, it's probably scientific."

The group looked at each other. Mumbles of, "Yeah, yeah, yeah. He's smart," rolled through them along with titters.

What a fucked-up group of piss ants he worked with. He needed to get away from the big city. Find someplace new where he could start over and she'd never find him. He couldn't take it any longer.

He wanted to get this gig done and over with and…what? What could he possibly do after being a punk gang member for so long? He'd never held a legitimate job. Didn't have anyone he could call a true friend. Just those who rode his coattails when he was on a paying job. Fuck.

Ratface left the idiots with him and went into the home's office and started pulling out drawers and dumping them. He searched for flash drives, files, papers, anything that looked suspicious.

From a closet, he pulled out an old shoebox and flipped the lid off. Inside, a pile of handwritten papers and some envelopes filled the space, one side to the other.

Could this be what they were looking for?

He pulled out a group of several pages

folded together. The writing was faded and in pencil. The pretty, looping cursive script flowed across the lines from top to bottom.

He straightened the wrinkled sheets and read the first page:

Dear Nicki,

Summer camp stinks. I wish...

That name struck a chord inside him. He knew a Nicki once. A long time ago. And damn, did he miss her.

The years with her were the happiest of his life. In fact, they were the only happy years he ever had.

They met the summer of her sixteenth year. Back then, there were no phones, no electronic hand-held games, no Facebook. Just person to person conversations.

She was coming in the door of a Kwiki Mart as he was walking out. They saw each other through the glass entrance. He was sure she was staring at his ugly face like everyone did.

He couldn't help the rodent-like features his face displayed in his hyena body. Somewhere in the family line, someone married or fucked a rat and he was paying the price for it.

Outside the Kwiki Mart, he lit up a cigarette from the pack he just purchased. He felt the rush as nicotine flooded his system and calmed him. He swore he was at the slowest gas pump in the world. It was taking forever to fill the gas tank of his souped-up Mustang.

He paced a few yards from the gas pumps. Not getting close because of the cigarette. He took a big drag into his lungs.

"Hey," a sweet, feminine voice said behind him, "groovy ride you got there."

He spun around to see the girl from the store. She held a Coke in one hand and dollar bills in the other.

"Thanks," he said, then hacked into a coughing fit from the smoke he'd forgotten to exhale.

She laughed and patted his back. "You okay, dude? You look like a fire-breathing dragon with all that smoke coming out."

He raised a brow at her. Fire-breathing dragon? "That's the nicest thing anyone has ever said to me," he replied. Most things he heard where rat jokes and negative comments on his looks.

She laughed again. So beautiful. "Dude, you need to hang around different peeps then."

She was right. He had just dropped out of school a year ago to hang full-time with the gang he belonged to. With them there were no rodent remarks or beatings. They were past that. Went on to other things for entertainment.

He couldn't get the girl out of his mind. He was so stupid—not getting her name or phone number or anything. He was sure he'd never see her again.

Nichola wasn't his true mate, but his human side loved her nevertheless. His hyena could get over it.

A couple days later, he and a buddy were sitting in a car waiting for the right time to go in and rob the mart. No guns or knives during that time. The amateurs never carried weapons in town. It just wasn't done. Fortunately, he had claws and sharp teeth if the need to defend himself ever arose.

Just before closing, there she was again—going inside. He was out of the car and in the store in a heartbeat. She stood in front of the chilled soft drink bottles, looking over the selection.

"You know," he said, coming up behind her, "the orange drink is pretty good without too much sweetness."

She swiveled in her long gypsy-style skirt

and loose-hanging shirt. Her hair was pulled back into a ponytail showing off her clear complexion.

When she turned and smiled at him, he was a goner. His heart would never belong to another. Needless to say, the robbery scheduled for that night didn't happen. He received a beating when he got back for botching the plan. But it was worth it. Because she was going to meet him the next day at the beach.

After her initial shock from learning about shifters, she was into the species and wanted to know everything about them. He thought that was so groovy. Until she found out about mates.

Her heartfelt need to be perfect for him became her downfall.

Sudden anger and sadness flooded him. He grabbed onto the closet door and ripped it off its hinges, throwing it across the room. A small two-drawer file cabinet sat next to him. He yanked that off the floor and launched it through the air.

His head tipped back and a lone howl erupted from his throat.

When he came back to himself, he noted the men had gathered around the door to the destroyed office. All looking at him with awe or stupidity. He wasn't sure which, nor did he care.

He pushed through them and headed out the front door, not caring what the neighbors saw. He was done there. What they were looking for wasn't in the house. He'd send another group to the lab tomorrow.

He wanted this "job" over and done with so he could go back to his self-destructive habits. That was the only way to keep the memories at bay.

Right now, he just wanted to be away from the looks. From the questions. From the heartache.

* * *

After four days of nonstop sex and food, they'd finally made it out of Julia's house Wednesday evening. Sophia had called her boss to take the rest of the week off to get over the...whatever was driving her body.

"You didn't need to come with me, you know," she protested when Chase drove them to her lab.

"Yes, I do," he said while holding the steering wheel in a death grip. They'd just left her house and were headed toward her lab in his black SUV.

When they arrived at her house, they found her front door open. Chase, the macho wolf, had made her sit in his car until he checked out her house and ensured there was no danger to her.

Her home office had been completely trashed. It had made her see red to know someone dared touch her stuff without her consent. Chase had called the sheriff, who happened to be a close friend, and told him about the break-in.

"So? Are you ever planning on telling me what you smelled in my house?" she demanded.

"Fine." His tone was grim when he explained how he scented multiple hyena shifters.

"What would they want with me?" Stunned that other shifters would tear her house apart, she turned to gape at Chase.

"I think someone found out about your research and knows what you can do." His fingers flexed on the wheel. "We need to make sure your work is secure. Maybe talk to your boss about what's going on."

"But...but I was careful with all my work. Every piece of paper I used was shredded and all my samples were stored in my private freezer or destroyed by my own hand."

"Somehow someone found out, and now they want to get their hands on it. Don't worry, love, I won't let anyone lay a hand on you." Determination lined his features.

She held back from smiling at his words for fear of offending him. He acted like she couldn't defend herself, but didn't Chase say she was a shifter now? Well, then she would kick some shifter ass if she needed to.

God, she hoped she would need to so she could finally see what the whole turning into an animal was all about. Get ready, bad guys, there was a new wolf-cat in town, and she was going to shred them to pieces first and ask questions later.

He parked in the back of the building. She noticed how few cars there were. It was after working hours, but most weekdays employees worked late into the night.

Once inside, they walked to her lab where she and Chase found no trace of any disturbance.

"Ew. What is that smell?" She wrinkled her noise in complaint at one of the not-so-fun shifter side effects, a great sense of smell.

"Bleach and ammonia. Someone was in

re." Chase looked around all her equipment, but she had already explained she was extremely careful with her samples and never left anything out so there was nothing to find.

They turned to her secured freezer, where she accessed the inside and pulled out a few vials and beakers and set them on the table workstation.

"Crap," she started, "I still need to write my notes from that night and add them." She pulled several loose-leaf sheets of paper with scratched writing on them from a shelf and set them next to the vials. She'd use her jotted down notes to jog her memory of the DNA compounds she played with before discovering the right combination.

"Everything looks fine, Chase." Sophia closed the vault's door.

A low noise filled the air. It sounded like a laugh and a whine mixed together.

She scanned the inside of her lab but couldn't see anyone in the large, dimly lit room. Chase tensed and moved to step between her and the lab entrance, giving her his back.

"What is it?" she whispered, unsure if she should be making any noise.

110

"Hyenas. They're already in animal form. I need to shift. We can connect through our wolves. Stay back and don't do anything to make me want to strangle you later, okay, sweetheart?"

Outraged, she fisted her hands on her hips and glared at the broad expanse of his sexy back while he removed his T-shirt. She didn't like how she was ready to drool at the sight of him shirtless.

She wished they weren't in danger so she could have him fuck her on one of her lab tables in clear view of anyone that went by. She wanted to slap herself to stop the erotic visuals that kept filling her head. *Focus, woman!* She was in danger of getting mauled in her lab, and all she could think of was getting fucked.

"You are one depraved, sick woman in need of mental help," she whispered to herself.

"You can tell me all about it later—and whatever it was that made that delicious scent come out of you." She could hear the smile in his voice.

She rolled her eyes and turned her back to him.

She glanced around again and thought

about what he had said earlier.

Wait a second, did he mean they could communicate via telepathy? She didn't get a chance to ask because when she turned to glare at his back, he'd already shifted into a large, black wolf.

She sucked in a sharp breath at the size of his animal. He had to be over six feet in length, with a massively muscular body surrounded by thick black fur, and paws as big as her face. Okay, maybe not that big, but he was huge.

Her inner wolf howled with pride, and wicked thoughts of him going feral to protect her brought a fresh flood of arousal.

"Chase?" she called out to him tentatively in her mind.

"Sophia, don't move from that spot, sweetheart. They will have to come through me to get to you."

"How many are there?" She worried her lower lip watching the entrance, scared for his safety.

"I see two coming down the hall, but smelled four."

She wished she could do something to help him.

"Chase, what if I shift —"

112

"No!" He growled so loud she winced. Well, crap!

"But why not? I mean I can help you – "

"No." Frustration and anger built inside her. He seemed to have sensed it because he sighed and then continued at a lower tone. *"You cannot shift, Sophia."*

"I can try," she urged, hoping he would change his mind. *"I mean, I know I haven't ever done it before, but I can give it a shot. I mean, how hard can it be, right? And maybe help you in the process."*

She could sense the tension he was feeling at her words.

"It's not safe for you to shift." His voice was soft but serious.

"Why?" Her question was drowned by a loud, piercing laugh. A large hyena dove through the air and went straight for Chase. The animal was big with black and brown coarse fur. The thing looked like a cross between a sick lion and a dog on steroids, so ugly, she was sure it had to be some kind of science experiment gone wrong.

Chase immediately crouched and leaped, catching the assailant mid-flight. His wide-open jaws clamped and locked on its front leg and then swung his prey out the door.

The hyena's body slapped against the white wall with a loud whine, creating a long bloody mark when it slid down to the floor. Another set of the ugly animals attempted to attack Chase, but he swiped his deadly claws, slicing through the enemies with ease.

He bit into the neck of one and crushed the bones, leaving the hyena in a messy pool of blood on the floor. The other assailant came back with the first aggressor and both attacked, clawing at Chase at the same time. They proved to be enough of a distraction to allow a fourth to break in through one of the lab windows.

Shocked into immobility, Sophia watched the man that stood across the room from her. This was a shifter in his human form. He was shorter than Chase but still a great deal bigger than her, with short black hair and dark brown skin.

The guy was not hard on the eyes either. He looked vaguely familiar. He walked forward, and she wondered again if she should try to shift.

SEVEN

"*D*on't do it, Sophia. It's too dangerous with two animals inside you. Your first shift should not be during a stressful situation like this one. If something goes wrong, it'd be a problem we don't need at this moment," Chase stated matter-of-factly in her head and continued to fight.

She bristled, hating how much sense he made. Her cat hissed, and her wolf growled.

He made a valid case for waiting. Still, maybe she could find a way to defend herself; she did have claws, and this guy didn't know that she was now a shifter.

There was enough blood being spilled that she knew he hadn't picked up her scent, and from what she could tell, hyenas weren't as sensitive as wolves and cats. She stood, patiently waiting. The intruder came closer.

"Dr. Sophia Reese, why don't you make this easy on the wolf and come with me now. We'll let him go, and he won't come to any harm." The man had a loud voice with a whiny pitch to it.

"Really? What will you do with me?"

She watched the man and knew he was assessing her, so she hunched her shoulders and tried to look scared.

"You won't come to any harm if you give us the experiment you've been working on." He seemed to relax which made her want to pounce on his dumb ass.

"I don't know what you mean, but I do know one thing. Chase is going to rip you all limb from limb." She gave him a happy smile.

She prayed one of the animals inside her body was willing to come to her aid. She envisioned her fingers shifting. The man made a grab for her arm. Long, razor-sharp claws stretched out of where her nails would normally be.

Not wasting a second, she turned her body into the man's, catching him unaware because of her sudden proximity and speed that, she had to admit, had impressed even her. Without a second thought, she buried her claws straight in his jugular, ripping his throat open when she yanked roughly on the soft flesh.

Blood sputtered and splattered all over her face. His shocked, wide eyes stared at her while his claws squeezed painfully into her arm. Fear that he might still hurt her engulfed her for a moment until she saw his large body slump to the floor by her feet.

Nausea rolled up her throat. She watched the man bleed to death.

"Sophia." Chase's growl snapped her out of her trance.

She jumped and turned horror-filled eyes to gawk at Chase's human body. Since he shifted, she was able to see the multiple cuts and bites that covered him.

She tried to swallow down the bile threatening to come out, but her stomach recoiled. For her, it was one thing to say she would kill someone, and quite another to actually do it. She darted past the bloody scene, her sneakers squeaking, and slid over a pool of blood and almost fell on her ass.

Sophia made it to the attached bathroom in the lab just in time to lose all the contents of her stomach in the toilet. Her body heaved until all she could do was gag when nothing else came out.

Chase walked in a moment later in his jeans.

After she rinsed her mouth, he helped her clean her face. He used wet paper towels to get rid of the spots of blood that had splashed her when she tore the hyena's throat out.

"Are you all right?" He spoke softly and caressed her cheek with a warm hand while his eyes took in her probably still green face.

"Yes, I…I've never done anything like that before. It was too much. All that blood, and something inside of me wanted to keeping going, to shred the man apart." She was filled with alarm at the thought.

He pulled her into his arms and held her for a moment. His warmth helped alleviate some of the panic inside her. He bent down and kissed her lightly.

"Come on. We need to get out of here before any others show up." He pulled her down the hallway and back to his car.

"I need to talk to my boss. We can't just leave the bodies there," she said.

"I've got that covered," he said. "Don't worry about it. Let's just get you out of here."

In the car, he buckled her in.

"Where are we going?" She leaned back on the headrest and closed her eyes, tuning out what had taken place a few moments before. She was too tired to dissect anything else for the night.

"To my house. It's a little farther down from River and Julia, but they'll be coming over in the morning to catch up." He pulled out his phone and thumbed his keys.

She felt like she'd run a marathon and needed a week's worth of sleep.

Sophia wondered who he was talking to on the phone. "I need a cleaning crew at the lab pronto. Multiple bodies. Mostly hyenas. One human." After a pause, he said, "Yes, I said hyenas."

She drifted, and the motion of the vehicle lulled her to sleep. The rest of Chase's conversation was lost on her.

Her stomach was burning and she was starving, but she refused to leave the soothing bliss she found in her dreamlike state. Soon she was lifted, and she curled into the heat of the man holding her.

Strong hands undressed and lowered her into a warm pool of water, washing her and almost pulling her awake, but it was too hard to open her eyes.

Afterward, she was placed on a big, soft bed. She snuggled into the pillow and blanket, and Chase's scent surrounded her. She sighed in contentment and allowed sleep to take over.

* * *

"Sophia." Chase's voice was low but firm. "Hmm?" She sounded more asleep than awake. "Wake up, love. You need to eat." He kissed her ear, licking the shell, and she moaned.

She blinked her eyes open, and he smiled at her sleepy look.

"What? What's wrong?" She sat up and peered around the room.

"You need to eat. Here, munch on this and I'll bring you some other stuff after." He helped fix pillows behind her back and set a tray on her lap. He brought her steak, chicken, and a bunch of side dishes. She gave him a sleepy look as she assessed the amount of food on her plate.

"I'll bring more in a moment, but you need to eat that first." He knew she'd eat that and more.

"Are you crazy? I couldn't possibly eat all

this. I'll turn into a cow," she grumbled but grabbed the fork and knife and cut into the steak.

She chewed through the entire tray full of food, and when he brought a second tray with fruit, chocolate cake, and warm bread, she dove through that as well.

After he took the tray away from her, he sat on the edge of the bed and looked at her with critical eyes. "How are you feeling?" He could see she had a hard time keeping her eyes open once her stomach was full.

"Sleepy…so tired." She yawned and leaned back, closing her eyes once again.

Chase watched as Sophia slept. He needed to figure out how to help her cope with her new situation. At least she'd eaten enough to not have to bother her for a while.

He stepped into his kitchen and glanced from Julia to River, who both looked troubled.

"So? Do we know why she's so tired?" River asked.

"Chase, she's been sleeping for over twelve hours. This can't be normal. Even I don't sleep that long and I'm pregnant." She toyed with her teacup as she spoke.

Chase didn't want to divulge his mate's

business to anyone but saw the need to add some insight into Sophia's situation. He'd already called in the pack doctor and asked enough questions to have a clear understanding of what was happening to her. She'd told him to call her if necessary, but he'd put that off unless things changed for the worse.

"Sophia has been through a lot. I think her body is finally shutting down and taking the rest it needs to handle the stress she's been through."

"Did she get hurt yesterday?" Julia's eyes flashed.

"Not physically. I think she was shocked at how bloodthirsty the animals she has can be. It will take her time to come to terms with it." He sat on a chair and ran a hand through his hair.

"I'm going to talk to our guys to find out who in that lab has hyena connections." Chase turned to look at Julia. "I'm going to ask you to stay here and watch her until we come back. I don't want her to go more than a few hours without eating."

"Of course, go and don't worry about her. I'll take care of sleeping beauty." She turned to her husband, gave him a stern look, and then glanced back to Chase. "Be careful, both of you. I don't want to have to explain to my sister why someone got hurt and make her feel like it's her fault. So bring your asses back here in one piece."

* * *

Sitting off to one corner at The Back Door with a couple of beers in front of them, Chase and River watched two of their pack members come toward their booth.

Being an hour past lunchtime, the bar was settling down from the throng of hungry patrons.

Riel and Seff slid into the booth across from River and Chase. Both were enforcers, but Seff tended to be a bit more strict and military, while Riel was a fun- loving guy who always got his job done.

Seff glanced from River to Chase and leaned forward on the table. "You needed to see us?"

"Yeah, first off, thanks for handling the clean-up at the lab. It got messy quickly," Chase said. "Did you get the vials and papers on the table before you left?"

The men looked at each other. Seff said, "There was nothing on any of the tables or counters. It was spotless, except for the blood and guts slung around."

"Oh no." Chase dropped his head into his hands. Someone had taken her work. The one thing they were trying to prevent happened anyway. One good thing about them getting the data was they would leave Sophia alone now. They didn't need her. That made his wolf almost giddy with relief.

Now, he just needed to find out who "they" were.

"Don't worry about it. Instead, I need you to get some information for me. I want to know who's in charge of the research facility, in front and behind the scenes. Shifter, human, witch, demon, everyone. I need this yesterday."

Riel's brows lifted at the request while Seff looked like he had been expecting it.

"Any particular reason?" the younger wolf queried.

River jumped in to answer. "Yes, my sister-in-law is the head researcher and top geneticist. Way too smart for her own good since she figured out how to suppress the shifting gene in our DNA."

Seff had a look of stunned disbelief.

"Why the hell would she do that? Is she crazy?" Riel burst out unthinking.

"My mate," Chase stated, "was trying to

do something nice by giving Julia the choice of changing back."

Seff stared at his leader, unwavering. "There's something else, though, isn't there?"

"Yes. In the process of separating the DNA strands she…had an accident. Sophia is now a dual shifter. She has two different female animals inside."

With their collective indrawn breaths, he knew they were taken aback.

Seff seemed to recover first from his shock. "Two different breeds? And are they both alphas?"

"Yes. Apparently, the pure cat and wolf strands bonded with her DNA so seamlessly, it's like she was born a pure-blood shifter. Both animals seem to be getting along. I'm not sure how long that's going to last, though."

His fear was that the stress on her body by her new physiology would kill her. The animals inside her were powerful and drained a lot of energy.

"So you've mated this woman?" Seff asked.

"Yes, her name is Dr. Sophia Reese. You'll both get an e-mail with her file so you can acquaint yourselves with her information." He ran a hand over the back of his neck and thought of Sophia's exhausted form. She was pale and had already lost weight.

"Don't worry, Chase, we'll find out what's going on at the lab right away." Seff grasped his forearm.

"That's all we have for now. I'm sure someone in that lab knows something and I want to know what's going on." He growled and fisted his hands on the table.

All three men nodded.

River cleared his throat and caught their attention. "Sophia is presently with Julia at Chase's. Chase and I will be taking turns with the women, while we dig around to find out more about these hyenas and hopefully find out who's behind them. Call either of us as soon as you know anything."

Chase's cell phone went off. He saw Julia's name and accepted the call immediately. "Julia?"

"She's awake. She's saying she's feeling better, but she looks pale, Chase. I fed her again. It seems that hunger is the only thing that wakes her. She's fighting off sleep until she sees you." Julia's panic came through the phone line.

"I'm on my way." Chase shut the call off and dropped the phone in his shirt pocket. He looked at the guys, wished them luck on their search, and reminded them this was their priority.

"One last thing, Chase," Seff said, holding him from leaving. "In the lab last night, there was a smell of a shifter we've never come across before."

"What?" Chase asked. How could that be?

"Yeah," Riel added, "We have no idea what type of shifter had been there."

Chase gave them a worried nod and hurried toward the bar's front door. Someone new was in his town and he needed to find out who and what they wanted.

* * *

"Where is Chase?" Sophia frowned, trying to clear her mind from the wave of exhaustion calling her back to sleep. She wondered what the hell was wrong with her body.

"He went to see what he could find out about the research lab and try to figure out who could be behind the attempt on your work. He'll be back really soon, baby girl. Are you still hungry?" Julia sat by the bed holding her hand.

Sophia smiled at her sister's use of the childhood pet name for her and shook her head at the question. "Yes, but I need a shower. I need to get rid of this sleep before it overwhelms me again. Give me a few minutes, and then we can have some coffee or something." She felt marginally better standing. She stretched tired muscles and headed to the shower for a nice, cool soak.

After the shower, she was less sleepy and finally felt she could function without dropping into an exhausted heap. She dressed in shorts and a tank top that she found lying on the bed, along with new underwear.

She made her way to the kitchen and finally took in the house that belonged to her mate.

Glancing around, she realized the house fit with him, and it really was Chase's space. It was clean, open, and uncluttered. The furniture was for comfort, not show. She fell in love with it.

And who was sitting on the sofa with her back Sophia? She breathed in a new scent as the person on the couch did the same. The woman turned with a smile. Tryx!

"OMG, girl," the baker extraordinaire said

to Sophia, "you've changed so much already!" She rushed around the furniture and gave Sophia a hug. "How are you feeling?"

Sophia shrugged. "Other than being tired, I'm okay."

Julia walked up behind her, a tray with mugs in her hands. "Just you wait and see what your new cousin brought with her."

Sophia followed the two into the living room and to the sofa. The grandest sight she'd seen in a long time greeted her, on the coffee table.

A large spread of delicatessens covered the glass top. Sweet breads, donuts, cream cake, sliced meats, rolls, did she mention donuts? There was also a huge variety of cheeses. Yum.

Sophia sat in front of the table and dug in. "Sorry if I'm being rude," she said, "but since this shifter thing, I've been constantly starving. It's like my body can't catch up with the energy it needs."

Tryx glanced at Julia. "That's to be expected," Tryx replied. "Your body is still adjusting to the changes. Until your metabolism finds its balance, you'll probably be craving food."

"No shit to that," Julia said. "I never ate half as much as she has. She could give River and Chase a run for their money when it comes to cleaning out the fridge." The girls laughed.

Tryx grabbed a piece of sliced roast beef. "I thought this smorgasbord might make a good snack for everyone."

"I fully agree," Sophia agreed. Everyone was quiet, ignoring the elephant—well, wolves—in the room.

Finally, Tryx said, "Sophia, you know there's a lot of great things about being a shifter. Shifting itself isn't the only thing."

"She's right," Julia continued, "you can smell who's around you without looking. Oh, and your glasses. You don't have them on."

"I didn't even realize I wasn't wearing them until after showering. It's better than Lasik. And free," Sophia added. "So, I'll admit it isn't as bad as I thought it would be."

"And," Tryx threw in, "you know when you've met your true mate by smell. No questioning, no dating needed. You're already perfect for each other."

Sophia asked, "Concerning mates, Tryx, why haven't you taken a mate?" She rationalized that if Tryx had someone to help her in the bakery, the woman wouldn't have to work so hard.

Tryx blushed and looked down. "I'm

holding out, hoping to find my true."

"Wait," Sophia questioned, "what happens if you don't meet him? I mean, how do you find one person in seven billion? You've been alone all these years?"

Tryx snorted. "All these years? How old do you think I am, lady?" Sophia's eyes widened. Did she just insult her new friend?

"Sorry," she said. "I—"

"You're fine, missy. I'm just giving you a hard time," Tryx replied. "Lighten up, girl." She snatched up a piece of cheese. "To answer your question, I haven't been alone all this time. For several years, I was with a human male.

"The man, Ernest, was an angel. He'd do anything for me. I loved him even though he wasn't my true mate. We enjoyed each other's company and he made me laugh. He was the next best thing to a true mate."

"What happened to him?" Julia asked.

Sophia threw a grape at her sister. "Julia, you don't ask people questions like that. You're being nosy."

Tryx laughed. "No, it's fine. It happened a long time ago. You're right to wonder how old I am. Shifters age differently than humans. Ernest died in his sixties from heart disease.

That was about twenty years ago."

"I'm sorry to hear that, Tryx," Sophia said. "Are you looking for someone else?"

The baker shook her head. "No. It hurt so much when I lost Ernest that I didn't want to go through it again. Plus, no one in Black Meadows does it for me."

"No hot and bothered from anyone?" Sophia asked? She couldn't believe she was asking such personal questions. Normally, she barely talked to anyone. She liked this type of interaction. Too bad she discovered that so late in life.

Tryx laughed. "No. No hot and bothered. Barely a 'warm and interested.' Who knows what will happen in the future. Maybe I'm not destined to meet him. You two are really lucky and the whole town is thrilled. You will make us stronger by controlling the men. Of course, the men don't know that, but the women do." She gave Sophia a wink.

Sophia gave the women a quizzical expression. "You both know these animals in my body are new for me, right?" Both ladies nodded. "Besides the general shifter stuff I already know from Julia, what else should I be aware of?"

Julia and Tryx shared a look.

Tryx turned to her. "I'm not sure what you mean?"

"You know, biological stuff that's embarrassing to talk about." Sophia rolled her eyes. The "old" her would never, ever bring up a topic like this, but the "new" her had no problem with it.

"Have you shifted into one of your animals yet?" Tryx asked.

Sophia gasped at the thought. At the lab, she so wanted to shift to help Chase. Since then, she hadn't even thought about it.

"Let's do it!" she said jumping to her feet, food forgotten.

Julia slowly stood. "I don't know about this, Tryx. I didn't do so well with my first shift. Maybe we should wait for Chase."

Tryx put a hand on Julia's shoulder. "You shouldn't have shifted so soon, Julia. Your body wasn't ready yet. Why your wolf pushed so hard, I'm not sure." The woman took a scared looking Julia into a hug. "Plus, you weren't prepared for what would happen. Sophia is more than ready to do this."

Sophia nodded in agreement. She was *so* ready. Julia stepped out of Tryx's embrace.

"You're right. Sophia is ready. Chase keeps saying her conversion was like she was born a shifter."

Sophia hugged her sister. "I love you, little sis. You know that." There wasn't anything she wouldn't do for her sibling. Hell, she'd given up the past six months of her life to find a way to stop exactly what she was getting ready to do. Ironic.

Julia sniffed. "Yes, I know. Now stop making me cry and let's get this done. Damn hormones." Julia laid a hand on her tiny baby bump.

Sophia snorted at that comment. She knew damn well hormones weren't the underlying factor. Can you say Drama Queen?

"Okay, I need to undress, right?" Sophia asked.

"If you don't want to ruin your clothes, sure," Tryx replied.

Julia pulled a blanket off the sofa. "Lie on the floor and cover up."

In seconds, a naked Sophia lay on her back, too excited to stay still. "Now what? How do I start it?"

Tryx's eyes widened and a sour smell floated in the air. Sophia took that scent to be fear.

"What's wrong, Tryx? I'm okay," Sophia

reassured.

"No, it's..." Tryx glanced at Julia. "To start, you just think about your animal and let them do their thing. But, Sophia, you have *two* animals. I don't know what will happen."

Understanding shone in Julia's eyes. "We're not doing this. Not without the alpha."

"Oh, this is such bull crap, and you know it," Sophia spit out. "I'll be fine. I can't be the only person who ever had dual shifters."

Both ladies looked at her with their brows raised.

"Okay," she conceded, "never mind. Just stand back and let me handle this."

Sophia closed her eyes and focused on the entities within her. As her conscience turned inward, an image of a golden lioness and grey/tan wolf appeared in her mind's eye. They lay beside each other looking up at her like she was a freak.

Could she talk to them in her mind? Only one way to find out.

Hi, gals. How's it going?

Two snuffs blew in her face.

Guess that means you're both doing great. She studied the two before her. *Look, ladies, I don't know how you want to handle this shifting thing.*

We're in uncharted territory here.

A word entered her head in a low whisper, and she instinctively knew it was her lioness speaking.

Choose.

Whoa, hold on a minute. I want both of you. Will one of you get mad if I pick the other? I mean, Julia hated when Mom let me go first because I was older.

Two more snuffs peppered her face. She swore she could feel the moisture on her skin.

This time, the wolf spoke. *We don't have penises to argue over whose is bigger. We work together like females do.*

Well, she knew who the feminist was in the group.

Great, let's get this going then.

Her heart rate picked up and her pulse pounded in her ears. Oh shit, she forgot to ask Tryx if this was going to hurt.

* * *

Suddenly, the animals were gone from Sophia's mind. Had they abandoned her because she wasn't a real shifter?

Blackness surrounded her. The only thing

136

she could hear was the blood pumping against her eardrums. Then the first sting hit her. Maybe a bit more than a sting. More like getting hit by a Mac truck.

Sophia sucked in a sharp breath and bit down on her tongue to keep from yelling out. Another Mac slammed into her.

Soft, warm hands cradled her cheeks. "Don't fight it, Sophia. The first time is hardest. Let it happen. Let it roll through you like standing under a waterfall."

A waterfall. What a beautiful image compared to the pain rocking her body. She took another breath and imagined herself under the falling water, naked. And Chase was there, walking toward her, naked, too. And his rod was not for fishing.

Hot damn, she liked where this was leading.

She felt her body racked with the pain that went along with it, but it was dulled back to the point she could handle it. The power of the mind was amazing. But still, she'd probably never shift again. Her pain tolerance was the size of her big toe.

Next she knew, she was looking up at Tryx and Julia. If she'd had her phone, she'd snap a photo of their faces and post it. They were so damn funny. She laughed, but it came out as a snuff.

What the fuck? She jumped to her feet, all four of them. *Oh my god*, she yelled in her excited mind. She had shifted into a... Wait, she wasn't sure what she was. Her two front legs were a golden color, but they weren't cat paws.

Mirror. She had to find a mirror. Bathroom. Go.

Her body moved so gracefully. She tried to watch how her feet didn't trip over each other. After hitting the recliner, she decided she didn't need to know. Her animals did and she was happy with that.

In the bathroom, she put her front paws on the counter and looked into the mirror. Well, her guess was that she was a lioness-colored wolf. Had a wolf ever had golden fur?

The bathroom light came on. She didn't even notice it was off. Wow.

"You're beautiful, Sophia," Tryx said. "I've never seen that color before on a wolf."

She smiled and glanced in the mirror. Shit, that was scary looking—all those teeth. She made a mental note not to smile in wolf form.

Outside, vehicle doors slammed shut. She heard the crunch of gravel as the visitors walked. Amazing.

"That must be the guys," Julia said, rushing out. Her sister stopped and turned to her. "Umm, don't come out yet. Let *me* tell Chase. He won't hurt a pregnant woman."

Sophia snorted. Chase would never hurt anyone unless they deserved it. Shifting did not fall in that category.

While the two women went to greet the men, she sneaked to the corner and peered around. River was kissing his wife as she held the door for Chase who was jogging to catch up.

Automatically, she dropped to a pounce position with her head lowered to the ground and butt in the air. She wiggled with anticipation. Waiting.

As soon as Chase was at the door, she tore from around the corner and launched into the air. Her mate caught her from reflex alone. His expression was confusion.

She took the moment to kiss him, which displayed in slobbery licks up the sides of his face. Then, she wiggled out of his hold and zoomed out the door.

Running as fast as she could, she made for the forest. The feelings flowing through her were incredible. She'd never felt so alive, so a part of the planet around her.

She glanced back to see if anyone was following her. Whoa—what was that? She wiggled her butt. OH MY GOD. She had a tail! Turning her upper body, she wanted to get a better look at it, but it kept moving out of her sight. She stepped toward it and it moved again. Dammit. Turning more, she almost got a good look until it slipped out of her vision again.

Shit. She'd look at it later. Time to go on.

Everything had a smell. Grass, dirt, air, dead leaves, pine needles, trees...bugs? She skidded to a stop and studied the tiny creatures scurrying at her feet. She heard their scuttle over the ground.

She dipped her head down until her snout hovered over the animals. Then took a deep breath, which was a mistake.

The small critters, very light in weight, went straight up her nasal passages. She stumbled backward, immediately sneezing several times. Dizzy from the sudden onslaught, she fell to a sitting position. Sitting for a wolf, which was partially standing up to her.

Laughter came from behind her. Her head whipped around, a low growl emanating from her chest. Her eyes scanned the trees, searching for the culprit. She hesitated sucking in another breath to catch the smell.

Then there he was, in all his wolfy glory. Her mate. Chase. His tongue hung out the side of his mouth. She recognized that as his gorgeous smile.

Springing to her feet, she jumped at him, nipping at his shoulders and bouncing around. In her head, this time, she heard Chase's human laugh.

"Calm down, my love."

No way, Jose. She bowled into his center, taking them both rolling to the ground. Then she was up and sprinting away.

"Catch me if you can!"

A devilish feeling entered her mind from Chase's thoughts. "Challenge accepted, little one. To the victor goes the spoils, which will be your body going to me."

"*If* you catch me." She was already out of sight of him. She knew he was back there, following her scent. That made her run faster.

Dodging trees and soaring over downed logs, Sophia felt as though she were flying.

What was that?

Off to the side, a squirrel jumped down

from a tree. Both animals inside her zeroed in on it. The little thing swallowed hard, then ran for its life.

Sophia peeled rubber trying to gain purchase to chase. Her animals chanted: gotta have it, get it, get it, get it. She wasn't sure what they'd do if they caught it, but if they ate it, she'd throw-up for days.

The small animal leapt for a tree, its feet grabbing ahold of the bark and scampered up.

Not a problem, her cat said. Her animal jumped for the tree.

What the hell are you doing? Wolves don't climb trees.

We aren't a wolf was the reply. Oh, so they were a lioness?

No.

No? What were they then?

We are that which has no name.

Oooh, how Voldemortish of you.

Just before her canine paws touched the tree, her feet morphed to that of a cat and strong claws dug into the bark and wood.

Holy shit! She clung. Not only that, but raced up the trunk after the critter. Sophia had forgotten about the squirrel already, too entranced with everything happening to her body.

The small animal skittered out a thin limb and jumped to another tree. Sophia came to a sudden stop. Even her adrenaline-filled companions knew they couldn't go out on that limb.

That's when she looked down.

Bad move.

A wave of dizziness hit her at how up she was. Thirty feet maybe? Enough to kill her if she fell. Sophia wrestled for control. She had to save them. Her cat and wolf fought like hell.

"Sophia, stop," Chase said in his human voice. She almost looked down at him, but changed her mind. Her mate probably wouldn't appreciate puke landing on his head right now.

"Sophia, don't fight your animal. Let her take charge. She knows what's she's doing."

But, but…

"Do you think you're the first wolf to get stuck in a tree?"

Yeah, she was thinking she probably was. She took a mental deep breath and stepped back. She'd trust her companions, until proven unwise. Her body descended while she held her breath.

A couple yards off the ground, her animal, whichever was in charge at that point, pushed away from the tree. The claws changed back to wolf paws in time for her mate to catch her again.

Her weight and momentum carried them backward and to the ground. She gave him a wet lick up the face and raced off. He didn't really catch her yet. And she had a head start while he collected himself and shifted.

This was the most fun she'd ever had in her life. Even her childhood couldn't measure up to this sense of freedom. No wonder Julia was okay with staying a shifter. If Sophia would've known, she wouldn't have wasted these past months locked up in the lab, looking for a cure.

She slowed when she came to a creek. The embankment was rather steep and she wasn't sure about getting we—

A heavy weight slammed into her and she tumbled down the side along with another body. Her nose told her it was her mate. Oh yeah, she'd almost forgotten about him in her elation.

With a huge splash, she and Chase landed in the water, drenched from head to paws.

She got to her feet and shook her body like

a canine would.

"Great," she said to his mind, "now I'm gonna smell like wet dog all day." She was sure he heard the playfulness in her tone.

He did. "Well, then," he said, "maybe you need to clean up better." At that, he jumped toward her, making her skip deeper into the water to not get squished.

"Chase!" she hollered, "this is not funny." But her animals thought it was. They recognized his wolf as her mate and the alpha of the pack. But he'd better not try to push the alpha thing too far or she'd have to bite his ass. Which sounded like a rather good idea.

He snapped his head up and eyed her. "You smell too edible, my love. What are you thinking? Hmm."

She laughed. "You haven't caught me yet." She doggy paddled to the other side and climbed the rocky mud wall only to be promptly mushed to the ground.

What the—

Teeth clamped down on her scruff, pinning her. A scorching heat seared her veins, feeling so delicious.

"No teasing with that smell, love," Chase said. "I will hunt you down and take what I want. And you will love it."

Oh God. She could come on the spot with the power of his words swirling in her. Except as a wolf, that seemed weird. Did animals have orgasms? She never thought about it before, for good reason. Sex would be confined to human form only.

The pressure on her back let up.

"Come," her mate said, "let me teach you some things."

She balked. Her animals knew what everything was. Her cat got her out of the tree, so...

"Well," he said in her head, "she didn't warn you not to inhale deeply when a pile of ants were under your nose."

If an animal could blush, hers would be right now. "Oh. You saw that?"

He gave her a lick up the side of her furry face.

"Yup. Funniest damn thing I'd seen in a long time."

A growl came out her throat. "Shut up! It's my first time."

"Exactly, love."

For the next several hours, he showed her the best way to stalk prey and hunt, put names to the new scents she experienced, and let her run after butterflies.

With an exhausted breath, she plopped onto the ground in a patch of sun. She was pooped. Chase settled and snuggled up to her.

"Enjoying being in nature in your shifted form?" he asked.

She glanced at him. "I've never been so elated in my life. Never felt so free, so in tune."

He chuckled. "I'm glad. You are absolutely stunning. The entire pack will be in awe of you."

That tweaked a bit of uneasiness in her stomach. That whole thing about being the center of attention, again.

"Why is that?" she asked.

"You should see you how I see you. I've never witnessed anything like it before."

"How so?" What was so different about her? Well, except the whole cat paws on a wolf body thing climbing the tree.

"Your animals — for lack of better word — have melded. You have a wolf body, but you're able to maneuver like a cat," he said.

"What's the difference?"

"It's huge," he answered. "Cats are much faster than any other animal. You noticed I didn't catch you when you were running."

"I just thought you were letting me get away to prolong the chase."

"Okay, you can think of it that way." He winked at her. He laid his head on his paws and stared at her with big, round puppy dog eyes.

She started feeling antsy and uncomfortable under such scrutiny. But he was damn adorable.

"It's okay, love," he said. "I'm just staring at your beauty. I can't get enough of you. It's like I want to squish you into my body so I can have all of you with me every second of the day."

Aww. She was going to cry. Nobody had ever said anything like that to her before. Growing up, she'd always been the geeky kid — short, overweight, glasses slipping down her nose, constantly reading a book, knowing all the answers on tests.

But now, she was like everyone else, in a way.

Another good thing — she was, for the first time in her life, a natural blonde.

You're welcome, her cat purred.

"I have something to confess," Chase

suddenly said. The worst went through Sophia's mind. He cheated on her already, he didn't love her, he didn't want her around anymore. She got a wet slap on the side of her face.

"Stop thinking about whatever you're thinking," he scolded. "It's not bad." He sighed. "I just want you to know that before you were a shifter, I wanted to get to know you as much as I do now."

"Oh," she said, "'get to know you' as in nonstop sex for days?"

"God, woman. You make me sound like a hound dog," he complained. "But, maybe, yes, sex crossed my mind a time or two...hundred."

She laughed. Men. She asked, "Then why didn't you say something?"

"Because every time I entered a room, you'd walk out. I thought you hated me for what happened to your sister."

Memories of Julia's attack came back. That seemed so long ago. A different lifetime.

"No, Chase," she said, "I never hated you for any reason. In fact, it was the opposite."

"What do you mean?"

"I left the room because I was so attracted

to you and knew you'd never want to spend time with someone like me."

"Why wouldn't I? You're freakin' perfect."

"Not compared to your last runway model girlfriend."

"Oh, her." She heard the resignation in his voice. "She was a nice person, but not my type. I had to attend a human function for networking and somehow River came up with her for a date for me. He said it wouldn't look good if I went alone."

"But I saw her with you another time," Sophia said.

"We hung out for a couple more days and figured out we weren't a match. She wanted the glitz and glamor. I wanted simple and easy. Plus, she was way too skinny. She looked horrible to me. Skeletal."

Sophia had to agree with that. "So you're saying I look good to you?"

He nosed her under her neck. "More than good, baby doll. More like scrumptious. How many times have I eaten you?"

Heat shot to her face. Thank God, he couldn't see the blush. He laughed, though.

Chase went on. "What I'm trying to say is you're the one for me, Sophia. My true mate. I want you to be with me till the day we draw our last breath."

Both her animals sighed in her head. "You are the only one for us. Always have been since the night I saw you at the hospital." Her stomach growled.

Chase laughed. "Your stomach is either agreeing or telling us to get our butts home for dinner."

She gave him a big lick and took off in a sprint. "Last one home has to go 'downtown' first."

Her mate gave chase, but didn't seem to mind coming in second place.

EIGHT

After dinner, Tryx said her goodbyes and Sophia and Chase bade her sister and River a good night to retire to their bedroom. The minute he got her upstairs he tried to tell her to go to sleep, but she would have none of it.

Stripping down to nothing, she started pulling off his clothes while he grumbled that she was tired and needed to rest. Still, he didn't try to stop her when she pushed him to lie on his back and straddled his hips.

She bent and rubbed her naked breasts on his chest while their mouths fused for a scorching kiss. His hands caressed her back in soft circles, trailing down to squeeze her ass cheeks.

She kissed his neck and slowly licked her way down to his nipples. Running her tongue in circles over the tight buds, she nipped lightly and blew cool air over the sensitive skin. He groaned.

Moving down, she licked and sucked her way to his hard cock. Her face was just inches from the thick, velvet-covered, steel pole. When she looked up, she saw him tensely gripping the comforter in his fists.

"I thought the loser had to go down first," he said.

"Eh," Sophia said, "I changed my mind. I didn't want to wait to taste you."

Licking her lips, she smiled up at him, noting the flare in his eyes. She wrapped a hand around his hard length and slowly pumped him from root to tip.

Chase moaned when she repeated the action, and a bead of liquid trickled from his slit. She spread the fluid as she pumped, lubricating his dick to a glossy shine. Then she lowered her lips to run her tongue in a slow circle over the crown of his cock.

God, but he tasted good. His flesh was hot and smooth. She inhaled his manly musky scent.

She moved her jaw and rubbed the underside of the plump head with her lips. His hips jerked, and he pushed his cock into her mouth. She kept a firm hold and slowly worked more of his hard length in until he hit the back of her throat.

Then she pulled him out and did it over again until he was slick. Her cheeks hollowed in tight suction while she slid him down her throat.

Her saliva slid down the sides of his cock as she continued to blow him. His hands had moved to hold her hair away from her face so he could watch her mouth. The entranced wonder on his face made her want to make it absolutely perfect for him. His eyes darkened when she took him in and hummed her pleasure in the back of her throat.

"Sophia, baby," he groaned. "You're fucking perfect but...you have to stop, or I'm gonna come in your mouth..."

She clamped her lips tighter and sucked harder while her hand pumped his lower half. His hands tightened in her hair, and his hips thrust his cock harder into her mouth.

That's what she wanted, for him to lose control. To let her pleasure him until he couldn't hold back. Her pussy soaked when she watched his reaction.

"Sweetheart…" he growled.

He tried to pull her head away, but she continued to pump his length and suck hard on him. She opened her throat more and took in as much of him as she could, curling her fingers around his ass and digging her nails into his cheeks.

The small, aggressive move was enough to take him over the edge. He came with a shout of her name and jerked in her mouth. She swallowed as much of his hot release as she could, but he kept coming, so she let go of him with her lips and moved his pulsating cock to spew over her breasts. His hot semen dripped down her front while her own juices soaked her thighs.

Chase stared in fascination when Sophia held his cock, licked his length, and then rubbed his seed over her breasts. The sight was so hot he became hard again while watching her.

One of her small hands massaged and tweaked a slippery nipple while the other rubbed the swollen lips of her cunt, dipping one finger into her sex. She looked into his eyes, and he could see the lust riding her.

She moaned in need. "Fuck me, Chase."

In the blink of an eye, she was on her

back. He thrust his cock into her slick cunt in one smooth move. She moaned with each hard thrust.

Desperation drove them both. Her nails dug into his shoulders. She pulled him farther in her and wrapped her legs tightly around his ass.

She lifted her hips off the bed, tilting her pelvis to bring him even deeper in her.

He growled and fucked her like the animal he had inside. With every thrust he slammed deep in her, moving her body up the bed and then hauling her back down to do it again. She whimpered and purred, coming closer to orgasm.

"Look at me. You're mine, Sophia," he growled.

Her gaze locked with his. "Yes, yours." Her head flew back, breaking eye contact with him.

"Who do you belong to?" His hands cushioned her head, pushing her to look at him once again.

"You, Chase. Only you," she moaned.

"Baby, you feel so good."

"Harder, Chase...please."

Her body tensed, and her legs started shaking. He rocked his hips, and his dick hit her at an angle that caused her breath to hitch. He moved a hand between her thighs and rubbed a thumb over her swollen nub. Once, twice, and on the third touch, he pinched her clit and rammed her pussy with his cock. She screamed and splintered into oblivion.

Her vaginal walls fluttered and contracted around his driving shaft. Above her, he groaned, stiffened, and jerked inside her, filling her with his semen. Her sex clenched and sucked his release deep into her womb.

She was exhausted and ready to fall into sleep.

She completely ignored the sticky mess she was covered in. He left and returned a few minutes later to carry her to the bathroom. He had drawn a bath. Then he washed them both and finally allowed her to get some rest.

* * *

"What do you mean the guy's dead?" Ratface asked his boss on the phone. "Was it the serum you used on him?"

"Of course, it was the serum, stupid ass," the boss yelled back. "What the fuck else would it be? I swear. Sometimes, you hyenas are so damn dumb."

Ratface cringed at the verbal abuse. Though he didn't know why. He should've been used to it by now. It brought up inner survival instincts he learned as a child to escape other kids when they meant to beat him.

"You said you took the scientist's stuff off the table in her lab yourself. What do you want me to do? I got the team in there like you wanted. We did our part and are leaving."

"Don't back talk me, you piece of shit." The boss was pissed beyond anything he'd ever seen. What were this data and sample stuff that was so important to have? "Whatever was on the table isn't the right serum. We have to find a way to get to the woman herself. Only she knows where the correct ones are."

Ratface smiled. "I know exactly how to do that with some help from her friends."

* * *

Sophia woke to the smell of food. Her stomach grumbled and cramped until hunger pangs dragged her out of bed. While she was dressing, she could hear voices coming from the kitchen.

There was Julia's soft pacifying tone, River's clear questions, and Chase's sexy deep growl. There were also two others she didn't recognize.

"Good, you're up. We were wondering if you were planning on showing up. Chase wouldn't let us eat until you came down. He said it was rude. I'm Riel, by the way." He winked at her when she walked into the kitchen, and she smiled at his easy charm.

They all sat around the dining room table talking over coffee and tea.

Chase stood to give her a kiss that was cut short after a few fake coughs and groans intruded. She felt her face flame and pulled up a chair to join them.

The two men whom she'd never met stood and bowed their heads.

Riel smiled. "It's an honor to meet our leader's chosen mate." He bowed and took a seat.

She smiled and blushed again. "Thank you. It's nice to meet you, too."

The other man, who seemed to be older and much more intense, had been watching her with a closed expression. He dipped his head. "It's my pleasure to welcome you into our pack, Dr. Reese. My name is Seff, and I am at your service." He kept his voice formal.

"Please, call me Sophia. It's nice to meet you, too, Seff." She smiled. She sat, and everyone started talking at once.

"So, tell me what you have learned." Chase spoke over the conversations and brought the discussion back to the main business of the lab.

The tension instantly filled the room. Whatever the men had to share wasn't good.

"The employees inside the lab have all been verified. We had to look deeper into their lives to see if there were any strange links. You know Dr. Warren?" Sophia nodded. "It seems he's got very little love for shifters and humans alike. He likes to believe he's going to discover the next big drug, so he takes exception to a young woman telling him what to do," Seff said, looking around the table. "Anyway, he's got witches and other shifters in the family, but no hyenas."

Riel took over and added what he knew. "We looked into Sophia's direct employees. All employees have shifters, witches, or humans in their families, but none have any hyena relations. Not sure where that link is coming in, but I'll look into everyone working in the lab and on the research." Riel lifted his coffee and took a sip.

"I've been trying to get access to the security footage from the night you both got attacked," River joined in. "It seems my guys can't find any evidence of a recording for that evening. Apparently, the system malfunctioned and stopped recording, making it impossible for us to see what happened."

"Did anyone find out why there was no one around when we got attacked?" Sophia asked. "That lab is extremely busy on a regular day, and even on evenings you'll find people working well into the night, waiting on some result or jotting down notes on their work. It was strange to see that nobody was there. It was as if everyone had been told to leave."

Seff said he'd find out more from employees and where they had gone off to while his leader and the doctor were attacked.

"So, all in all, we have nothing," Julia stated. "What happens to your storage when someone attempts to open it?" Riel asked.

"It's set up in a way that it locks down after a finger and voice recognition failure. What that means is that it resets and you have to wait twelve hours before you can attempt again. It's my backup."

"When someone tries to access your

storage, does it have any alarms or does it send any notice to the building security? I'm trying to gather more information so I can interrogate the guards," Seff said.

Chewing on her lower lip, she considered the question. She'd been asked if she wanted alarms but always felt they could be disabled, so she had dismissed the idea in favor of the finger and voice recognition with a shutdown backup.

"Not that I'm aware of. I specifically declined the alarms. They wouldn't know if someone was trying to get to my research unless I notified them." She gave him an apologetic smile. "I'm sorry. I guess that brings us to another dead end."

Sophia turned to Chase and leaned her head on his shoulder. "Since no one can access it, I think the cold storage is the best place for my work right now. Don't you think?" She looked up at him. His eyes reflected sorrow and he looked away from her.

"Yes, I do now. Until we can figure out who wants your work, it's safest inside the locked space," Chase answered.

"Chase," she said, "what's wrong? What are you not telling me?" The others looked at her then back to him.

He ran a hand over his face, back through his hair. "Sophia, after the attack, someone took what you pulled out of the storage room before my guys got there to get it."

She shrugged. "That's fine. Not a big deal."

Chase nearly jumped from his chair. "What do you mean that's fine? You know what someone can do with your data? Wipe out the entire shifter race."

Sophia smiled. "Not with what I pulled out. They were old tests. I was going to destroy them because they were taking up space."

The four males deflated on the spot. The tension squeezing the space disappeared.

"So, you're telling me your work is still in the vault?" Chase verified.

"And safe," Sophia said and kissed him on the cheek. "We're all good."

"Unless they can get their hands on you," Riel stated, ratcheting up the tension once again around the table with his words.

Seff, Chase, and River turned to glare at him. "Sorry to say it, but it's true. The samples are safe unless they can get their hands on Sophia to get the vault opened. This means she can't be left alone without protection."

River sighed and turned to Chase. "He's right. I'm sure by now they've realized they can't get the storage opened without her. They're going to want her soon, which means she's not to be left alone."

"What do you mean I can't be left alone? What am I, four?" Outraged, she looked at River and gave him an angry glare.

"We'll all take turns until we get rid of the threat—" River broke off as Riel's cell phone rang.

The enforcer looked at the number and stood to answer the call away from the table. Meanwhile, Chase continued to pile more food onto Sophia's plate. She wondered if he was trying to turn her into a cow.

Here she was trying not to eat them out of everything they had, and he just kept adding stuff to her plate thinking she wasn't paying attention. She rolled her eyes but continued eating.

Riel returned, concern written on his face. "That was Tryx's phone. The caller wasn't Tryx. Not sure who it was, but it's clear they

MILLY TAIDEN

have her. They stated she was fine for the moment, but they want Sophia if we want her back."

He hadn't finished speaking when the other three men stood, ready to take action.

"We can't let anything happen to her. Do you have her phone's GPS turned on?" Seff asked.

"Everyone in the pack has an active GPS on their cell phone. If hers is working, they want us to find her. It might be a trap," Riel said.

"I hope so. I need to get my hands on whoever is behind all this and finish it once and for all." Chase's voice had deepened to an almost unintelligible growl.

"Who stays with Sophia?" Riel asked.

River stood and walked toward Chase's open home office. Everyone quickly followed as the men gathered weapons, and Riel sat to access the mapping of Tryx's phone location from Chase's laptop.

None of the men said anything about who would babysit her. Anger built.

"Oh, for God's sake. Give me a frigging break and just go. I'm safe. They'd think I'm with you looking for my friend." Sophia's rage had been simmering since they started talking of watching over her like she was some newborn, and now that someone actually needed all of them, they were still debating who would stay with her.

"Absolutely not." Chase turned and pulled her into his arms. He held her tightly to him. "I'm not taking any chances with your life."

His concern soothed her, and she leaned into his body. The fear she saw in his eyes was enough to stop her ranting.

"Riel, you stay and track the signal while we find Tryx."

* * *

Seff drove Chase's SUV while the alpha called two other enforcers, Kane and Troy. The men were working the streets as cleaners to ensure resolution of any problems the pack members got into with humans. They were usually left to work on their own.

"Riel, this is River. We've called Kane and Troy. Their phones will track with ours. Keep an eye on their signals."

"Got it. Bringing them up now. Signal is strong. We're good," Riel said.

"Any movement from Tryx's original

location?" River asked.

"Nothing. It keeps flashing, there, in the middle of nowhere."

Chase spoke up, hearing Riel's side of the conversation as well as River could. "How're the girls?"

"They've calmed down. They're in the other room. I must say, Alpha, you've got yourself a handful."

A growl erupted from Chase. No one made fun of his mate. Unfortunately, the growl didn't transfer down the phone line.

Riel continued. "She'll be the perfect female alpha for us. Brave and willing to risk her own safety for her pack. Even though lab made, you got a winner."

His anger dropped, replaced by worry. "That's what concerns me. She's too willing to jump right into things without knowing what's going on. I have to protect her from herself sometimes."

River laughed. "Finally, someone's giving you shit now. I told you to wait until your mate came along. Now you know exactly what I've been talking about since I met Julia."

Yeah, he did. And damn, if he didn't love it.

"Gotta go, Riel. Meeting the other two in a minute. Call if anything happens." River pushed the end call icon and dropped the phone on the seat between them.

"I don't like this, bro. What do you think?" River asked.

"I don't know what to think," he answered. Unease rolled through him. Their pack had never had this kind of trouble before. Hyenas weren't welcome anywhere. Trouble always followed. If this was because of them, he'd hunt down every one and destroy them.

He saw his men's truck sitting at a crossroad. He flashed his headlights and they pulled out behind him. Then a thought occurred.

"Goddammit. River, call Tryx's shop to make sure she isn't there. This had better not be a fake kidnapping."

That had been happening a lot lately. The news had been reporting that supposed abductors called up the victim's family and demanded money for their return. While all along, the family member was safe and clueless somewhere else.

River hung up. "Her assistant said she's not at the shop. Didn't know where she was. Of course, she couldn't reach her by phone."

"Fuck," he mumbled. It was looking to be the real deal.

A mile from the target signal, they hid their vehicles off the road behind a group of thick trees.

Chase laid his mini iPad on the truck's hood while the others gathered around.

"Here's how it's going down," he said. He pointed out the route each would take to encircle the phone and hopefully Tryx.

Splitting into groups, they shifted out of their skin and set out in a large circle around the area, slowly closing in on the coordinates Riel had passed along.

In the center of the clearing lay a woman bound and gagged with a cell phone next to her. Her clothes had been torn, and cut marks dripping blood were visible on her arms and legs. The woman's blonde hair was covered with dirt and leaves. There was no one else around, and she resembled Tryx, but as they neared her, they realized she wasn't Chase's cousin.

Once they reached the unmoving body, Chase scented her and knew she was human. Kane picked up the female and carried her toward the trucks. Growls sounded around the group. Their display of aggravation made

Chase wonder why they were called out here.

They returned to their vehicles and called Riel, but he didn't answer. Concern made Chase's heart beat faster in his chest, and he tried Julia and Sophia's phones with no success.

* * *

Riel left Sophia and Julia sitting in the living room and went into Chase's office.

"This is all my fault," Sophia said.

Julia laid a hand on her shoulder. "Don't think that. What these people do, you have no say over."

"Yeah," she said, "but if they had the vials, they never would've taken Tryx. They are still after me, still after my tests."

Julia asked, "What exactly did you create, Sophia? Why do they want it so badly?"

She paced in front of the window, keeping an eye out for the men even though they just left.

"That night you were bitten and in the hospital, I was so scared I'd lose you. With Mom and Dad gone, I couldn't stand the thought I'd be completely alone." A sob caught in her throat. "But you woke up and kept

170

breathing. I almost cried in relief. But then you shifted and it was horrible."

Sophia wiped at her eyes. "My God, Julia, I thought you were going to die all over again. The sound of your bones breaking, your screams, and me not able to do anything to help you. I felt so useless."

Julia wrapped her in a hug. "It's all right, Soph. I'm okay now."

"But you weren't then. I made a promise to myself that you'd never have to go through that again. As my little sister, I'd protect you like I was supposed to."

Julia pushed her to arm's length. "It is not your job to babysit me, Soph. I'm an adult."

She waved the words away. "Whatever. I will always do what I have to, to keep you safe."

"Keep me safe? Are you kidding?" Julia popped her fists onto her waist. "Do you remember as kids you told me the jalapenos in the garden were pickles and I took a huge bite?"

Sophia burst out laughing.

"I could've died from an asthma attack," she continued.

"No, you wouldn't have," Sophia said. "You didn't have asthma until years later."

Julia lifted her chin and sniffed. "Well, it

could've started with that."

"You got me back, though," Sophia said, remembering the incident.

"I did?" Julia replied. "What did I do?"

Sophia snorted. "Seriously? You don't recall picking out all the chocolate marshmallows in the cereal box of Count Chocula?"

Her sister let out a cackle. "Why in the world would I do that?"

"Because that's the only part I ate. I didn't like the crunchy bits, so you left those." Both girls laughed. "Mom wouldn't buy another box until I finished that one without marshmallows. I never ate another bite of them."

"You deserved that after convincing me I was adopted," Julia answered.

She rolled her eyes. "That was so easy. You never even looked like me. I died laughing when I heard you'd asked the mailman if he was your father."

"Oh, shit," Julia heaved between laughs, "I thought Mom was going to kill me."

"And the demon teddy bears. Oh my god. Do you remember those?"

Julia gasped then threw a sofa pillow at her. "That *was* you!"

Sophia fell back laughing, slapping her thigh. "I never told you. But after you fell asleep, I snuck into your room, took the stuffed animals, and staged them to look like they were doing their own things."

"Damn, for the longest time I swore they were possessed and could move on their own." Julia shook her head.

"I told you not to watch *The Exorcist*, but nooo. You didn't listen."

"Yeah, but now, I have my own possessed animal hottie." A smile plastered on her sister's face.

"I realize that now," Sophia said. "After shifting and experiencing nature through my animals, I see it's a gift, not a curse like I thought."

Julia smiled at her the same way their mother used to. That brought tears to her eyes.

"Hey," Julia leaned toward the curtained window, "who's that outside?"

"The guards are walking around."

"I know what they look like and they aren't skinny," Julia replied.

Sophia turned and pulled back the sheer covering the pane. Off to the side, bodies were moving, but the thing she noted was a device on the door that had a bunch of wires running through it.

* * *

When an explosion rocked the front of the house, Riel lifted his gaze from the computer screen in Chase's office to see the women running into the office. Not wasting any time, he clicked a button that unlatched a column in the wall.

Sophia and Julia both gasped when a piece of the wall slid, giving way to a small hallway. He immediately jostled both in, and with a finger over his lips, indicated for them to be quiet. Then he locked them inside.

Riel shoved a filing cabinet in front of the column and ripped his clothes off. He shifted seconds before the door was torn open and two hyenas crowded the entrance. He snarled and lowered his head, showing them his fangs.

Their whiny laughter grated on his nerves. He watched a female and a male stroll into the large office. The female, known for being aggressive and hostile, came in ready to fight. She shoved the male out of the way in her attempt to get at Riel.

The female opened her jaws and showed him her fangs in the silly smile hyenas were known to have. She went for his face and used her paws to scratch at his neck. Riel dodged and tried to get space between the two of them. Undeterred by her smaller body or his massive claws, she attempted to sink her claws into his face once again.

Riel's powerful claw slashed across the female's face, and he shoved her away. She hit a chair, the wood splintering, and landed on her side.

Her whiny growl became louder, and she turned her head toward the inactive male. Riel guessed she was trying to get the male's attention.

Both animals zigzagged around Riel. The male jumped over a table and landed on Riel's back, biting repeatedly into his shoulder and clawing at him while the female tried to cut into his face once again.

What was it with the woman and his face? He growled and shook the male off. The hyena hit the wall in a loud whine.

Riel's focus turned to the female, and he bit into one of her paws as hard as possible. Then he jerked her roughly and threw her across the room, breaking a glass coffee table in the process.

She picked her bleeding body up off

the floor, whining loudly.

The male came at Riel once again but only got as far as biting into Riel's hind leg before Riel shoved him against the oak desk, bit him on the back of the neck, and tossed him through a window.

Riel heard the other hyenas whining outside as well as the distant roar of an engine. The female limped toward the broken window, growled at him one last time, and jumped out. The urge to chase made Riel take a step in the direction of the window, but he stayed firmly in front of the filing cabinet he'd placed before the hidden door.

Maneuvering the SUV up the driveway to Chase's home, Seff waited until they were closer to the house before he slowed enough to allow Chase and River to get out of the vehicle. Chase saw the torn front door and rushed toward his home.

Multiple windows from his office were broken, and blood covered the lower panes. Two animals moved away from the house, limped into a large van, and took off.

Chase and River headed into the house while Seff stayed in the SUV and followed the van. Rushing inside the house with River, Chase was ready to tear the place apart. When they entered the office, they came face to face with a snarling Riel.

"Stand down!" Chase growled.

Riel's wolf lowered his head and whimpered. Blood covered his brown fur. He panted, trying to regain his human form. Once he was back in his skin, he groaned and landed on a chair, struggling to get his bearings.

"Sophia and Julia?" Chase asked, knowing his enforcer wouldn't dare let anyone take their women and then stay behind.

"In the safe room. I locked them in before they got to them." Riel groaned and shifted to his wolf to allow for faster healing of his wounds. Chase watched as Riel shifted, making sure the injured wolf was able to complete the process.

Chase moved the filing cabinet out of the way and unlocked the hidden passage with the secret code. He stepped back when he heard the hiss of the sliding wall. Inside, Sophia was holding Julia in her arms as the other woman sobbed on her shoulder.

River stepped in front of Chase and pulled Julia toward him. He picked her up in his arms, soothing her with soft words while he carried her to a sofa.

Sophia ran out of the tight space and launched herself into Chase's arms. While he held her, she buried her face in his neck and used his shirt to muffle her cries.

It broke his heart to see her that way, and he wasn't sure what to do to help. He rubbed her back and kissed the top of her head, hoping she'd tell him how to make her distress go away.

"Where...where's Riel?" she inquired into his shoulder.

"On the floor." He ran a hand through her hair, trying to find her face under the messy tangle.

"Oh God." She hiccupped, and her sobs grew louder. "He was out here all alone, and we couldn't help him. We tried, but the door was locked, and then we...we heard all the fighting and the growling. I...I feel so bad. He was so young." She spoke in a low murmur, describing how the poor man had gotten killed trying to defend them, and they'd done nothing to help.

"Sweetheart, he's on the floor recuperating, he's not dead," Chase said softly into her hair.

She lifted tear-stained eyes to his face

178

and then turned to see the bloody, brown wolf lying on the floor panting, his tongue lolling out of his open mouth.

She pulled out of Chase's arms, crouched down next to Riel's animal form, and petted the big furry head. She looked him in the eye, her tears falling on his brown fur, and kissed the top of his head.

"Thank you," she whispered in his fuzzy ear and then stood.

Chase helped her back up and into his arms. "How long does he have to stay like that?"

Chase noticed how scared she was when she stared at the still animal. Riel's only sign of life was the movement of his chest when he took slow, even breaths.

"Not long. His wounds will heal and close within a few hours, and then he'll be able to shift and speak to us." He was proud of Riel. He'd proven himself once again to be able to be a commendable defender.

"We can't just leave him here. Come on, you and River can carry him into one of the bedrooms. If he has to be lying down, it should be on a bed," she ordered them.

Julia had also calmed once she realized the brown wolf was alive and soon to be well.

They carried him to one of the lower level bedrooms and then left him alone to rest. The men were in the process of calling the cleanup crew when Seff showed up in Chase's vehicle.

Shortly thereafter, the cleanup crew arrived and installed heavy-duty metal doors in the front and back entrances of the house.

The windows were replaced. A group of four would stay the night to secure the premises. River had insisted they alternate with another set of enforcers to ensure maximum protection.

In the kitchen, Julia cooked a meal to keep some semblance of order while Sophia quietly dissected the personnel in her lab, over and over again.

NINE

In the dining room, everyone spoke at the same time, telling what happened from their own point of view. Sophia sat quietly, internally reviewing every interaction she'd had with the members of the lab for some clue as to who could be behind the attacks.

Everyone was staying the night. Chase and River thought it would be easier to keep the women safe with the security patrolling outside. Seff stayed in the room next to Riel's, while Julia and River took the room at the end of the hall opposite Chase and Sophia.

Once inside their room, Chase pulled her in for a kiss. They removed their clothes slowly, moving their kisses and foreplay to the shower.

First, he washed her and himself. After they'd both rinsed the soap off their bodies, he pulled her back into his arms. He nipped and licked every inch of her warm skin, branding her all over again.

Her hands glided over his muscles, her nails caressing his shoulders and biting into the hard planes of his chest and abs. She threaded her fingers in his wet hair and tugged, bringing him closer to her hungry lips.

He carried her to the bed where she watched him lick the drops of water clinging to her tightly puckered nipples. He devoured the tips, sucking them into the hot cavern of his mouth while she moaned her encouragement.

Her pussy throbbed with every bite on her skin.

His finger speared into her swollen cunt, doubling the pleasure already streaming inside her body. He kissed her stomach and moved down until his head was between her legs.

Electric currents ran through her, pooling heat to her sex and racking shudders down her body. His head lowered, and he licked and sucked his way up and down her pussy. He dipped his wicked tongue into her slick sex and fucked her mercilessly.

She pinched her nipples to increase the pleasure while he rubbed his lips over her engorged clit. She glanced down to see him watching her. Her breath hitched, and she bit her lip in a whimper while her fingers rolled and tweaked the tight buds harder.

She rocked her lower body on his face. He inserted two of his digits into her wet cunt while his tongue lapped at her. He curved his fingers to rub the upper wall of her channel, making her head roll back and her back bow as she tried to ride his face harder.

His lips clamped over her nubbin. He moved his fingers faster in and out while drawing circles on her clit with his tongue. Her legs locked in tension, her toes curled on the back of his shoulders, and she came screaming his name in a sob.

Her legs dropped to either side of him while she tried to catch her breath. He kissed his way back up her body. Her hands fisted in his hair and pulled him up for a kiss. She ran one of her hands down his front and grasped his cock, squeezing it and making him jerk in her hand.

She guided the hard length into her wet entrance and whimpered at the delicious feel of him filling her. He was so deep she could hardly breathe. She wrapped her legs around his hips, the balls of her feet digging into his muscled ass.

Thrusting in and out of her slowly, he kissed her lips, her jaw, and her neck, and sucked on the curve of her shoulder. Every slap of skin created a higher wave of tension inside her clenching sex. Her hands ran over his shoulders and down his back, pulling him in deeper.

"Chase, oh god, oh god, oh god..." she chanted as he increased the tempo of their mating.

"Oh, baby. You feel so fucking good," he growled and ran a hand between their bodies to rub a thumb over her clit, roughly pinching the sensitive nub.

She licked the curve of his shoulder and clamped her teeth on him, marking him as her own. He jerked inside her when her tongue licked the tiny pricks of blood.

"Mine," she growled into his neck.

She dropped back on the bed, still licking her lips. Her head thrashed as she curled her nails into his biceps. Her climax hit her in a giant wave of ecstasy. She was caught in absolute bliss and barely noticed her body trembling or the scream that tore through her.

When her mind had cleared from her

pleasure-induced coma, Chase had curled her into his side and was raining kisses over her face.

"I love you. I never want to lose you," he growled and held her tightly to him.

She smiled and sighed. Exhaustion dragged her down.

"I love you, too," she whispered and let sleep claim her.

Chase stopped breathing for a moment. She'd marked him and told him she loved him. He wanted to shout it to the world, to wake her up and demand she say it again to his face, but most of all, he wanted to make love to her again and again. He ran his hand down the curve of her spine and smiled when she snuggled closer into him.

The following morning, he walked into the bedroom, aware he'd let Sophia sleep longer than he expected. He sat down by the bed and watched as she breathed evenly. He tried to rouse her from sleep.

After multiple attempts of trying to shake her awake only to get a grumble and then have her fall into a deep sleep, he became alarmed.

He called the pack doctor. The woman showed up sooner than he deserved, considering he had growled at her on the phone and demanded her immediate appearance.

She took Sophia's vitals and told him his mate just needed rest. She stressed the need to allow Sophia time to recharge her energy. Her body was coping well with her change, and Sophia would soon be able to handle her new physiology without the need for so much sleep.

The doctor pointedly told him that if he exhausted her with draining amorous activities, she would need longer sleep.

* * *

Sophia knew she was dreaming. She looked around and couldn't figure out where she was. There were flowers, rolling hills, and green trees as far as the eye could see, without a building or home in sight. Turning in a full circle, she didn't see anyone else.

Giggles caught her attention. She smiled at the childish laughter. Walking toward the noise, she came upon a large tree. Crouching down, she peeked behind it and saw two toddlers, a boy and a girl, playing on the grass.

The little girl blew unsuccessfully at fat brown curls that kept falling over her eyes. The little boy grinned mischievously and used a small stick to dig a hole in the grass. Concerned for the children's safety, she walked around the tree to ask the whereabouts of their mother. They looked up at her and smiled.

"Mommy!" they yelled and ran toward her. Their soft, chubby little hands pulled her down on the grass, and they climbed onto her lap.

The little girl's gray eyes twinkled when she smiled impishly at Sophia, while the little boy lifted a chubby hand to pat Sophia's face and pulled one of her long brown curls to play with. He leaned his head onto the curve of her neck.

The little girl, feeling left out, also grabbed a curl and twirled it in her fingers, copying her brother and leaning onto Sophia's other shoulder. Love and joy filled her heart while she held the two precious bodies.

Sophia woke up with a strong sense of wellbeing and happiness that she couldn't contain. She smiled and turned to look at Chase. Instead of seeing happiness reflected back from him, he was watching her warily.

"What's wrong?" she asked, losing some of the contentment surrounding her just seconds before.

"How do you feel?" he asked her quietly, brushing her hair from her face.

"Good. Hungry, but good. Actually, not hungry, I'm starved. Why?" She sat up on the bed, noticing she wore a cotton sleeping gown. She clearly remembered falling asleep naked in Chase's arms.

There was a knock at the door, and Chase moved to open it, letting Julia in. Her sister's worried gaze increased the anxiety Sophia felt.

"Thank god, you're finally awake." Julia rushed to sit by the bed.

"Of course, I'm awake. What's going on?" she demanded a little more frantically.

"Sweetheart, you were sleeping for a long time, and we were worried about you." Chase moved to the other side of the bed and held her hand in his.

"What do you mean for a long time? How long was I asleep?"

Chase and Julia looked at each other. Then Chase nodded and Julia replied, "Two days."

"What? That's impossible. I mean I was...we were..." She turned to Chase for some help, knowing her face had turned red.

"Yeah, well after you fell asleep, we were

unable to wake you up. We called the shifter doctor in, but all she said was to let you rest and that you would come around once you weren't so worn-out."

His eyes kept roaming over her face as if worried she'd keel over in sleep any second.

"Well, I'm not sure why I slept so long, but I feel incredibly rested. So where's the food?" She winced at the cramping in her stomach.

She enjoyed the conversation around her while they ate, and thought of how she'd love to check out her blood under a microscope. Wondering what lay behind the bouts of exhaustion she was experiencing, she wished she could pick apart her cells and look at the impact the shifter gene had had on her system.

Once again, Chase, Seff and Riel went off to look for Tryx. After two days of searching, every clue they'd gotten had seen no results. They were starting to wonder if she'd been taken out of the state or if she'd been killed. Sophia refused to believe the sweet wolf was dead.

Julia went home with River after he made a comment over how tired she looked.

Sophia was on her own inside while two men secured the outside of the house. Because she was tempted to sleep, she decided to use Chase's computer to access her work email instead.

The last thing she needed was to take a nap and wake up a week later. In her email, she found a request by one of the directors for their monthly meeting. Cringing at the fact the email was days old, she typed up a reply suggesting a date and time.

A new message arrived from a generic email address she didn't recognize. Thinking of all the kinds of computer viruses she could give Chase's system, she debated opening it. She gave in to temptation, took the risk, and opened it to find a web link. It clicked open to a site that showed a video that was being streamlined live.

There was a woman dangling from a set of metal chains in thick manacles. Her body was bloody, and her face showed her anger at being tied up. Sophia's eyes watered when she realized the woman was Tryx.

Scanning the screen, she noticed Tryx was in a basement somewhere. Nothing stood out to give Sophia any inkling as to where they could be.

A small chat icon popped open on the screen, and her eyes left the image of Tryx to look down at the message.

User 1: *If you give us the samples you can save her life.*

She stared at the words for what seemed like an eternity and then used shaky fingers to type up a response.

Guest: *How do I know you're not lying?*

The response came back immediately.

User 1: *You don't, but we don't want to hurt a helpless female. We just want your work. You have two hours to decide if she lives or dies. Call this number when you're ready to make a trade.*

Be careful of sharing the information with your wolf, or the woman dies. We'll know if you use your phone. The deal will be off, and she'll die. Once you are ready, call. We know where you are and will take care of the two shifters guarding you.

Guest: *You mean you're going to kill the wolves?*

User 1: *Two hours.*

The pop-up closed, indicating the other person had gone off-line. She paced around the office, wondering how to let Chase know what just happened.

She concentrated on the link she had used with him at the lab. Mentally picturing his wolf and hoping she successfully got through to him in human form, she screamed out to him.

* * *

Chase was in The Back Door talking to a group of men while planning a new search mission for Tryx. A nagging in his head made his wolf pace restlessly. He tried to take over his body, and Chase had to haul the animal back to keep the skin.

The wolf became agitated and fought his restraint. He'd never had this happen before. The animal knew who was in charge but was currently fighting for dominance.

He turned to River with a frown, and they stepped in one of the back offices.

"What's going on?"

"I...don't...know." He clenched his teeth while rubbing his hand on his forehead and fighting the animal for control. His wolf must've been sensing something wrong. Breathing deeply, he focused on his link with the animal. There was something just beyond his reach, and it sounded very much like Sophia's soft voice calling out to his wolf in the distance.

"Chase, just let him out and find out what he wants. It won't do us any good to have you fighting to keep the skin. Release him," River suggested.

Chase reluctantly let the animal have control over his body. As soon as he let the wolf loose, he heard Sophia's call clearly.

"Chase? Chase? I hope this works. Chase...I need you."

TEN

His heart beat painfully loudly. He thought of all the things that likely happened to make her reach out to him in this way. He tore off his clothes and shifted. While he could communicate with Sophia in the flesh, their wolves were the ones with the mental link. So if he wanted a clear connection with her, one of them needed to be shifted into their animal.

"What happened?" he roared in his mind. *"Where are you? Are you okay?"*

"Oh, thank God! You can hear me," she squealed. *"I used your computer to check my email and there was this strange link that showed me a video stream of Tryx tied up by a chain hanging from a roof in some dark cellar-type place."*

194

"Where?"

"That's the thing, I don't know…"

He could hear the uncertainty and concern in her voice and wished he could reach out and soothe her worry.

"Then this message popped up and told me that I could save her life if I just turn my research over. They gave me two hours to call a number. They'll come get me and take me in place of Tryx."

"Like hell!" he yelled.

"Chase, listen to me, I don't want to go with them, but I want to help find Tryx. Maybe we can go with their plan until we reach whatever destination it is they're keeping her and then you and your guys can get us out of there?"

"No!" he ordered in a loud growl.

"Yes!" she growled right back.

He knew she didn't appreciate his dismissal of her idea. It would've been a perfect plan if it was anyone but his mate.

"Sophia, we're not having this conversation," he insisted in a rigid tone.

"Yes, we are. Your guys haven't found a single trace of where she could be. This is our one chance to get her back. So you either help me do this or…I swear, I'll call those guys right now and go without you."

"Baby, be reasonable." He tried to keep her from doing anything dangerous.

"No." The anger in her came through loud and clear. *"You be reasonable. That's your cousin out there. Wouldn't you do the same thing for me if I was the one being held somewhere and no one could find me?"*

He remained quiet for a moment and thought of ways to dissuade her from her crazy plan. She continued to talk as if he'd already agreed with her.

"Chase, listen to me. We have about an hour and a half to figure out how to do this. I'm going to give you an hour, but you can't call me. They have my phone tapped, and they're watching the house, which means whatever you do, you're going to have to follow from far away."

"Sophia —"

"We can't ruin the whole operation because you guys stray too close. They're not going to do anything to me until they have their hands on my work, which means at some point they are taking me back to the lab."

His heart sped up in his chest. *"I'm not letting you put yourself in danger."*

"I'm not going to be in danger. You'll follow behind us. I'm not going to do anything stupid to get either of us hurt. Since they don't know I only need to use my fingerprint and voice command to

open the safe, I am going to work them to take me to her so we're together. That will give you guys a chance to stop this once and for all." Her soft voice tried to pacify him, but he knew things she didn't.

"Sophia, if anything happens to you —"

"Chase, stop. Nothing is going to happen to me, because you will make sure of it. I'm going to call them in exactly one hour to give you guys enough time to be in place before they come for me."

He snarled.

"Chase? I...I love you. If anything does happen, I just want you to know," she whispered and broke off the communication with him.

Chase shifted into his human form and growled. "Well?" River asked once Chase had changed.

"Sophia was contacted by whoever has Tryx. They want her in exchange. She wants to do it and for us to follow from far away until they reach wherever she's being held so we can retrieve them both at once. The foolish woman is walking right into their clutches, and nothing I said would change her mind." He ran a shaky hand through his hair.

He tried to dress quickly, but his hands shook and made things slower.

River stood quiet for a moment. "This is the best chance we've had so far of finding Tryx." He clasped Chase on the shoulder. "Don't worry. We'll make sure nothing happens to your mate."

Chase lifted panic-filled eyes to his brother. "It's not just her I'm worried about."

River lifted his brows, waiting for him to elaborate.

"She's pregnant. It's what has made it harder for her body to adjust to her change." He wished there was something else he could do to keep her safe. Some way he could take her place and keep her and their children from harm.

Tightly gripping the chair in front of him, River's eyes widened. "Does she know?"

Chase shook his head. "No. She just conceived two days ago. That's why she slept so long. It's been so difficult for her body to adjust without me throwing in that she's going to be a mother, too." He paced around the confines of the room.

River's face paled. Determination quickly replaced the worry that lined his features. "Then we need to make sure we do this right. Let's call everyone and get in place." He smacked his brother on the back and pushed him out of the room to join the others and make plans.

* * *

Sophia hated how far she'd pushed Chase, but the man needed to learn she had a brain. They were supposed to be mates, which implied a partnership. So far, he'd told her what to do at every turn, and she'd followed along because his judgment made sense.

Now, it was time to follow her lead.

He contacted her through his wolf. He told her they were in place and to go ahead and make the call.

He got her to promise not to do anything to get herself hurt and to leave all the fighting to them. Then he implicitly told her not to try to shift, to which she mostly agreed. What she didn't tell him was that if the need did arise, she would suffer the pain and to hell with the consequences.

She picked up the phone and made the call at the time she'd been instructed to by Chase.

"Dr. Reese. We're going to—"

"Hold on a second." She tried to calm her nerves and remember what she was supposed to say. "I am not giving you my work until you take me to the wolf and let me see her. I want to make sure she's still alive and not hurt. You'll have to bring her with us when we go to my lab."

"You are pushing your luck, Doctor."

"Tough. You want my research, I want Tryx. So you take me to her and I will gladly give you all my samples, plus my written data without complaint or any trouble," she promised.

"Very well, since you are agreeing to be of assistance, I see no reason why we must make things difficult. We will take you to see the wolf first. My men will be there to get you in a few minutes. Be ready to walk outside with no weapons or electronic devices."

The line went dead.

Sophia had to take a deep breath to calm the sickening pain in her stomach. She ran to the kitchen and grabbed a sandwich, hoping the food would calm the cramps. As a last thought, she darted to her room and gave herself a spritz with a body spray she'd stopped using. She hoped to confuse their sense of smell. She was glad Chase had a lot of her stuff brought to his place, and she was able to use the body spray.

Almost gagging at the strong scent, she

tried to adjust by walking away from the fumes. She knew she would either have to put up with it or wash it off. After the majority dissipated, she was able to handle the clinging scent on her body. It was not something she'd be using again after this.

Ten minutes later, she heard the roar of engines pull up. She brushed her sweaty palms on the sides of her jeans and walked out of the house. She saw two wolves on the ground outside the door with darts protruding from their necks. She looked at each of their chests and noticed the faint rise and fall, indicating they lived. She walked away feeling marginally better.

Four large men stood by a black delivery van and a green pickup was parked right next to it. She walked slowly and steadily, holding her head up. She looked each man in the eye.

She stood in front of the one she figured was in charge and lifted her chin. "Let's go," she ordered, putting her hands on her hips.

The man looked her over and then sniffed the air around her. His eyes narrowed, and she lifted haughty brows at him.

"What? I smell like the wolves you guys hate so much? I have been staying with a bunch of them in case you hadn't noticed, genius." She prayed her words were enough to keep the man from taking any closer sniffs of her.

He considered her for what was surely too long, causing her palms to perspire once again. She kept herself calm, knowing they could sense it if she was nervous or lying.

He opened the van door and allowed her to sit inside. There was one large man to her right and another to her left. She assumed it was to ensure her cooperation.

* * *

Chase and his men were located on a cliff overlooking his house. It made it easy for them to watch what was happening without being scented by the enemy.

His heart had frozen for a moment when the hyena had taken a whiff of her scent. He should've told her about her condition, but he knew that keeping it from her would prevent her from lying and then getting caught from it.

Through his binoculars, Chase had seen Sophia say something. The man had stared at her and then opened the door to allow her inside.

Exhaling a sigh of relief, Chase watched the van take off. He contacted one of the five teams he was working with.

They made their way slowly down the cliff, giving the vehicles ahead of them enough room not to call attention to themselves.

His eyes never veered off the van carrying his mate. He listened to the voice through the walkie giving updates on the roads and exits their target was taking.

He was going to spank Sophia's delectable ass for putting herself in this kind of danger. Grinding his teeth, he focused his body into combat zone.

Everything inside him cleared of all emotions other than aggression and cold-blooded calculation.

* * *

The black van carrying Sophia arrived at a small building that sat on an empty lot. There was nothing in the surrounding area. She peered at the dilapidated green structure and shuddered. She hoped they really had brought her to meet up with Tryx, or she was sure this was all going to have been for nothing.

Taking deep breaths helped her keep her calm. The man whom she had spoken with opened the door for her to exit. He tightened his hold to keep her from falling on her face, and she gave him a small smile.

Inside the building, there were two men. They opened a door and motioned for her to go down the hallway.

So far, she had counted six men in total that Chase and his team would have to get rid of.

Slowly making her way down the dark, dank passage, she came to a large room with multiple windows. It had the look and feel of a basement but was just a regular room. The plastic covering the windows was what gave it the dark dungeon feel.

Realization dawned that she was at the same place she had seen in the video. She gazed around the corner of the dingy room and found Tryx gagged and tied with a chain to a chair. Next to her, a big man stood by and kept watch over Tryx. Sophia walked until she stood a few yards in front of them and stopped.

"Dr. Reese, it's so good of you to join us." The man was clearly a hyena shifter with his whiny voice, but he had to have a rat in there somewhere because his kind of ugly face didn't happen naturally.

She didn't care what anybody said, not even a mother could call *that* cute. He had beady, red eyes and a pointy nose. His big ears really didn't help him with his attempt to look mean.

She would have laughed at how ridiculous his face looked had it not been for the gun he held in his hand.

"Yes, well, a promise is a promise. So I am ready when you are. Just let her go, and then we can go to my lab." She hoped he didn't get a whiff of her, although from what she knew, rats had an amazing sense of smell.

"This here is a dangerous animal, Dr. Reese. I couldn't possibly let her go." He stared at her, and she wanted to slap the leer off his face.

"Look, let me talk to her. I promise you I can get her to behave if you give me a second alone with her, and if she does, we can take her with us. If not, then I guess you can just let her loose after you get what you want from me."

She looked at the man with the biggest, most innocent eyes she could muster.

The man jerked his chin toward the video camera in the room, and she turned to look. Once he saw that she'd noticed their every move was being recorded, he continued walking. He got to the door and stopped.

At the entrance, he told her there would be someone watching the cameras in case they thought to escape. He told her he would unlock the chains when he returned if he believed the wolf would really behave.

He took a deep breath, leveled his eyes on her, and frowned. His eyes darted to her stomach, then his expression softened and his fingers massaged his temples.

"Nothing is simple, anymore, is it, Dr. Reese?" Ratface said. Sophia didn't know how to respond to that. What was wrong with her stomach? Did she have something on her shirt? "Just do as we ask and no one will get hurt."

He sighed heavily and tilted his head back. "I am so sorry, Nichola. This is not what I wanted." With that, he walked out the door, locking it behind him.

Sophia moved to stand in front of Tryx and removed the gag from her lips. There wasn't time to analyze what Ratface had said.

"Sophia, what are you doing here?" Tryx sniffed her and horror filled her face. "Does Chase know you're here?" she hissed.

"Shhh, yes, he does," she whispered so low she knew only Tryx could hear her.

"How could he let you come here in your

condition?" The pixie wolf growled in anger. She muttered how stupid her cousin was for such an intelligent man.

"What are you going on about? I'm better now. Be quiet and listen. Here's the plan. Chase and his guys are probably outside now. We're going to be good little girls until they get us out of here, and if the need arises then I'll shift and help him out."

"Are you insane? You can't shift!" The little wolf almost bit her head off with her growl.

"And why not?" She wondered why everyone kept telling her the same thing. She was getting really tired of being ordered around.

"Because..." Tryx sputtered, "You're pregnant."

"What?!" she yelled. A bout of dizziness overwhelmed her and made her legs weak. She sat on the floor and lowered her head to her knees while taking deep, calming breaths.

"Shhh. You're pregnant, didn't you know?" The surprise in Tryx's voice shocked her even more than the question. How could she have known that unless she was a freaking clairvoyant?

"You can tell? How the hell can you tell

and I can't? How would I have known?" Something wasn't adding up.

"Well, maybe you wouldn't have, but Chase sure would have. I mean he's like a damned bloodhound," she muttered under her breath. "His sense of smell is so acute he could probably tell you were pregnant the minute you conceived. The only reason I can tell is because my sense of smell is almost as good as his. Not to mention you've got two strong babies in there, and their scent is drifting and mingling with yours."

Sophia shook her head in a negative while Tryx nodded gloomily.

"No, no way. Chase wouldn't have kept that from me."

She thought back to their conversations. He insisted it wouldn't be a good idea for her to try to shift because they wouldn't know how her body would react to two animals.

Always pushing for her to wait, and then he'd even made her promise not to shift… He wouldn't have withheld from her that she had two very precious tiny lives inside…would he?

"That son of a bitch!" she growled.

What if she had attempted to shift with

no one around? She had been all alone earlier, and thank goodness she hadn't thought to try, but what if she had? She could've hurt her babies.

"Calm down, Sophia. Anger isn't good for one baby, much less two."

Sophia's head jerked up and she peered at Tryx while she tried to piece it all together. "So do you think they're the reason why I've been so hungry every couple of hours and so exhausted that I've slept for days?" She hoped it wasn't anything that would put her children in danger.

Tryx smiled and nodded. "Absolutely, being a shifter can be draining when you first change until your body adjusts, but you have two animals so it's probably even more so. Add to that the fact you now have two babies draining you more, I'm surprised you haven't passed out and fallen on the floor yet. And yes, you should be shoveling food down your throat every few hours."

Tryx laughed when Sophia lifted her brows in suspicion. "It's true. We shifters eat a ton since our metabolism is much faster than that of a pure human. I'm sure you've noticed you've not gained any weight with all the extra eating you've been doing.

"But when a female is pregnant she eats

even more than normal, so again to add to your case, you've got two babies draining your body of energy as they grow. You'd be putting yourself and them in danger if you didn't eat enough to supply them with the nutrition they need to develop."

Relieved, Sophia sighed. "Oh, thank God. I'm always starving, and it was starting to worry me. That being the reason, I've got no problem eating a horse if necessary, as long as it keeps my babies safe. You did say it was two, correct?"

She and Chase were going to be parents. A growl worked its way up her throat. It was still up in the air if he would live long enough to see his children grow, but it was so exciting, she felt a stupid grin working its way onto her face.

Tryx sniffed her and smiled. "Yes, a boy and a girl. Congratulations, although this is probably not the right time for this. I still can't believe Chase let you come here." She frowned again.

Sophia glanced down and kept her voice low, "I didn't give him much of a choice. I told him he either cooperated or I was coming on my own. No wonder he was so angry with me."

It made her feel better to know he wasn't just trying to tell her what to do. He was worried for her and their offspring. It didn't stop her from being angry with him for not telling her about her babies.

The door rattled, and the big hyena man walked back inside with several other men. Their time was up.

ELEVEN

Seff, Chase, and a group of pack members and enforcers broke into two teams. Eight of them stayed in skin, weapons ready. The other seven shifted and took the lead. From the layout they'd gathered of the place, Chase mentioned he had a feeling Sophia and Tryx were located somewhere on the ground floor.

They swarmed the place through multiple entrances at once. Blasts of gunfire erupted when the men inside started shooting at the intruders. Seff and Chase did a full walk around the building to see if either could scent Sophia and Tryx.

When Chase moved to a side entrance, Seff's wolf readied for combat. Down a hallway, Seff heard faint screams and quickened his steps. He scented both women and male shifters inside the room. Using hand signals, Chase motioned for Seff to go ahead inside. Chase indicated he would go through one of the outer windows in a surprise attack.

When Seff broke down the door, he found a large hyena and rat mix shifter between both women. A few others scattered around the room.

The rat pulled and held a gun to Sophia's head. Tryx was tied down by heavy chains.

"Goddammit," Ratface said. "If you'd have waited a few more minutes…" The rat pushed the gun into her hair. "Come any closer and they're both dead."

"Let them go. They don't have what you want," Seff said while scanning the windows for movement.

He turned his gaze back to the enemy. If necessary, he would tear the man limb from limb. However, there was no way to ensure the women would not be hurt or killed if he attacked the rat shifter.

Seff watched the rat grab a hold of Sophia's arm. "You're right. This one has what they want. I'm taking her with me."

He saw her wince when the rat squeezed

her arm roughly. Seff growled and took a step forward only to stop when the man jerked back, holding her tightly. The others took a step closer to the lone wolf. "Stop, or I'll shoot her and drag her out of here bleeding."

All of a sudden, Chase jumped through the window, breaking glass and creating a loud ruckus. In an automatic reaction, the man turned to look toward the unexpected noise and in the process released Sophia's arm long enough for her to quickly step away. Seff, who was prepared for Chase, pulled Sophia out of harm's way.

Seff released his claws and swiped at the hand holding the gun. The sharp cuts forced the rat to release the weapon with a yelp.

Another man rushed Seff and he pushed the hyena with so much force, it propelled him right into Chase.

Seff watched as Chase's large canines and massive claws cut into the mangy dog.

Chase's wolf snarled and went for another man's neck, tearing at the hands that tried to block the attack. The man kicked and shoved his bloody arms, but the fight went out of him and he fell to the ground. The remaining men bugged out, pushing through the door.

MILLY TAIDEN

Seff removed the heavy chain holding down Tryx. He watched the two women embrace and hold each other. Now that Chase had dismembered the last threat, Sophia would be safe.

Off to the side, Seff watched Chase change back into his skin and shrug into a pair of jeans. Riel walked into the room and stopped next to him. Both watched the alpha walk straight to Sophia and stop when she glared angrily at him.

"Sweetheart?" Chase frowned, and Seff wondered at the awkward reunion.

Curious over her obvious anger, Seff watched Sophia take a few steps to stand in front of Chase. She gave him a slow smile and then punched him hard in the stomach.

"Ow!" Chase grunted and rubbed his stomach while watching her. Sophia threw him a disgusted look. What the heck had the alpha done to his mate? Seff and Riel snickered over Chase's woman trouble and continued to watch the show.

"That was for being such a closemouthed jerk," she hissed and then twined her arms around Chase's neck.

Chase stood unmoving, warily watching

Sophia. "And this is for coming to our rescue."
She yanked his head down and kissed him.
Seff looked away and smiled when the other
men in the group laughed, whistled, and
catcalled at the make-out scene in front of
them.

When Chase had enough, he growled
and his men quieted. He instructed his
beta to search the rest of the building then
blow it up. He didn't want the place being
used by anyone again.

On their way back, Seff watched Sophia sit
stiffly next to Chase. He'd never understand
women. She kissed him and then refused to
speak to him. Chase looked confused, and Seff
did not envy him. Women were more trouble
than they were worth. When Chase lifted his
hands in question to Tryx, the tiny female
glared at him and turned her face away.

If only women trouble was the single
problem they had. In the melee inside, the
hyena with the rat face had disappeared.

* * *

Sophia stepped into the house and went
straight for the shower, slamming the door so
hard it rocked the panel, causing it to crack. She
wanted to ensure he knew how pissed she was

216

with him.

Turning the lock at the last second, she allowed herself some alone time in the bathroom while she undressed. Let him stew over that one. She took a nice warm shower and washed her hair, making sure to take twice as long as usual in the bathroom. It allowed her to release some of the tension and frustration running through her.

At the end of her long shower, she massaged lotion over every part of her body. She stared at her abdomen in the bathroom mirror. She smiled, remembering her dream, and tentatively touched her belly.

She put on her robe and left the serenity of the quiet bathroom behind. Barefoot, she walked through the bedroom and out to the balcony. She took a deep breath and sat on the edge of a cushioned lounger.

The night air was warm as it caressed her skin. In the distance, she could see the lights from the closest neighbor's house.

Chase's house was not as isolated as River and Julia's. In Chase's case, his neighbors were close enough that she was able to look into their windows with her new shifter vision. She wondered if they could do the same back into Chase's windows.

His scent drifted from right outside their balcony door. She knew he was probably wondering what was wrong with her, but she'd been hurt by his actions.

"You can come out here, Chase," she said softly, knowing he heard her.

His bulky mass filled the exit and then moved to stand before her. He'd obviously showered in one of the other rooms; his hair was wet, and he smelled clean and fresh.

When her eyes roamed his sexy body, heat traveled through her and curled into a ball of arousal in the pit of her stomach. His cargo shorts and white T-shirt complemented the bronze of his muscled skin, making him look ideal for the cover of an outdoor magazine.

Sitting on the seat next to her, he pulled one of her hands into his grasp and lifted dark, anxious eyes to her face. "What did I do? Tell me. I swear I'll fix it."

She raised a hand to his face, cupped his cheek, and glanced away. "I'm not sure it's something you can fix. You either trust me, or you don't." He could claim they were mates all he wanted, but trust was more important to her than any animal attraction linking them together.

"I trust you, Sophia."

He said the words with so much conviction, she wondered if she'd been wrong.

Wanting to believe him, she peered at him from under her lashes. "Why didn't you tell me I was pregnant? Tryx said you knew from the moment of conception, and you didn't think it was important to tell me? What if I would have decided to ignore my promise to you and shift?" Her voice wobbled, and she blinked back tears.

"I'm sorry, love. I never meant for you to feel like I don't trust you. I wanted to give your brain a chance to adjust to being a shifter before you had to deal with the fact that you're going to be a mother. I just thought it might have been too much to handle in one shot."

He crouched in front of her and gave her a sorrowful look. He lifted her hands to his lips, kissed them, and then placed them over his heart. "I swear to you, I will never keep anything important from you again, sweetheart. Just please don't...don't go," he pleaded softly, his voice full of emotion.

She saw the sincerity in his eyes. Sliding off the lounger, she sat on the floor with him.

Her hands cupped his face, and she smiled. "We'll start fresh... No withholding of anything between us, because if you ever do that again I may have to kill you."

"Never." He moved his head down to lock his lips with hers.

She threaded her fingers into his hair and held him in place while their tongues mated. His hand moved to caress her cheek, her jaw, and then curl around her neck.

She smiled and hugged him tightly. "We're going to have two babies, Chase. Can you believe it?"

He smiled and moved a hand to settle it over her abdomen. "Yes, we are. You up for it?"

When she blew a raspberry, he laughed. "Are you kidding me? I'm going to be a fantastic mother. I excel at everything I do," she boasted.

"That, you do. You're already perfect. There's nothing you can't do."

Guilt riddled her a bit at this statement. One day she'd have to tell him about her attempt to play the violin.

When she surfed across Lindsey Stirling on YouTube fiddling and dancing in a steampunk/Mad Max-like video, she was hooked.

She so loved the smooth, melodic sound

the string instrument made. She spent hours in the lab, blasting classical and new age music featuring her favorite intonations.

Eventually, she wanted to make her own music. How hard could it be? You just dragged a wand up and down the strings, moving it back and forth every once in a while. Right?

Talk about epic fail. Not only did the screeching chase away all the birds as she played it on the back porch one night, but dogs blocks away began howling in long, sad cries.

No. She couldn't do everything. Having brains didn't mean you could play a musical instrument.

Both got up from the floor and stood in front of each other. Once on their feet, he pulled on the satin tie holding her robe together.

Their gazes locked, and he removed the robe. His clothes came next. Then he proceeded to kiss her neck. His lips traveled down her collarbone to her breasts and stopped to lavish nips and kisses on her nipples. Her eyes lifted to look at the stars, and the warm night air caressed her overheated skin.

She grabbed his hands and pushed him to sit back on the lounger. Once he was seated, she straddled his thighs. She rocked her body over him in a sensuous slide of skin on skin and licked the shell of his ear.

"Chase, I can't wait to have you inside me." She nipped the lobe. He groaned, and she ground her hips into his cock. "I want you to fuck me hard and fast. Right here, right now."

"Baby. You're making me lose my mind," he growled.

She scored his shoulders with her nails and licked the soft area behind his ear, causing him to shiver. He became more forceful, his hands squeezing her breasts and pinching her nipples. She whimpered.

"Oh, please, Chase, fuck me already." Her body burned with the need to be filled by him.

"Whatever my mate desires." He lifted her body up and placed the head of his heavy shaft at her entrance.

She slammed her body down, allowing him to fill her in one smooth thrust. They groaned in pleasure. She rode him hard and fast, his hands lifting and lowering her body on him repeatedly.

Moaning loudly, she pleaded for him to make her come. Rocking her hips, she felt him stiffen. He moved his fingers between her thighs to flick on her sensitive clit while his lips latched on to her breast and sucked mercilessly on the taut tip. He bit down and pinched at the same time. Tension coiled at the pit of her womb.

Her movements became jerky, and his hands tightened around her. He continued to slam her body over him again and again until she tensed.

Pleasure exploded, and a scream tore out of her. He gripped her hips tightly, gave a purely male groan of satisfaction, and warm semen filled her womb when he came.

She lay draped limply over him, her head tucked into his neck. He massaged her back in slow circular motions, and she purred in contentment. Lifting her into his arms, he carried her inside.

Belatedly she remembered the open windows and lighted rooms from across the way where the occupants may have seen and heard what was going on. Oh well, now she was an exhibitionist, too. She smiled at the thought that Chase had turned her from a geek into a full-blown, sex-starved nymphomaniac.

TWELVE

A week later, Sophia knocked on the office door that had the title *Facility Director* on it for her delayed meeting. For the first time since she started working here, they were meeting in her boss's office.

Tori Winchester gave permission to enter.

Making her way toward the center of the room, she noticed it was decorated in warm and inviting tones.

"Oh, Sophia. It is so good to see you," Tori said.

Sophia looked at the chairs in the office. "Are you expecting someone? I can come back later. I'm early."

"I am, but come in. He can wait since he's late," Tori assured her. "I was starting to get worried after your message about being sick. Are you feeling better now? Never mind, I can probably answer my own question since you look fabulous."

Sophia knew she looked more like she'd been on vacation than sick, but that was all thanks to her new genes. Her gaze roamed the credenza behind the older woman. The last time she'd been there, she'd been unable to see the pictures on it clearly. With her poor vision and her need for constant squinting, even while wearing her glasses, the images on the credenza had been blurry. Now that she was able to, her gaze took in everything on the large mantle.

"I feel so much better now. I think I just needed some time off after burning the candle at both ends of the stick. In fact, I—" Her eyes focused on a framed photo of two men and a woman.

There was a dark-skinned, good-looking man, a young woman, and another much uglier man. Her heartbeat slowed to a crawl when she recognized the dark man in the picture as the same one whose throat she'd ripped open in the attack at the lab.

"Dear, are you all right?" The older woman's previously warm voice forged itself into sharp steel.

Sophia's eyes snapped to Tori and then back to the picture.

Tori opened a drawer and reached in, but Sophia was too stunned to notice what she pulled out.

Recognizing the second male as the rat-man made her eyes widen in shock.

Tori's expression of a warm, soft, elderly sweetheart slipped to show a hard and bitter face. The edges around her eyes deepened, and her lips compressed into a straight line.

"I'm...I'm sorry, I guess...I'm not feeling as well as I thought. Maybe it'd be best if I came back at another—" Sophia stopped short when she noticed the gun pointed her way.

"No, I don't think that would be best." The woman's no-nonsense voice filled Sophia with dread.

Her hands folded protectively over her belly. She frantically tried to think of a way out of this situation. She couldn't help but gape at the previously sweet Mrs. Winchester and wondered what the hell was going on.

"I see you noticed the photo of my beautiful Nichola," she sighed sadly. "She was a beauty, wasn't she?" The angry question required an answer as Tori's extremely steady hand held the gun up toward Sophia's face.

"Yes, she was quite lovely." Sophia darted another look at the photo, taking better stock of the woman in the middle. The girl in the picture was young, probably a teenager in the shot. She had a wide smile and blonde hair parted in the center with the '70s trademark feathered waves. The girl was clothed in bell-bottom jeans and resembled Farrah Fawcett in *Charlie's Angels*.

Hoping to buy some time, Sophia decided to ask the obvious question. "What happened to her?"

Tori seemed to gauge the sincerity of her question before she answered. "It was quite tragic, the story of my Nichola."

Outwardly calm, Sophia screamed out for Chase in her mind, knowing he waited for her in the car and might not hear her in his human form. She hoped that even though the call would be faint, he'd still be able to sense something was wrong.

"She fell in love with a wolf shifter." Sophia let her eyes go wide, pretending to be clueless. "Oh, don't look at me like you don't know what I'm referring to. Your sister is married to one of them." Tori spat the words as if they were burning her tongue in distaste.

"I'm sorry. I just don't understand what you're talking about," she said, hoping the woman would elaborate on her bizarre tale.

"Well, of course, you wouldn't, I haven't told you the whole story yet. As I was saying, she fell in love with one of those shifters. I tried to explain to her how dangerous those animals could be, but she refused to listen to me.

"She was obsessed with becoming one of them so she could be her lover's *true* mate. At least the wolf told her he wouldn't change her because it was too dangerous." Her eyes grew distant. "Her entire life lay before her, and she wanted to waste it on that…that animal! Since the shifter she loved refused to bite her, she went to one of her close friends for help. A fucking rat face found someone willing to turn her for money. A wolf shifter bit her, but her body couldn't handle the change and it killed her."

"I'm…I'm so sorry for your loss." She hoped Tori would put the gun down if she showed her some sympathy.

Sophia sat completely still, unwilling to push the obviously disturbed woman over the edge and have her pull the trigger in her craze. "How…how long ago did this happen?"

"Forty years ago." Tori's enraged features made it seem like it had just happened.

"But, how old was she?" Sophia tried putting two and two together, only she was coming up with more than four.

"She was barely sixteen and still just a baby in my eyes." The woman's temper seemed to be cooling.

Sophia's mind raced. She processed the information. "But...she couldn't have been your daughter. You told me you're sixty years old."

Tori's green eyes glowed with rage. "She wasn't my daughter, she was my baby sister."

Shocked speechless once again, Sophia was quiet on the outside while inwardly screaming out to Chase.

Tori lowered the gun. It pointed at the middle of Sophia's chest.

"Those two young men in the pictures, they were her supposed best friends before that wolf killed her. Friends don't get other friends killed. I'm sure you remember becoming acquainted with them recently. I will make them pay until the day they die for what they did." Tori stood, continued to point the gun in Sophia's direction and walked around her desk. Sophia wondered how she never noticed

Tori's insanity before.

Tori stopped in front of Sophia and motioned with the gun hand for her to stand. "Sadly, they weren't as successful as they anticipated in retrieving those samples from you for me. Now that I have you here, you're going to hand them over so I can give them to someone who will finally put an end to the shape-shifting gene. Get up."

Sophia stood and continued to fold her arms over her belly.

Tori cocked her head toward the door. "Let's go down to that lab of yours and get those samples before I lose my patience."

Sophia turned to walk to the lab, and the pointy steel was pushed into her back.

Chase was restless. His wolf was hounding him again. Pushing to take over and shift out of his skin. His hands gripped the steering wheel. He looked around the deserted parking lot.

Sophia was meeting with her boss. After her meeting, she was supposed to destroy the samples in storage and meet him back in the car. He glanced around and realized there were no other cars in the lot. Other than his SUV, the parking area was empty. Unease settled over him.

It was the end of the day, the sun was setting, and it was too goddamned quiet. He concentrated on calming his distressed animal until he recalled the last time that had happened. He decided not to wait around for Sophia.

Opening the door to walk into the facility, the urge to run and ensure her safety overwhelmed him. There was no guard at the entrance, which made his discomfort level rise. He followed Sophia's scent down the hall.

He heard her soft voice. She was speaking to someone and heading toward her lab. Cautiously alert, he moved with the grace of the predator he was.

When he neared the entrance to her work place, Chase could see Sophia and a woman standing a few feet behind her. The woman held a gun to Sophia's lower back.

Sophia unlocked her cold storage and disabled the security on the file system, then moved a few steps away.

"Pull them out of the storage and place them on this table for me," the woman ordered.

Sophia walked into the storage room and moments later walked out with vials and files. She walked back to the table the old woman indicated and put the research down.

"Now, I'm sorry I have to do this, Sophia, I really like you. You're so intelligent. No one ever came even half as close as you to the results you've achieved in the past six months, which makes this really difficult. You should have just handed them over the first time I sent the hyenas for them. It would have saved us all so much wasted time, and could've kept you from this type of end." She lifted the gun toward Sophia's chest.

Anger surged inside Chase. He let the wolf loose and shifted out of his skin, muscles and bones popping too slowly for his liking. The only thought consuming him was to destroy the woman who was holding a gun on Sophia.

He growled and launched his body like a missile at the woman. Having heard his growl, the woman tightened her grip on the weapon. His jaws bit into her neck as her hand squeezed on the trigger repeatedly. Sophia scurried and crouched behind a table.

Loud screaming filled the air as Chase's wolf mauled at the woman's throat. Blood spurted. Her shrieks were soon cut off, and her delicate flesh lay torn open, bleeding on the floor.

Slipping back into his skin, Chase rushed to the side of the table that Sophia had ducked behind. He found her curled into a small ball on the floor, passed out. Her hands were protectively covering her belly.

He turned her over and noticed blood covering her chest. His heart stopped. His hands shook when his eyes found the small bullet hole on her right shoulder.

Lifting her unconscious body carefully off the floor, he ran for his vehicle. He placed her in the back seat and called the shifter doctor to ensure she was ready when he arrived.

He tossed a pair of sweatpants and T-shirt into the front seat from the gym bag he always kept in his truck for emergencies.

Spinning tires out of the lab's parking lot, he made a call to River.

"Sophia's been shot," Chase said. "I'm taking her to the hospital before she bleeds out. Her animals are too weak to heal her in time."

"Shit. What do you need us to do?" River asked.

"Need another cleaning at her lab. Her fucking boss has been behind all this."

"Seriously?"

"Damn bitch shot Soph when I attacked her. And make sure the cleaners get all the papers and stuff on the counter by the vault. This time, it's the real stuff. Don't need someone getting their hands on it." He'd had enough of that the last go around.

His nerves stretched taut. She lay pale and limp on the seat behind him, bright red blood trickling from her gunshot wound. Driving like the devil was on his tail, he arrived at the small private clinic reserved for his pack members.

He carried her inside in a frantic rush. The pack doctor met him at the entrance in her operating gear. He followed her to the surgical room and lay Sophia on a bed. After that, he was dragged outside to allow them to work.

His wolf was quiet and sad, seemingly mourning his mate and his children, something Chase refused to do. Sophia was going to be fine, she had to be, or his life would end along with hers.

As he paced in the waiting room, his phone rang.

"Yeah, River, what you got?" Chase asked.

"We're at the lab…"

"Good. Any problems?"

"Well, only if you call no body and no vials on the table a problem."

* * *

Sophia opened her eyes and winced at the burning in her shoulder. She squinted until she could see clearly. She turned to scan the room and came face to face with a sleeping Chase.

He was sitting on a chair, his hand holding hers, keeping them connected even while he slept. She smiled at the sight of her mate. God, she loved that man. Moving her fingers in his hold, she squeezed his hand, and he jerked awake. He looked like shit.

"How are you feeling?" His voice was hoarse. His other hand lifted to brush a lock of hair behind her ear.

"Thirsty. Little ones?" She tried to talk past the sand in her throat.

Her hand traveled to her tummy, feeling the bump that hadn't been there before. Her smile widened, knowing she was still nurturing their two precious bundles.

"They're good, healthy." He sat beside her on the bed and helped her take a sip of water. Then he fixed the pillows behind her back, allowing her to sit up.

"Sophia...I—"

She watched him swallow.

"I almost lost you. I-I can't lose you." His voice broke. "I love you."

She smiled and pulled him down for a soft kiss. "I love you, too. So much sometimes, I think I'm going even crazier than I normally am, but I wouldn't trade my feelings for anything in the world." She looked into his eyes solemnly. "I'm not going anywhere."

She grinned, and he hugged her tightly, carefully ensuring her injury wasn't bothered.

She smiled to herself. Who would've thought she'd end up with her very own FBA, man-candy Chase? Apparently, fantasies did come true, even for geeky scientists.

A nurse came in with a tray of stainless steel things. One had a needle. Chase's face paled. She laughed at him as his phone rang in his pocket. He pulled it out and glanced at the caller ID.

"It's River. I lost the phone signal with him earlier. I need to take this outside," he said, tilting his head toward the door. She had a feeling it could've been a solicitor call and he'd take it outside.

"How are you feeling, Ms. Reese?" the nurse asked.

Sophia took a moment to take stock of her aches and pains. Besides her shoulder, which didn't even hurt that much, she felt fine.

"Everything feels fine. Just a dull sting on the shoulder and that's it."

"Good. The doctor will probably release you shortly," the nurse replied, writing on the chart.

"Was it really that bad? I mean, aren't shifters supposed to heal themselves? I'm surprised I'm here."

"Normally, yes, the shifter part heals the human body on its own. But Alpha said you were newly turned and didn't want to take a chance. You were losing blood quickly."

Wow. She could've died. And of all the people, one she truly trusted and liked was the one who shot her.

The only good thing about all this was she was finally safe. It was over.

* * *

"I don't give a fuck," Ratface said, talking into his cell phone. "I'm out. She's dead and I don't owe you one goddamn thing. I don't even know who the hell you are."

"Listen to me, you ugly fucker," the man

said, "the job isn't done. I need the girl."

"Then get her yourself. My guys and I are leaving. I hate this too-quiet town." Ratface looked out the window of Tori's home. He hated that the woman was dead, but he wasn't going to complain either.

When rushing into the lab hours earlier and seeing Tori's mauled body after hearing gunshots, he couldn't believe the sight. Nichola's older sister was finally out of his life.

The bitch had made his life hell since Nichola's death years ago. She'd hounded him, stalked him, never giving him a moment of peace, believing he was the reason Nicki had died.

He was and wasn't the reason. If he'd known earlier what the girl had planned on doing, he would've stopped it. But he hadn't known. She wanted to surprise him.

Then he smelled the little change in her chemistry that tore out his heart.

He shook his head to clear those memories. That part of his life was now over. He could move on, though he didn't have anywhere to move on to.

"Fine, then," the man said. "Leave. I'll hire someone else."

The line went quiet and Ratface slammed

the phone onto the carpet. Plopping into the chair behind the desk in Tori's home office, he stared at the pictures lining the front edge. The beautiful, young face he dreamed of every night for so very long stared back at him. A smile graced her lovely face.

His head dropped into his hands. How did things get so wrong? How did he let Tori talk him into this stupid-ass job? It was supposed to be easy and she'd promised to leave him alone if he got the research from someone in the lab.

Someone who happened to be a new wolf and newly pregnant, if his nose told him right during the time they were in the room with the kidnapped older wolf.

Yeah, he knew what he had to do. He couldn't let more innocents die. Question was, would he be killed before doing it?

THIRTEEN

"What do you mean there's no body?" Chase growled through the phone. He paced the hallway outside Sophia's recovery room at the clinic. If his phone hadn't lost reception earlier, this would've been solved already.

"Just that," River said, "there is no body or blood. But the air stinks of strong cleaning products freshly used."

"You think someone else cleaned up for us?" Chase pondered out loud.

"Unless there are clean-freak zombies," River replied, "then someone took care of the dead woman."

What the hell was going on? Would this never end?

"And the tubes and papers aren't on the table?" Chase asked.

"Nope," River said, "didn't see anything."

Shit, shit, shit. "Did you see anybody or talk to anyone?"

River sighed. "Trebir let me and the guys in the back and gave us white lab coats. We didn't have any problems getting in. Do you want us to ask employees? Few are here, though."

Chase's brows drew in. "What? You gonna ask if anyone's seen a dead body lying around?"

"Does sound bad, when you put it that way," River answered.

Fuck, sometimes he wondered if his brother came from the mailman.

"Oh," River chimed in, "I did meet the facility director."

"How did you know he was the director?" Chase asked.

"We ran into him coming out of his office as we were leaving." His brother's voice turned snarky. "And before you give me the third degree, the title on the door read Facility

Director. That's how I know who he was."

"Did you talk with him?"

"Shortly. He didn't give any hint to being aware of anything going on. Nice guy. He's a shifter, but I've never smelled his animal before."

"Did you ask what he was?" Chase asked.

"No, I didn't want to get personal with the man and have him start asking me questions."

"Good call," Chase said. "What's the man's name? Why don't I know him? I would've remembered meeting someone with an exotic side."

"Name's Jake Schnake." River laughed. "Jake the Snake. He's probably heard that a million fucking times in his life. Poor guy."

Chase wondered if it was too simple to think Jake was a snake shifter. Chase still didn't remember meeting the man. Usually, he eventually met every new shifter who came to town.

"Okay, anything else?" Chase asked.

"Nope. Unless you want us to do anything more, we're done. It's up to the facility or family to question police. Do you need me to talk to the chief?"

"No," Chase said, "I've got to talk to him

about the break-in to Sophia's house."

"You don't think that's taken care of now?" his brother asked. "Wasn't the dead woman in charge of the hyenas trying to get your mate's work?"

"She was, but...I don't know." Chase still had a feeling something wasn't right. Maybe he was being paranoid since this was his mate he was trying to protect.

Shit. He felt like a first-day alpha with no experience. He hated being indecisive. Logic versus intuition.

The doctor entered the hall from her office, stethoscope around her neck.

"River, the doc's out. I'll talk to you later." He pocketed his phone. "What's the verdict, Doctor?" he queried.

"She looks good," the doctor said. "Scans show the hole has healed in the middle of the muscles already. She shouldn't have any problems making a full recovery. She'll have a slight scar, though."

"Eh, scars are sexy on a woman," Chase said, thinking with one head more than the other now that they were talking about his mate.

The doctor laughed. "As long as you think so, Alpha."

This having a mate thing was still a bit new for him. He had to watch who he was talking to. And with which part of the body he was talking with.

Chase followed the doctor into Sophia's room.

"Hello, Miss Sophia." Doc maneuvered around the nurse and placed the end of the stethoscope on Sophia's chest.

Chase wondered at that. "Can't you hear her heart without that thing if you got closer?"

Doc looked up at him. "Of course, but how would it look if I went around with the side of my face attached to everyone's chest?"

Point proven. Though, he wouldn't mind putting his ear to his mate's chest. It'd put his mouth right at nipple height.

"Chase," Doc said, "if you insist on thinking whatever it is causing that smell, I'm going to kick you out."

It didn't help his case when he watched his mate's tongue swipe across her bottom lip. He groaned when the nurse grabbed his arm and dragged him out.

"Wait," he said, "when can I take her home?"

"After I'm done examining her," Doc

answered. "Ten minutes."

"Thank God," he mumbled.

"Congrats on finding your mate, Alpha," the nurse said.

"Thanks, Marcy," he replied. "Finding my other half is better than I ever thought, if I can keep her out of trouble."

FOURTEEN

Sophia lay in bed snuggled up to her mate. It was so nice being home and safe. And hot. This man was a freaking heater on high. Now that her body was working overtime growing babies, she generated her own warmth.

From the bedside, Chase's phone rang. The distinctive ring informed them it was his brother calling. Anyone else she would've balked at, but River usually didn't call unless something was up. He was always too busy taking care of his drama queen.

Chase rolled over with a growl and slapped a hand on the bedside table.

"This had better be good," he said.

Sophia reached back and smacked his ass before rolling away.

"Quit being grouchy and talk to your brother. We'll call him tomorrow morning to get back at him."

She listened to her mate greet his sibling as she meandered into the bathroom. Nature always called her when waking. With two more tiny bladders being added, that need would soon become even more necessary.

After the morning ritual of teeth brushing and showering, she realized she needed more clothes or had to do laundry more often. She opted for more clothes. At least, more underwear. She could wear the same sweatpants a couple days before washing.

The scent of coffee dragged her out of the bedroom and into the kitchen. God, she was starving.

Chase was still on the phone, but had eggs, sausage, ham, and bread for toast on the counter for breakfast.

As she filled a cup with java, fingers snaked their way to her backside and grabbed a handful of ass. She playfully batted away his hand and smiled at him. That was something she definitely wasn't expecting. But she could get used to it.

With a mug of hot coffee in hand, she plopped on the stool behind the island counter, waiting for Chase to finish his conversation.

Finally, he set his phone on the counter.

"What did River want so early?" she asked.

Chase seemed hesitant to answer. She knew he was keeping something from her to protect her. Again.

"Chase," she said, "no holding back info to spare me."

Her mate sighed deeply. "You're right. We agreed to that. At least, you did." He gave her a wink then poured scrambled eggs into the frying pan.

"River checked out the compound where we found you and Tryx. Looks abandoned in a hurry. But we need to make sure the threat to you is fully neutralized before you go about gallivanting around town," he said.

"I don't *gallivant*, for your information." She rolled her eyes. "My sister does enough for both of us."

His serious eyes met hers. "You know what I mean."

She sighed. "Yes, I do, love. And thank you for watching out for me. But isn't this over? Tori was doing all this." She thought back to last night. "What happened to her after she shot me?"

He stepped back from the stove, running a hand through his shaggy hair. She remembered how she snagged her fingers in it when she came not too long ago. Her insides heated.

With a deep breath, Chase's eyes snapped to hers. Hot lust shone, sending a thrill through her. But her stomach growled, throwing cold water on them both.

"Babies first, I guess," she said.

Chase spun her stool around and pushed her knees apart. After sliding between her thighs and pressing the head of his hard cock on her covered entrance, he pulled her head back and kissed her. Good and wet.

"From now on," he said, pulling away an inch, "this is the first thing that happens. No talking until I get a deep, hot kiss. Got it, woman?"

She rubbed her pussy up and down his length, eliciting a groan from him.

"You got it, mister." She teased as much as she could. She loved seeing him lose control.

"But my eggs are burning."

He jumped back. "Oh, shit." With a couple steps, he was at the stove lifting the pan from the heat. "That was close."

She laughed, watching his muscles ripple with the movement. All those yummy muscles.

"Now, no more distracting me," she said. "Everything is back to normal for us, right?"

Chase raised a brow. "We've experienced normal?"

True. Nothing had been normal since she stuck herself with the two sharps in the lab. She waved a hand in the air. "You know what I mean."

He dumped eggs into a bowl and laid meat in the pan. "I still have questions I want answered before I let all this go."

"Like what?" she asked.

"Like what was that woman's end game?"

"Her name was Victoria. Tori, to me," Sophia said. A touch of sadness entered her heart, but didn't stay too long considering the woman almost killed her.

Sophia recalled Tori's story. "Her little sister was purposefully bitten. Her body didn't take the change well and she didn't survive it."

"What was her sister's name?"

"Nichola Winchester."

Chase looked over his shoulder at her. "I remember people talking about it when I was young. It happened before I was born. She lived in a town over, but one of the wolves belonged to our pack."

"Well, seems Tori wanted revenge. She wanted to create a serum that would destroy all the shifters or something like that."

Chase remained quiet. She understood why. Genocide was nothing to take lightly. But it was over. She'd destroy her work and not think about it again.

She said, "Let's go to the lab after this so I can get rid of everything. I hate the thought of it sitting around."

He flipped meat onto a platter and dropped bread into toaster slots. "Uh, about that…"

That did not sound good to her. "What about it?"

Chase turned the burner off and moved the skillet back. "I called for a cleaning crew on our way to the clinic last night." He paused.

"And," she said.

"River called to say the things you set on

251

the table…" He paused again.

Irritation started in. She prompted, "The vials and documents of my work, what about it?"

"Seems it's missing," he finished.

"Missing?" She sat straighter on the stool. "What do you mean missing? It was right there."

"River said somebody took the body and your work before he got there."

"The bod—Tori? Somebody stole her body? How can that happen?" She was ready to come out of her skin.

"Calm down, love," he consoled. "We're working on it. I'm calling the sheriff after we eat and we'll make a plan to figure this out."

What the hell? Why would somebody take a dead body and hide it?

"Are we sure it wasn't one of our guys? Someone at the lab?" she asked. The only people she thought were at the lab were Tori and the man she had an appointment with who was running late.

She wondered who that was.

"Could be someone who was there. We're not sure yet." Chase set a plate piled with food in front of her. Breakfast went into her mouth while her brain processed the new facts.

Two scenarios existed: One was a coworker witnessed what happened and hid her work for her until she came back. Took the body, too? Eh, her workers were lab techs not morticians. They'd get blisters if using shovels to bury a body.

Two, nobody knew what was in the vials, so why take them? To analyze and sell? To whom? No scientist would know what the material was, much less what to do with it. That option seemed very unlikely.

"Chase, I think one of the guys at the lab must've hid my stuff, waiting for me to get back. That's the most logical," she said.

"You think?" He looked skeptical, but she was learning that was his job.

"I do. I bet when I go in next, one of my coworkers will search me out to hand it over. We watch out for each other." She hoped, anyway.

He nodded. "That could likely be the solution. I want you to rest at least one day before going in." He set his fork on his plate. "Your body is under a lot of stress. I don't want the babies to suffer for it."

She snorted. "Way to play the baby card, butthead. Now there's no way I'm doing anything."

He smiled at her. He knew what he was doing, butthead indeed.

She did tell him, "I will go to Julia's, though. Tryx is staying there for a while and I want to be there for her."

"That's a good idea. See, you're owning the female alpha role already." He kissed her on the forehead while she chewed. "I knew you'd be awesome."

His phone rang. He glanced at the caller ID and frowned.

"What's up, Sheriff?" Chase asked, pointedly looking at her. His silent message that he was concerned.

She stopped eating to listen to both sides of the conversation.

"Hey, Chase. I've gotten a couple reports about hyenas around the car plant. Could these be the same as those who broke into your mate's home?"

"Could be, Sheriff. Though, I thought they would've left town. Guess not. You want to meet me there? See what can be sniffed out?"

"That would be great. When can you be there?" the sheriff asked.

"Fifteen minutes. Need to get dressed then

I'll leave."

Sophia was putting breakfast dishes in the washer when her mate came up behind her. He put his arms around her.

"I need to go," he said, kissing her neck. She snuggled back into him, wiggling her ass along the front of his pants. She loved the growl that came from him. "Wait till I get back, Miss Tease."

She laughed. "I'll be at Julia's. Can't do anything at their place."

"Didn't stop us the first time." He swatted her ass and headed out the kitchen door to his truck.

She couldn't believe how happy she was. After all these years of being shy and staying in the background, her life ended up in a place where she needed to shine to protect her pack.

Her pack.

Those words were new. And felt good, felt like home.

She glanced at her watch. It was too early to visit Julia and Tryx. Knowing her sister, she wouldn't be out of bed for another hour. And then it'd take another hour for her to wake up.

Now would be a good time to stop by her home and pack up some things to bring back.

Clothes for sure. Maybe some books and definitely all her bathing accoutrements. Men know nothing about taking a real bath.

She plucked her purse from the table by the front door and pulled out her keys. When she placed her hand on the door, the floor shook. The new windows that had been installed a short time ago popped and cracked as the walls rattled.

What the hell was going on?

She opened the front door to a man with his hand raised, ready to knock, and his head turned, looking over his shoulder. Over the forest of trees that separated the house from town, a mushroom of fire and smoke soared into the air.

The man turned back to her, a smile on his face. She gasped.

"Hello, my love." Holding an aerosol spray, his hand lifted in front of her face. "Good to see you again." A mist from the canister covered her face, going down her nose and throat, choking her air.

His name hit her memory before blacking out: Jake Asshole Schnake.

FIFTEEN

Chase chuckled to himself on the way out of the house. He felt sure he was going to enjoy the rest of his life with his mate. After watching River turn to goo when around Julia, he worried he would look weak with his mate.

But he felt just the opposite. He could take on the world with her beside him. Damn he fell hard and fast. Almost a disgrace if they weren't shifters and that being the norm.

As he traveled the paved road away from the pack community, a queasy feeling took over his stomach. He was being paranoid again. Had to be.

Sophia would be fine. The hyenas were

gone, the mastermind behind Tryx's kidnapping and the break-ins had been taken care of (even if her body was currently missing), and a coworker was keeping the DNA samples safe for Sophia.

What else was there?

Turning onto the main road leading in, a vibration from his truck snapped him from his thoughts. On the far side town, above the buildings and shop roofs, a fireball of flames and smoke lifted into the air, followed by another smaller explosion.

If he didn't know better, he'd think the car plant had blown up. That was where he was headed to meet the sheriff. Where hyenas had been spotted.

Chase floored the accelerator and zipped through the downtown streets, running a yellow stoplight, and coming to a stop outside the burning plant's fence line.

He had to sit a second to take in what his eyes were seeing. Thick black ash floated over the upper portions of the plant, resembling a thundercloud filled with black ink. More smoke continued to pour from broken office windows.

Doors on the first floor were open, people exiting on feet, knees, or over someone's shoulder—any way they could. Many were covered in ash, keeping their identities hidden.

Chase punched the truck's engine, ramming through the guard shack's single arm barrier, flying toward the main production line building where most of the smoke hovered.

He was out of his vehicle and inside the door before his brain caught up with his actions. His instincts were to save and protect. Half his pack worked in the plant. It was the main moneymaker in the small town.

People flowed past him in a heavy stream. It was too dark, smoke too thick to see much of anything. Someone yelled to him, "Alpha, second floor. Help."

That was all he needed. When he was younger, he spent several years working in the plant side by side with members of his pack. Here, he'd gained the trust and respect of many of his fellow wolves with his strict work ethic and willingness to go out of the way for others.

Taking the stairs three at a time, he was on the second floor swiftly. His lungs were already overcome with the toxic air. Even though wearing his favorite pair of jeans, he shifted, tearing all material on his body to shreds, which he quickly shed.

In his wolf, he moved much faster, closer to the ground where the air was better.

The upper floor consisted mainly of admin offices and conference rooms. Along the back wall of the building, a section in the middle from ground floor to second-level ceiling was blown inward like a missile had been shot from a fighter jet.

A long pile of shattered wood and debris stretched from one side to the other. Chase's heart squeezed. How could anyone have survived this?

Yet through the chaos and uproar, his senses picked up heartbeats and groans. He shifted to human form and starting chucking pieces of furniture, file cabinets, and drywall every direction to get to those alive.

He dug his way through to an unconscious female, one of his pack. She was bleeding profusely from deep gashes. Summoning his alpha voice, which he didn't often have to use, he ordered the unconscious woman to shift.

Her inner wolf had no choice but to obey, transforming and mostly healing her fragile flesh. He lifted the animal and carried it to the stair landing, the safest place on the burning level.

The next he smelled was a human male,

but there was no heartbeat from him. His wolf cried out inside for the loss of life while he continued through the smoldering fragments.

Others on the floor had found their way from under the wreckage, most confused and in shock. Chase let out a shrieking whistle, drawing their attention. In various zombie-like stages, they made their way toward him. The more coherent helping those worse off.

Behind him, first responders rushed forward, finally reaching the upper floor. He saw Seff and Riel making their way along a different path through the debris. Of course, they had their clothes on, still. Wussies.

A smaller explosion rocked the structure, sending portions crashing to the bottom level. A woman's scream turned his head.

A female dangled, holding on to exposed wires over the hole that had opened from the blast. Burning remnants were below and above her. The only way to reach her was from a snapped two-by-four sticking out over the gaping maw.

With no thought of his safety, Chase launched himself through flames to the board. He discovered that piece of wood was about two feet long. Not enough space for both of them if he pulled her up with him. There was only one way to do this.

After quickly explaining the plan to the woman, he stretched out and grabbed her wrist. On the count of three, Chase yanked the woman up to the board he lay on, giving her his position of safety. As he fell into the fire below, he prayed one day Sophia would forgive him for abandoning her and the children.

SIXTEEN

Sophia woke slowly, which wasn't normal for her. The smells of the room registered in her brain before her eyes even opened.

Without moving, she let her other senses inform her of her surroundings.

The air was chilly and damp, a bit musty as if in an underground room or basement.

Light buzzing noises, like appliances or small machines, were the only sounds.

The surface she lay on was hard, but gave to the bend of her body. A cot maybe. Definitely not Tempurpedic like Chase's mattress.

She smelled fruit and bread, faintly. And of course, her stomach growled, making itself the squeaky wheel.

Opening her eyes, she rose to a sitting position. Looking around, she saw her senses were correct, but her guess on where she was, was far from being right.

If she believed in time travel, she would've thought she was in a 1960's bunker. A secret lab not only hidden, but forgotten.

The room was done in white and teal tiled walls and floors like those in her parents' old elementary school pictures. Army green lockers lined one of the walls and a door that had a sign that said *restroom* sat next to those.

What was surprising was the new lab equipment sitting on a center island. Nothing state-of-the-art, but updated and solid gear.

So, where in the hell was she?

Then the image of her abductor popped into her head. Jake Asshole Schnake. Anger erupted in her chest.

"Hey, prick. Why are you here?" she hollered, not afraid of his reaction to her name calling. She dropped her feet over the side of the cot and stretched her back.

From a corner, she heard his voice.

"My, my. How the princess has changed. I wouldn't have believed it if not seeing with my own eyes," he said. She heard him, but didn't see him. Glancing up the wall, she noted a small monitor with a camera below it. His damn smug face filled the screen.

"Shut the hell up and take me home, you bastard. I told you I never wanted to see you again. And the courts agreed."

"The courts have no control over me," he said, narrowing his eyes, studying her. His voice was calm and calculated, which she knew happened when he was upset. So the justice system had done its job on him. Unfortunately, insane assholes seemed immune to changing for the better.

"Fine, Jake. What do you want?" He didn't reply. That worried her. Jake had always known what he wanted and he made sure everyone around him knew also. No one was getting in his way. Except his own idiotic, non-intelligent self.

When Sophia had first arrived at the CDC viral lab, she kept to herself and did her work as her shy withdrawn personality dictated then.

Jake was a hotshot at the lab who, in her opinion, was a social butterfly dipping into every female's flower to find the tastiest fruit.

He was a nobody to her.

She'd happened upon a discovery she was keeping to herself until she was absolutely, positively certain her data and experiments were correct. She didn't want to go through showing her work and someone finding it to be faulty and wrong.

She was too old to hide in the closet anymore.

Then one day, Jake introduced himself and asked if she'd like to get a cup of coffee. Of course, she said no, but was flattered to hell that he noticed her.

The next day, he brought coffee to her and so she was forced to sit and talk with him. Turned out he wasn't that bad. He sounded intelligent, but he was a research tech so he should've been. His smile was hot enough to melt panties off any woman.

And talk about hot, the man sizzled in the thin white T-shirts he wore under his lab coat. Broad shoulders and pants that hugged his thighs and perfect ass. Mmm, mmm. Eye candy galore.

Sophia couldn't believe he paid her any attention, especially the friendly kind. Before long, he'd wiggled his way into working with her at the lab, and eventually, in the bedroom.

Needless to say, he was much better in bed than he was in the lab. He even introduced her to blindfolds and light bondage. She never enjoyed restraints and such with him. Something inside her didn't completely trust Jake Schnake.

Her suspicions were proven correct. The morning she was to give the presentation on the discovery, Jake had tied her to the bed, stripped her naked, and took pictures with his phone.

He left her tied while he demonstrated her work and took accolades for himself. He knew the shy Sophia would do nothing.

To prove Jake's wrongdoing, she'd have to show the pictures of her naked self sprawled over the bed. Sophia would *never* let that happened.

As a secondary plan, Jake had erased all information related to the project from her computer. If she didn't have the history of data, then it made sense she couldn't have made the discovery.

The only thing that saved her was a backup of her computer onto a flash drive she had in her purse. After losing important info several times due to system crashes and stolen laptops, she got into the habit of having an alternative place to store her stuff.

267

That thumb drive along with testimony from coworkers were enough to convince a judge to award her the case.

She took the money she received in damages and got the hell out of the city, dragging her sister with her.

And now, here she was again, trapped by the dick. Luckily, she was smart enough to not let him slither his claws into her.

"What do I want?" he echoed. "I want everything, Sophia."

Yeah, that was so Jake. "What do you want with me, dipshit?" she said, growing tired of him already. She was being bold, but with shifters inside her, she was stronger and faster than any human. She wasn't afraid of him.

He studied her more from the monitor, quietly. The old Sophia would be huddled under the cot by now, scared of others finding out she was in trouble.

New Sophia wanted to bust out a fang. But did Jake know she was a shifter? He couldn't possibly have a clue. She'd never heard of shifters before her sister was bitten.

She looked at the monitor and saw an empty chair at a desk. He was gone. The sound of metal against metal turned her head and a heavy-duty steel door opened to reveal her captor.

The first thing that hit her was his smell. Holy hell in a basket! He was a shifter. She hadn't known. Then the significance of his name slapped her upside the head.

"You're seriously a snake shifter? Not just an asshole?" she blurted.

He crossed his arms over his chest and leaned against the door. "You were always a bit slow when it came to things outside the lab," he sneered.

She snorted. "Yeah, fuck you, too, dickwad."

A laughed burst from him, surprising her. "I like this new you much better than the other one," he commented. "Unpredictable."

"Ha," she grunted, "You ain't seen shit, yet. Now, I'll ask again, what do you want with me?"

"I want your shifter DNA research," he said.

Why was she not surprised by his answer? Once a liar and thief, always a liar and thief.

She recalled the last conversation she had with Tori, facility director. She said she was waiting for a male. "Are you working with Tori? You part of her scheme?"

"For your information, it's *my* scheme. Winchester played along because she had a bone to pick with the shifter race. One word about getting revenge and she was all in," he answered.

That made sense. Her boss said as much that night the woman was killed. Wait—Chase said the samples on the table were taken and the body missing.

She asked, "What did you do with Tori's body? You'd better do right by her."

Again, he laughed. "Maybe you're smarter than I gave you credit for. Don't worry about Winchester."

"Someone will find her and evidence will link you to her," she said.

Jake laughed. "No, nobody will find her body. I guarantee it."

"This is shifter country, Jake. Someone will smell the decay before—"

"Trust me, Sophia," he sneered, "*no one* will find her body. It's physically impossible."

The man really was stupid. "How could it be impossible—"

"I disposed of her body, but it isn't buried," he huffed. "She's not your concern. You're going to be busy."

Sophia patiently waited for him to continue. He smiled. The little prick was purposefully baiting her. Damn. She'd forgotten how annoying he could be.

"Tell me, Jake, what will I be busy doing?" she asked.

"You will be creating a serum to make supershifters," he answered.

"What?" Did she hear correctly? "Supershifters? As in Superman-like shifters? Being several times stronger than humans isn't enough for you?" Good God. What would it take to please this man?

"You got it, love," he replied.

The side of her top lip lifted in disgust. "I am not your 'love.'"

His eyes darted to her stomach as he smirked. Instinctively, she covered her lower belly.

"Guess you're right. Fucking you to get your research won't work this time. I'm impressed you're screwing the alpha. Went straight to the top, didn't you?"

A growl vibrated in her chest. Jake stiffened and pulled out a gun from his lab coat pocket.

"I suggest you calm yourself and your

animals. I believe you were shot not too long ago."

Her inner companions backed off, but weren't happy about it.

Jake tilted his head to the side, toward a counter. "You have food and water in the fridge. And there's a restroom. You're not leaving this room until I have a working serum in hand. Your research is in the walk-in cooler in the back. Feel free to get started anytime." He slipped out the door, making loud clanking sounds as he locked up behind him.

She plopped down on the cot. Was this truly happening? First, Tori wanted to get rid of every shifter in existence, and this asshole wanted to be Captain America.

If her boss was still alive, she wondered which plan would've overcome? Knowing Jake, he would've done something to Tori. Seemed he was prepared to get rid of her body.

Looking around, she blew out a breath and wondered where to start. No windows, one exit door, she wasn't crawling through AC ducts in the ceiling. She made her way toward the food. Might as well check it out and see the offerings.

No filet mignon, but better than cheese and crackers.

"Oh, by the way," his voice came from the monitor on the wall, "your computer and research are on the counter next to the microscope."

She looked over her shoulder to find where he was talking about. Yup, that was her laptop she locked in her office. Tori made everything easy for him.

Taking a handful of grapes, she moseyed to her computer and opened it, making it look like she was working even though escaping was at the top of her thought list.

She needed to focus to try to reach Chase with their telepathic wave in the sky, radar love thing. Hopefully, he was at a place where he could communicate with her.

SEVENTEEN

Chase glanced up at the woman balanced on the two-by-four he was on less than a second ago in the burning car plant. At least she was safe. His death by fire wouldn't be in vain.

His only regret was that he wouldn't get to see his children. Well, he believed in an afterlife, so maybe he'd see his children from wherever he ended up.

Suddenly, his body was slammed into by something cold, hard, and...wet?

He flew sideways through the air and crashed onto the concrete floor away from the main fire. Sitting up, he shook water from his drenched hair.

"Sorry, Alpha." A firefighter on the other side of the blown-open wall held a firehose on the flames. "Didn't see you coming down."

Chase raised a wave to him. "No problem, Eli," he called out. Getting to his feet, he chuckled to himself. "No problem at all."

With a cough, he headed toward the closest exit, which was where he'd parked his truck earlier. He had a pair of shorts stuffed somewhere in the back that he could slide on.

He was comfortable in his nakedness, like most shifters were. But there were humans outside, and of course, being in cold water always caused shrinkage, and he didn't want anyone to think he was usually this size...not that size mattered...well...

Outside, fire trucks, ambulances, and other flashing lights filled the parking lot in front of the building. Responders and factory employees bustled in different directions. Some handing out blankets to those in need, others helping the injured to medical personnel.

"Chase," River hollered from somewhere among the crowd. Of all times for his beta to open his mouth and draw attention. Chase hurried to his truck before everyone and their brother saw him—all of him.

"Hey, man," River said, "you okay? What's going on?"

Chase pulled a black pair of workout shorts from under the back seat and slid them on. "Hell if I know. But I'm thinking hyenas had something to do with it. You demolished that shack where Tryx was held, right?"

"Yeah," River responded, "last week. Same day we rescued Tryx and your mate. Cleared the place then leveled it." Julia came up beside his beta.

Chase nodded. Speaking of mates, he searched the crowd for his.

"I take it Sophia hadn't made it to your house yet," he asked Julia.

She shook her head. "No. You want me to call her?" Julia asked.

"No," he said. "If she's at home, that's fine. I don't need her worrying over anything."

Sheriff Hurley tapped the hood of the SUV as he came around the front side. Soot and ash covered his uniform and face.

"Glad you're all right, Chase," the sheriff said. "Scared the shit out of me for a second."

Chase bobbed his head, a little embarrassed by the concern from another respected male.

River and Julia eyed him. "What happened?" River asked.

"Nothing," Chase said, cutting off any response of the sheriff. "Just doing my job protecting lives." He pointedly stared at the officer beside him. He didn't need any glorified stories getting started when he did what anyone else would've done.

The man lifted his hands. "Whatever you say. My official report will read otherwise," the sheriff replied with a smile.

"I'd like a copy of that report," River said.

Chase snorted. "Not on your life." He turned to the town's peacekeeper. "What do you think happened? Accident on the plant's part?"

The sheriff rubbed his chin, staring at the smoking remains of the structure. "Not sure. I'm inclined to say it wasn't a coincidence that the hyenas were spotted around here, but who knows?"

"I don't get it," River said. "Why would hyenas mess with the plant? It has nothing to do with Sophia."

That was a good question. One Chase didn't have an answer to. From the corner of the building, a fireman yelled out for the sheriff. Hurley motioned for Chase and River to follow. Julia stayed with the truck.

The back side of the facility was demolished. Chase immediately smelled gunpowder in the air. "Explosives," he said.

"Shit." The sheriff kept walking, now with a frown on his face.

River took a deep breath. "Yeah, I'm picking up hyena stench under the smoke. They were here."

The guys stood behind the firemen as they hosed down the second floor. Seff and Riel edged out from the ragged opening, both soaked through. Chase laid a hand on each of their shoulders as a gesture of a job well done. As alpha, he complimented the good as well as disciplining the bad.

"How many didn't make it?" he asked Seff.

"I smelled two, but the smoke interfered a lot," his enforcer replied.

Chase nodded. It could've been much worse.

What was the purpose for all this destruction, he wondered.

Sheriff Hurley slapped Chase on the back. "Go on home, Alpha. I think every emergency responder in the county is here right now. Not much you can do."

Chase agreed. He wanted to get back before his mate left the house. River walked with him to his truck where Julia was looking at her phone and frowning.

She glanced at Chase. "Soph isn't answering her phone."

Alarm raced through his already adrenaline-laced blood. Then his brain kicked in. "She might be outside or in the laundry room."

Julia's face drained of color. Whatever was going through the drama queen's head wasn't good. Chase glanced at his brother. River gathered his mate to him.

"I'm sure your sister is fine," he cooed, walking her away.

Julia replied, "But the hyenas—"

Chase pulled the truck door closed on her last word. Hyenas. They were still around. Could this have been a distraction to get him away from the house so she would be vulnerable?

The wheels on his SUV spun on the wet pavement as he tore out of the parking lot. He didn't care that others stared openly at him speeding away. The only thing he cared about was his mate.

If the bastard dogs were still around, waiting to get his mate, where had they been holed up all this time? There was a lot of forested area they could've hunted and survived in their animal forms. But where did the explosives come from?

By the time he passed his beta's home on the way to his, his wolf was ready to explode from his chest. It wanted to find their mate now. To have her next to them now.

Swinging into his driveway recklessly, he saw her car and nearly melted with relief. She was home. Sleeping, he bet. She was just napping and didn't hear the phone.

He entered through the kitchen door a bit too hastily, bouncing it off the wall.

"Sweetheart, are you home?" he called out. Steps quickly carried him to their bedroom. The sheets and comforter had been pulled up and folded back, ready for tonight. But no Sophia.

"Sophia," he called out again. Backtracking, he walked by the front entrance and saw her purse and keys on the floor. He lunged at the door and nearly ripped it off its hinges opening it to look out.

Standing there, he breathed in traces of a

pungent, musty odor, typical for inhalant anesthesia.

They came right to his fucking front door and took her.

He fell to his knees in a panic so consuming, it blocked out everything around him. That's when he heard her. She'd communicated telepathically with him through their animals a couple times already. How had he forgotten about that?

Shifting into his animal, her wavelength came in louder and clearer.

"Chase? I need you. Hear me, please."

"I'm here, baby. Where are you?"

"Chase! Oh my god. You're there."

She sounded in hysterics. *"Calm down, love."* Like he should be the one telling her to calm down from the state of mind he was in a second ago. *"Tell me where you are."*

"I don't know. A room without any windows. It's like a basement. I can't get out."

"Okay, love, tell me how you got there."

He felt rage surge on the connection between them. She said, *"By an asshole, shithead, fucking prick dick."*

"I take it you know this person," he replied to her description.

"*A jerk from my past. Jake Schnake. It's a long story.*"

He'd heard that name before. When was that?

"*How are you? Did he hurt you?*"

"*I'm fine. A little nauseated from the spray he used to knock me out, but okay other than that.*"

"*Good. Sit tight. I have to find a way to get to you.*"

"*How? I don't even know where I –* " she stopped for a second.

"*Sophia?*"

"*The bastard is talking to me. I have to go.*"

"*Stay safe. I will find you.*" He shifted back to his human form and lay on the floor. Panic was grasping for him again. How was he going to find her? Where did he start?

The man's name, Jake Schnake. River had mentioned that name just this morning. His brother said the man was the facility director at the lab Sophia worked at. Chase began to doubt that was who he really was.

If the guy was the director, Chase would've met him at least once by now. And for the director to have an animal River had never come across? That didn't seem likely. Time to meet this guy.

He grabbed his keys off the kitchen counter then realized he was buck naked from the shift a moment ago. Shit.

Finally properly clothed, he headed to the research lab for lack of any other place to look for clues of his mate's whereabouts.

In the distance, black smoke rose high into the sky, the dark column then bending toward the east with the air currents.

Coming around the corner to the lab's main parking lot entrance, Chase glanced at a person standing in the shadows. The face he instantly recognized and slammed on the brakes. The truck was barely in park when he flew out the door.

In seconds, he had the rat-faced hyena around the neck.

"Where is she?" No preamble of polite words, straight to the heart of it. He only wanted one answer.

Ratface's face bloomed red, unable to breathe. His long, skinny fingers scrabbled at the fingers around his neck. His mouth moved, though no words issued. Chase wanted it that way, just to get his point across. Answer or death.

When the piece of shit was turning dark purple, Chase released his hand and the bastard fell to the ground, gasping.

Glaring down at the scum, Chase had to control his wolf from taking charge and mauling the guy. "Give me one reason not to kill you where you sit."

Fearful eyes turned up to him. "I know where he took your mate."

Chase grabbed the hyena by the back of his shirt and hauled him to the passenger's side of his truck and shoved him in. As soon as he closed the driver's door, Chase demanded, "Which direction?"

Ratface pointed to the left. Chase skidded tires onto the main drag.

As they passed the car plant, Chase asked, "You in charge of that?"

Rat snorted. "Tried to stop it. Unsuccessfully, obviously."

Chase really looked at the hyena for the first time. The man's shirt was ripped in places and blood stains splotched the material. His face had scratches and dried blood on it. His pants and shoes were covered in dirt and grass stains.

"Why would you do that?" Chase asked.

Ratface shrugged and stared out the window. "Had no purpose to do it." Chase glanced at him. What did he mean by that? "Turn here."

He slowed and cornered onto a side street that led to the town's reservoir. The road was seldom traveled as far as he knew. And nothing was back there.

"If this doesn't take us straight to her, I'm killing you and dumping your body for the animals to feed on."

Ratface sighed. "It'll get us there."

They remained quiet while he navigated the little maintained road until Chase asked, "You gotta name?"

"Mickey," Ratface said.

Chase held back a retort. "As in…"

"Yes," Mickey replied, "as in *mouse*." Sadness and shame wafted from the shifter. Chase wondered what kind of childhood someone like this guy had. Couldn't have been normal. He couldn't imagine a rodent/hyena mix. That was fucked up.

"So, Mickey," Chase said, "what the hell is this all about? Why are you after my mate?"

With a sigh, the dog rubbed a hand over his head. "Long story, for the most part."

"Give me the cliff notes," the alpha ordered.

"Yeah, fine. Some snake shifter came to Victoria Winchester, the lab's facility director, and gave her the opportunity she'd been looking for to destroy the shifter population."

"Why would she do that?" Chase asked.

"You want the cliff notes or the audiobook?" Mickey said.

Chase grimaced. "Keep going."

"Anyway, all she had to do was get him the work of this Dr. Reese and he'd create a solution for her. But for her to do that, she had to find a way not to implicate herself, if she wanted to keep her job. That's where I came in."

"And the other dogs with you?" Chase clarified.

Mickey nodded. "Members of the group I belong to. We were tasked with getting the research. Unfortunately, Tori didn't know that Reese setup the safe's security features. Before, it was just used as storage with no locks. Things didn't go as smoothly as she thought."

Chase grunted. "I'd say."

At the end of the paved pathway, a car sat partially hidden behind brush.

"Stop here. We walk the rest of the way."

Chase eyed the shifter next to him, but

MILLY TAIDEN

didn't question the directions. He didn't smell deceit.

After passing the reservoir's dam on foot, curiosity got to Chase. "Why are you helping me? All this time you've been trying to take my mate. Why the change?"

Mickey pushed through wild brush, swatting tree limbs away from his face. He was silent for so long, Chase thought he wasn't going to answer.

But then he started. "I was in love once, a long time ago." He snorted at his own words. "Yes, someone who looks like me actually found a woman willing to see past the facade.

"As you can imagine, my growing up wasn't the happiest of situations. Kids are cruel even at that young of an age. If you're not pretty or skinny, you're not part of the 'in' group.

"And I was really fucking far from the 'in' group. Grew up fighting to stay alive. Shifter teens are worse than humans. Got into the wrong crowds, done things I shouldn't have to be accepted, to feel like I belonged. Then all that changed when I met Nichola.

"She was a beauty straight from heaven. Knew how bad I was, but saw how much I hurt inside from the life I'd chosen."

He laughed. "The woman must've been blind or something 'cause she never once frowned with disgust when looking at me or cringed away from touching me.

"Hard to believe she came from the family her bitch older sister came from. The Winchesters. They had money and power, but no family love. Talk about dysfunctional. The gangs I ran around with had more love than her parents.

"I loved her, but she didn't love me. She had eyes only for my best friend. For the longest time, it was the three of us, hanging out, playing video games, eating pizza. Then suddenly, Nichola decided she had to be one of us—shifter. She wanted to do everything she could to belong. Ron, the one Nichola loved, told her it was too dangerous, and he refused to change her.

"She begged me to help her. Pleaded with me. Told me her heart would be forever broken if she couldn't be Ron's true mate. What could I do? I loved her secretly. Had for years. I couldn't stand to see her so unhappy. I would've done anything for her. And I did.

"I looked for a wolf who would change her. But she found one herself first—a piece of trash who would do it for a lot of money. How Nichola came up with it, I don't know. Not caring about her life one bit, the bastard took the money and mauled her. I found her minutes before she bled out. I held her in my arms until she took her last breath."

Chase's heart went out to the guy. He currently understood what it felt like to have the only person who mattered ripped away with no hope of getting them back.

The men tramped through forest with little sound but leaves crunching underfoot. The tiny critters whose short lives made the cycle of life spin continued on their way of collecting food and carrying it back to the mound or hive.

Mama birds brought food to their nests filled with open beaks. And squirrels buried nuggets of goodies for when the snow covered the ground.

Life went on even though one precious light was snuffed too early.

Mickey had finished his story, apparently. Chase didn't want to know any more of it. Seemed Tori Winchester, Nichola's sister, either guilted or blackmailed Mickey into helping her get Sophia's work.

But it still didn't explain why the hyena was helping him get his mate back. Maybe it didn't matter. Maybe people could change when faced with the truth of their lives.

Mickey ducked behind a bush and lifted his arm to stop Chase. The alpha crouched in behind him.

"What?" he whispered.

"The camera watching over the entrance is ahead."

Chase leaned to the side, peeking through the pile of brush in front of them. Whatever entrance they were headed for, he didn't see. Even with shifter eyesight.

Mickey said over his shoulder, "Stay here. I'll be back."

Chase watched as the man skittered from tree to tree, then climbed a sturdy ash. After a minute, Mickey jumped down and signaled for him to come out.

Chase looked up the tree and saw chewed wires dangling from a small camera. He raised a brow at Mickey.

The shifter shrugged. "It's what rodents do. Chew on wires and never get shocked. Beats me how we do it." He knelt at a metal sheet lying on the ground. It looked strange. Like someone just set it there and left.

Mickey wrapped his fingers into an indentation Chase didn't see at first and pulled. Nothing happened.

The hyena blushed and quickly stepped away. "You can open this better than I can." He pointed to the finger hold. "Normally, a remote would signal the plate to slide, but you'll have to force it either back or off completely."

"Okay." Chase got down on a knee and grasped the indent. He'd use his body weight and try to wrench the plate completely off. Bracing his legs and feet, he leaned back and pulled with everything he had. If this was the way in to his mate, by god, it was going to open.

Fortunately, the sheet metal wasn't as strong as it looked, or his shifter lent him a big paw. Either way, the piece of steel ripped from the automated track it was on and flew backward, out of Chase's hands. It embedded itself in a tree trunk, slicing halfway through.

Good thing Mickey ducked or he would've been divided into two smaller pieces.

"Jesus, dude, that was close." Mickey ran a shaky hand over his hair. "I about shit my pants."

"Sorry, man," Chase said, looking down the newly revealed hole. "What is this?"

Mick shrugged. "Some kind of underground military facility. Some throwback to the Cuban Missile Crisis. Has its own self-destruct button, even. The Snake brought us here to work out of until he got what he wanted. It's been abandoned for decades."

"Go in first?" Chase asked.

"Nah," Mick shook his head, "this is as far as I go. Follow the hall to the end and turn left. That'll take you to the living quarters. He's got a lab setup. She's probably there."

Alarms screamed in Chase's head, but he smelled no treachery, only...regret? Still, he'd have to be on his guard.

He held his hand out to the one-time enemy. Mick stared at it, then turned glassy eyes to Chase.

The alpha said, "Still don't know why you're helping me, but I appreciate it more than you know."

Mickey grasped the outstretched peace offering. "Maybe by saving the lives of your two unborn, it'll make up for the tiny one I lost along with their mother when all she did was love me." He slipped into the trees and was gone.

EIGHTEEN

Sophia stood in the military laboratory, staring at her blank laptop screen while focusing on Chase's telepathic link with her. She felt so useless. She couldn't tell him where she was, how long she'd been there, or even how she got there.

She heard Jake talking to her from his monitored position in another room. If she didn't answer him, he'd know something was up. Did he even know she was mated to Chase and could communicate with him?

She told Chase she had to go and hoped he discovered a way to find her. If not, she could be there a long time. And no way in hell was she giving birth in a sixty-year-old abandoned bunker.

Her name echoed in her ears.

"What?" she hollered back. "Quit yelling. I can hear you."

"Then why aren't you answering me?" he shot back.

"Because I'm trying to think, which requires ignoring you," she replied. "Do you think I'm just gonna pull this outta my ass or something? This has never been done before."

He smirked on the screen. "No funny business, now. I'm trying your serum on you first. If it kills, then you go without me."

He wanted to play shitty, did he? Bring it on. "Well, let's see here. You had my work for a week and I don't see any advancement here. Could it be that you couldn't even figure out what I did, even though it was right here in front of you?"

His smirk dropped from his face. Anger glared at her. "Oh, wait. That is why you kidnapped me, because you're too much of an idiot to know what the fuck makes up a DNA strand."

She was on a roll now. "That makes me wonder how you graduated with your degree. Did you fuck your way through classes, Jake?

That's the only part of you worth anything. God knows your personality sucks."

The image on the screen became distorted, or was Jake himself becoming distorted?

She continued her poking and prodding. "Don't you see when you enter a room that others quickly look for a way out? They don't want to listen to you BS about your great accomplishments when they know you're so full of shit, you could be your own fertilizer company. Just open your mouth and the shit spews everywhere."

Strange noises came from the speaker. Pops and snapping that sounded a bit like when Chase shifted to and from his animal.

Stepping closer to the TV on the wall, she couldn't believe her eyes. Jake's body had grown taller, and much thinner. What was happening to him? His neck stretched toward the webcam port, like a giraffe reaching for the leaves at the top of the tree.

His head narrowed, pupils turned to slits, and a long, forked tongue flitted out of his mouth.

Sophia slapped a hand over her mouth to dampen her scream. Snakes, especially pythons, were not on her favorites list. She swallowed hard.

"Hey, dude. Chill the fuck out," she said. "I'm just giving you a hard time. You used to razz me all the time about shit. I'm just returning the favor."

Jake the Snake pulled back from the camera. His neck shortened and eyes turned back to human.

"Man," Sophia said, "if you're going to rule the planet as super snake shifter, you need to build a thicker skin." She cringed at her words. "No pun intended."

His body continued to fill out his clothes where they had become baggy and hanging on him.

"Why don't you check on me in a couple days to see if I've come up with anything. I've got enough food until then. Take a break and rattle around elsewhere. Maybe curl up and take a nap under a rock." Shit. She needed to close her mouth.

Jake left the desk where the webcam was setup. She prayed he wasn't coming to the lab. She'd completely squig out if he slithered into the room.

Not wanting to keep her feet on the floor, she hopped up on counter and scooted back against the wall. She popped a grape into her mouth.

She wondered how she would go about creating a super shifter shot that would make a shifter better than they already were.

First question was what constituted "better"? Being stronger, bigger, faster, smarter? Dinosaurs were big but didn't last. They could've eaten them out of food after so long. Cats were some of the fastest, but they still weren't top of the food chain. Humans were the smartest, well, supposedly.

Who was it that said humans would need to get off the planet in a thousand years? Stephen Hawking, she thought. Then he said if people continue developing AI, it would overrun humans in a hundred years.

Damn, none of that sounded "better."

Maybe what comprised of survival wasn't a supremeness, but the ability to adapt, to change to the environment.

Like when she was in the tree in her wolf form. Her inner ladies put their heads, or paws, together and gave her what was needed to capture her prey.

That was an interesting thought. What if the answer was combining traits instead of magnifying what already existed?

She hopped off the counter and organized her work area. Pulling microscopes, spinners, separators, beakers, burners, and pipets, she set up for quick experiments.

Coming back from the cold storage, she set her pure lioness DNA vial and her pure wolf vial carefully in the rack. With a drop of cat on a glass plate, she slid it under the microscope. Then with a steady hand, she added a drop of wolf onto the feline.

The reaction was incredible. She'd never seen anything like it in her life. The two species attacked each other, virtually swallowing smaller cells until only bigger cells existed, but those cells were now a combination of both DNAs.

So now, only the strongest, biggest of both reproduced. Was that what her insides looked like? She wanted to know.

In a glass container, she created a mixture of half-cat, half-wolf and filled a syringe.

Looking around for something to poke her finger with, she felt a sting in the nail tip. She glanced down to see a needle-sharp claw protruding.

"Nice." She punctured another finger and squeezed a drop onto a glass slide. Placing it under the scope, she looked into the eyepieces. Surprisingly, they were different.

Why was that? Perhaps the way the cells

were introduced to the human DNA made the difference. She had pure samples of both injected at the same time. Not a mixed portion.

She dropped one cc of the combined DNAs onto her blood.

As she watched, the hybrid potion separated into the feline and wolf parts and rejoined with similar cells in her blood.

That made some sense. All the material was from the same base source. What she didn't know was how the serum would react when introduced to a shifter with its own animal.

Would the cells battle it out to the strongest, or would they combine to create something new? She could only theorize the end result.

"Sophia." She gasped as Chase's voice came into her head. Her eyes darted to the monitor. Jake wasn't watching or at his desk.

"I'm here. Where are you?" she asked.

"I'm where you are," he replied.

Sophia slapped her hand over her mouth to keep her outcry quiet. He was here. He found her. She wasn't going to question how, just accept and do what she could to get out.

"Love, it's a maze. I need help to find your

location," her mate said.

Her head whipped around looking for something that would help. A pair of heavy metal tongs sat on a counter. Snatching those up, she made her way to the iron door.

She banged out the "Shave and a Haircut" ditty, minus the last two knocks. Bum-diddy-bum-bum… Glancing at the monitor, she didn't see Jake at his desk.

Where could he be? Not knowing about his location worried her.

"Chase," she said telepathically, *"watch for Jake. He could be anywhere."* Just then a red light in a corner began to flash. That couldn't be a good thing.

"Gotcha. Bang again. I think I'm close." Tool in hand, she beat bum-diddy-bum-bum, bum-bum. She added the last two beats.

Next thing she heard were sounds coming from the other side of the door. It opened to reveal a naked Chase. She loved this shifting thing, as long as it wasn't her shifting. That shit hurt.

He scooped her into his arms and swung her in a circle. "You ready to go?" Chase asked.

Sophia looked over her shoulder at her workstation then broke away from him.

"I have to either take the samples or get rid of them somehow."

At her setup, she put the cap on the end of the syringe needle containing the DNA mixture of both animals. Where could she keep it in a safe place? The securest location on her body was between her plump boobs. As good as any. She slid the container down her bra, needle side facing down. Though it didn't matter; her tests show the mixed DNA didn't affect her.

Chase set a hand on her waist. "Are these two the vials you need to get rid of?" he asked.

She nodded. "There isn't a place here to properly dispose of the material."

"You mean, like this?" Chase said as he lifted the glass vial from the rack and thrust it onto the concrete floor.

"Chase!" Sophia couldn't believe what he just did. Then again, the DNA wasn't toxic, not usable, unless injected.

Chase picked up the second vial and repeated the action. He grabbed her hand. "Come on, let's get out of here. The flashing light doesn't give me a good feeling." Every other second, the room was washed in red illuminance. She felt the same.

Together, they ran through the complex.

"Need to find a plain wood door that leads to the long hallway."

Chase followed his scent, but he probably went down many wrong turns before finding her. He opened a door to reveal what looked to be a control room.

The first thing she noticed was how big all the individual stations were. Nowadays, a thin laptop and portable printer worked in a space smaller than a TV tray.

The room felt old, like a place where ghosts gathered. The only things that appeared modern were the desk in the corner with a monitor hooked up to wires pulled down through the ceiling. The background was the one she saw in the single monitor in her room.

Sophia hurried into the room and stood behind the desk. Like she suspected, the lab was on the screen.

Across the room, Chase gasped. "Shit."

"What?" she asked as she walked toward him.

"We have to hurry." He grabbed her hand again. She looked over her shoulder to see a countdown ticker at fifty, forty-nine, forty-eight, below a red button.

"What's that?" she asked. Probably a

dumb question, but what did she know about old military installations?

Chase said, "If it's what I think, it's a countdown to self-destruction."

"Self-destruction? Shit! Let's go," she hollered as she yanked him through the door.

The next wood door they came to opened to the dim path that led out. Made sense. Whoever started the pending apocalypse would've wanted to get the hell out as fast as he could.

What Chase failed to understand was that big beautiful women didn't flat out run long distances. But she understood his reason for rushing. Life or death.

She wrapped her arm under her breasts to keep everything from flopping with each step. She was able to pick up her speed with those babies being controlled.

A swath of light cut through the dimness ahead of them. When they reached the spot, she saw Chase's clothes on the floor at the base of ladder-like steps going up the wall. This was where he entered and undressed before shifting. How did he find this entrance? They had to be miles from nowhere.

"Go." Chase lifted her to the third ring. With a little squeak, she grabbed the next rung and climbed. She pulled herself out, Chase right behind her.

He picked her up by the waist and ran along a treeless path. She trusted he knew what he was doing.

The ground shook violently, causing Chase to lose his footing and go down with her. She heard an explosion, and another, and another. Good God, how big was the place they just vacated?

Chase helped her up. "You okay?" he asked.

"Yeah, fine," she replied. "Where are we?"

"Behind the town's reservoir. I bet the compound was hooked into the water. Probably the reason the government built it."

She noticed he had his clothes on again. Darn, he'd dressed while she made her way up the ladder. Oh well, still damn good-looking.

Walking along the path, she felt bad about leaving her work behind but now it was buried in the lab under tons of concrete. And without it, no one would want anything from her.

"Do you think Jake was still inside?" she asked Chase. The dirt path was ruddy with grass growing through most of it. It would've been somewhat hard to find if not knowing where to look.

The forest lined the sides and the canopy covered it, so it wasn't noticeable in the air.

"No, I think Jake set the alarm and fled. Once he figured out the compound was breached, he probably high-tailed it out of there. I think this is over."

Suddenly, she was jerked toward Chase as he was tugged away from her. His hand broke from hers as he was lifted off the ground.

She ogled him as the camouflage-marked snake, hanging off a tree limb, twisted further around Chase's body. She thought it was a snake but it was as round as a small blown-up beach ball. It had to be Jake. And Jake was a python who could eat a human after suffocating him.

Oh my god. She realized why no one would find Tori's body. In snake form, Jake had — she would've thrown up on the spot if her mate wasn't in a life or death situation.

"Chase!" The snake had completely encircled Chase, arms pinned to his body. The python squeezed her shifter. With each of Chase's exhales, the animal constricted. Eventually, Chase wouldn't be able to breathe in and would suffocate.

If Chase shifted into his wolf, the snake would wrap around it. He'd be in no better shape.

It was up to her to save him. But how? She searched for a downed tree limb.

Chase wiggled and kicked to no avail. With his arms trapped, he couldn't do anything.

There were no weapons there for Sophia to battle with. The end of her fingers tingled then stung. She looked down to see sharp as shit claws. Those would work well.

Good thing. Chase's face had turned red. He had seconds left.

Arms extended, Sophia swiped at the lowest twist of snake. The skin split, revealing bright-red blood and pure muscle.

A hiss echoed in the air. The damaged tail end of the snake snapped around and punched her backward where she fell. She got up and charged, claws out and ready. The tail whipped around again, socking her before she even got close.

What else could she do? Chase was turning purple. "Jake, let him go. I'll give you the serum. I figured it out," she cried out. It was possible the mix of the DNAs was the solution.

Jake didn't seem to loosen his hold on her mate. Chase's head nodded. He was dying.

The sample syringe in her bra came to mind. She had wondered what would happen when introduced to a shifter. She was about to find out. It was her last hope.

She pulled the syringe from between her boobs and took off the needle's safety cap. Climbing to her feet, she kept the needle hidden in her hand.

"Jake, please." She stepped forward. "Let's negotiate. What do you want?" To talk, he'd have to shift, thus releasing Chase. He wasn't falling for it. Apparently, he wanted to kill her mate first. She took another step, now within arm's reach of the flesh.

Her thumb rested on the syringe plunger. She took a deep breath, trying to keep her emotions right so Jake wouldn't smell anything.

With a lunge forward, Sophia stabbed the needle through the thick skin, her thumb pushing as hard as it could. Once again, the end smacked her away.

Sophia watched the snake's face for any sign of problems.

Suddenly, it dropped Chase. He landed on the side of the path with a *thud*. He sucked in a loud breath and coughed.

Sophia ran and grabbed him by the arm,

dragging him to other side of the trail. The snake fell in a heap, its eyes meeting hers. Confusion overpowered the angry vibes he gave off. Then his slit pupils glazed over.

The snake's head widened, neck shortening. He was turning into his human shape. Wait—his arms and legs were shifting to those of a wolf. His face spouted golden hairs as his mouth opened, but no sound came out.

Now, its back legs and hips looked like they melted into the browns and olives of the snake. From the cat whiskers, a canine snout pushed out.

His torso rotated between gold, grey, and camo pattern, one after another...

Suddenly, Jake was in his human form, lying on his back, eyes closed. Before Sophia could say anything to him, his body morphed into a pile of water that instantly spread out and soaked into the dirt.

Both she and Chase stared at the wet spot on the ground, mouths gaping. Chase was the first to stand and he pulled her up and away from the dark spot.

"What happened to him?" he asked. "What was all that weird changing he was doing?"

She had theorized correctly earlier. "I think the DNA from the three shifters fought for dominance. None being strong enough to take over." She stared at the gravesite. "I'm guessing his human form couldn't take the stress of the battle and his cells...returned to their original state of matter."

He nodded. "Ashes to ashes." Perfect analogy. "Let's go," he said. "I think this is over."

Sophia slapped his hand holding hers. "Don't say that. The last time you did, a snake picked up your ass and tried to kill you."

"No worries, love," he wheezed. "I've got you to keep my ass safe."

Sophia smirked. "You got that right. It's all mine."

THE END

WAIT! Keep reading for your free, limited-time, copy of Pack Princess! If you haven't read it yet, you're going to love it.

MILLY TAIDEN

PACK PRINCESS

DEVIL RIDERS MC

NEW YORK TIMES and USA TODAY
BESTSELLING AUTHORS

MILLY TAIDEN

&

MINA CARTER

This Copy Published By

Latin Goddess Press

Winter Springs, FL 32708

http://millytaiden.com

Pack Princess

Originally Published By

Blue Hedgehog Press

A single night of passion, or the one meant to be…

Evva Castillo knows she's a pack princess. Duty to her family and her pack will always come first. But duty turns to hardship when she's ordered to marry someone she doesn't want. Can her hope for a night away from the packs' prying eyes bring her the courage to go through with her job?

Razor is the leader of the Devil Riders MC. They're rough, tough, and dangerous enough that no one would risk entering their sanctuary. Until a daring princess shows up to cause trouble, stir his libido and give him a run for his money. But when the time comes to let her go, he'll either have to watch her walk away or finally face the past he's been running from…

PACK PRINCESS

— For our readers

We all need a sexy biker to love. Fall for one of the Devil Riders.

PACK PRINCESS

ONE

T *hump! Crack!*

"Argh!"

"Evva Castillo! What in the world do you think you're doing?" Evva's best friend, Giselle, stood at her bedroom door.

Giselle's eyes widened, snapping to the pieces of colorful wood all over the floor. Ten seconds before, Evva had done her best pitcher move and threw the box against the wall, cracking it on impact. The delicate wooden case was a gift during her last birthday from her father.

Father, hah!

He'd gone ahead and put her in such a position that royally screwed her. How could he think that marrying her off to some man she barely knew was a good idea? All for a stupid merging of the packs.

A growl built up her throat. She gripped the glass penguin he'd given her for Christmas, ready to add it to the pile of rubble on the floor.

Evva flipped a long curl over her shoulder and stuck out her bottom lip. "Did you miss the conversation downstairs? The one where I casually found out about marrying what's his name—Chip something or other?"

"Dale Rasmussen," Giselle winced, rubbing her hands on the sides of her jeans. "I know it's hard to understand, but he's a handsome guy who's stepping up as Alpha of his pack. Doing this will not just be a solid way to unite the packs, but to ensure we thrive."

Evva rolled her eyes. "And what about what I want? I don't know him from a can of paint. Come on. And that last name? Seriously? I hope they don't expect me to take it. I can't even say it right."

"It can't be that bad." Giselle stopped the maid at the door and took the trash scooper out of her hands. "I got it, Mayra."

Giselle shut the door to the room and headed for the broken mess. Why couldn't she have said no? Heck, why didn't she have the ultimate tantrum and tell him it wasn't going to happen? Respect. Responsibility. She knew that her father only wanted the best for their pack and that meant she had to swallow her pride and abide by his decisions. Even if it meant losing the precious control she had on her life.

"Stop that, Gigi. You don't have to clean up after me," Evva sighed, putting the glass penguin back on her nightstand.

Giselle grinned and squatted down. "Well, you look like you want to hurl these pieces at the wall all over again."

"Maybe just a little," Evva grabbed Giselle's hand, stopping her mid-sweep. "Wouldn't you hate to have the choice taken out of your hands?"

Giselle's shoulders slumped. "I would. I just think you're going overboard with this. He's a nice guy with a good pack. And come on, he's hot. What else do you want?"

Okay, so maybe Chip wasn't fugly. He did dress impeccably with his tailor-made suits and hair perfectly in place. He kind of looked like a woman's wet dream come true, but there was something about him that screamed weak. That alone was enough for Evva to forget all about his pretty boy smiles and not want anything to do with him.

"Oh, I don't know. Maybe to not be ordered to marry someone. To be allowed a choice. Now father has put me in a position with no other choice. There's a contract in place. No tantrum or feelings will change a thing. He gave my word, and he knows I stand by my responsibilities."

"You're your father's daughter. The most precious and probably most spoiled pack princess."

"Gee, thanks."

It was true. She was spoiled. Anything she wanted, she got. Being the daughter to a wealthy pack meant she was treated as a princess. Which was why she was so angry over being dictated to about something so important. Who cared if the groom resembled Mr. Big from *Sex and the City?* She wanted to make her own choice!

Stupid pack laws.

"You know you are, so cut it out."

"It still doesn't make it right," Evva grumbled.

Giselle picked up the last of the broken music box pieces and stood. She

4

gave Evva one of her teacher-type glares she gave the kids in her class. "You're too big for tantrums. You didn't do them as a child, don't start now. It's beneath you."

"Fine. So I should just accept all this and be miserable for the rest of my life?" she growled. Dammit, that's exactly what she'd have to do.

Giselle took a deep breath before answering. "Why not try to learn to adjust to your new life. Give it a chance. I'm sure it won't be as bad as you think. Dale seems like such a nice guy."

Evva snorted. "You're just as bad as our other friends. All infatuated with Chip and his pretty-boy appearance. That's not my thing, Gigi. I like my men to be harder. Scruffier. With the kind of face that will make you wonder if he'll spank you or kiss you."

Giselle's jaw dropped. "Wow. Where the hell do I find one like that?"

Damned if Evva knew.

She needed to get out of there. To breathe and forget all about that stupid wedding even if only for a few hours. Tomorrow would be time enough to get back to it. For now, she needed a few drinks and to get the hell out of the mansion.

"I have an idea," Evva tugged off the engagement ring her father had handed her on behalf of her fiancée, placing it in one of the drawers of her five-foot tall jewelry box. She didn't dare shove it into one of the ones with her bejeweled toys for fear of Gigi's reaction. Besides, a princess needed her bling.

"What's your idea?" Curiosity and a hint of excitement sounded in Giselle's voice.

"A girls night out," Evva answered nonchalantly. "To say goodbye to my single life, but more importantly, to help me cope with this upcoming change."

"Wait, like a bachelorette party?" Giselle gasped. Hell. Gigi seemed like she might pass out.

"No! No. Nothing like that. There will be no strippers. Maybe just a night at the bar going for a few drinks with the girls. You know?"

"Oh!" Giselle slapped a hand on her chest. "You scared the crap out of me. You know your dad would kill us if he found out you'd gone and done something like that knowing you're engaged."

What her father didn't know...

"What do you say?" Evva asked, hoping

6

to encourage Giselle into agreeing.

"Is that what you really want?" She sat on the chair across from Evva's bed and frowned.

Evva clenched her teeth, glancing down at her lap before lifting her gaze to meet Giselle's. "No. What I really want is to choose my own husband, but since that was taken out of my hands. This is probably the next-best thing. I need some way to relax after the news."

Giselle nodded sympathetically. "I'll get the girls together, and we can go out a last time to help you relax. Give me a few hours to get everyone."

"Thanks. I think this will at least help me unwind. Maybe even be more agreeable." When she died. The poor bastard had no idea what he had coming. If he expected some docile wife, he should've married Giselle. Evva was so far from docile it was laughable. That's probably why her father decided to choose her husband for her. She tended to give most men a run for their money with her sarcastic wit and sharp tongue.

It didn't matter. She needed some time away from her father. He'd made a decision without her input and that was something she had a hard time getting over. Tonight, she'd hang out with the girls and have a few drinks.

Maybe even some fun. She knew there was no escaping her reality, even if just for a few hours, she could pretend she still controlled her life. Then she'd go off and do her duty to her pack. Her husband might hate her within a week, but she'd marry him. It wasn't her fault he chose an alpha princess with a short temper for stupidity. He'd just need to learn to adjust to *her* ways.

* * *

Evva would kill her friends slowly. Each and every one of them. How could they think for even a second that this bar filled with her father's friends would be fun?

She needed to get the hell out if she was actually going to be able to chill tonight and take her mind off things. First things first. Everyone had to be distracted, or they would notice her escape. She smiled at the other girls who would not— no matter how much she mentally begged them to—stop gushing over Chip and how handsome he was.

She was pretty dramatic, but acting as if she were actually enjoying herself was turning out to be harder than she thought. Her smile kept slipping, and her brows wanted to dip down in a scowl. What was the obsession with Chip? He could double as a damn Ken doll.

All perfectly put together. Any man who was prettier than her was not her type.

"So, are you and Dale going on a honeymoon?" her friend, Ann, asked.

Evva's other cousin Lainie clapped excitedly and bounced in her seat. "Oooh! Yes, tell us about the wedding."

Frickin' hell.

What she wanted was to tell them to shut the hell up about Chip and his baby face or his perfectly cropped hair. The eye-twitch she was known for was going to be a dead giveaway on how angry she truly was.

"Ladies and gentlemen," the person on stage spoke. "Let's begin our Karaoke night!"

The crowd broke into screams and claps.

Wonderful. She so needed to get out of there, yesterday. A light bulb turned on in her head. "Oh my gosh!" she turned to her friends. "Go sing Super Freak for me."

Giselle giggled and sipped on her drink. "You're crazy."

"Come on! You know we used to sing that all the time while we were in college. It will be fun. I'll be here cheering you on." Evva grinned. Her cheeks hurt from how hard she tried to keep the smile going.

Frantically nodding, she shooed them toward the stage. "Do it for me. It'll mean so much."

Giselle smiled with genuine amusement.

For a moment, Evva felt like the world's biggest jerk, but then she remembered how Giselle would get to pick her own groom. Evva wouldn't.

"Alright," Giselle agreed, and the women headed for the stage. "Come on, girls. Let's give our bride to be a show."

Evva waited until they were busy answering the DJ's questions before making a mad dash for the door. Her heels clicked on the pavement, drumming away the tightness in her chest and breaking the door to the wonderful freedom she'd wanted.

Now, all she had to do was find a place to drink a little, or a lot, without any of her family or friends telling her what a wonderful thing it was to merge packs.

Scuffling and voices sounded behind her. They grew closer. Louder. Adrenaline rushed through her, urging her to move her ass. She made a quick turn down an alley.

Palms slick with sweat, she leaned against the back of the building, surrounded by darkness. God, she hoped leaning so close to a dirty building would keep her from getting caught. She didn't want to think of the years of grime on the wall rubbing her bare back.

After a few moments of holding her breath, she listened hard but didn't hear anyone enter the alley. Then raucous laughter, music, and cursing drew her attention further into the darkness. She followed the sounds deeper into the alley and to a plain, metal door.

She pushed it open and smiled. Now this was more like it. The room was dark, but she could still see clearly. One of the benefits of her nature. It was a bar, but that was where the similarities with the place she'd left her friends ended.

There was a bar at one end of the room, true, but if any of the chairs crowded haphazardly around the tables matched, then she'd have been very much surprised. Several of them showed signs of repair, as battle-worn and battered as the tables they sat around. The floor underfoot stuck to the soles of her shoes as she ventured further in. There was a lot of leather on show. Not the cutesy, designer sort of leather she was used to seeing. This was more worn-in, worn-all-the-time leather that belonged on the back of a bike.

Shit. She'd walked smack-bang into a damn biker bar. Blinking, she backed up a few steps. A girl like her *so* should not be in a place like this.

She eyed them warily. Bikers, these sort of bikers anyway, were so far removed from her daily existence that they might as well be aliens. She caught sight of herself in a mirror on the wall opposite and forced her spine straight. She was Evva Castillo. She didn't cower and run, not from anyone. Ever.

Her walk took on a sassy sway as she made her way through the bar, checking out the talent. She'd always dismissed biker's as hairy, old, and fat. Motorcycles being something men purchased during a mid-life crisis to try and reclaim some of their youth. Only, there wasn't an ounce of fat on any of the men falling silent as she passed them.

Hunger replaced the surprise in their gazes, but not one of them moved to intercept her. She eyed all the man-candy on display. What was this? Had she walked onto some film-set about sexy-ass bikers? Or perhaps she'd been hit by a truck in that alley, and this was her version of heaven.

"Hey there, Princess. You gone got yourself lost?"

She turned at the voice, almost running smack into the middle of a very broad, very male, very *naked,* chest.

She peeked up, then up some more. The owner of that voice was nice — real soft on the eyes — but not what she was looking for. She hadn't wanted a man. Not really. She'd wanted a way to get away from the pressures of the pack. "Why? Are you going to give me directions?"

He winged an eyebrow up, the expression as scary as hell, but she held her ground. "Someone needs to, before a pretty princess like you gets hurt. Door's that way, sweet stuff. I'd use it before someone takes a liking to you."

She was so out of her depth it wasn't even funny. Should she go? Hell yes. Was she going to? Not in this lifetime. "Thanks, but in case you didn't notice, I'm a big girl. I can take care of myself."

"What Cuffs is saying, Darlin', is that you walk now, or you'll be walking funny come morning," a new voice drawled behind her.

She jerked around and had to crane her neck to stare smack into a pair of silver eyes. Holy hotness. Red, flashing, danger lights blinked on and off in her head. She swallowed hard, adopting a bored expression to cover her reaction. "That's got to be the worst pick up line I've ever heard."

"Princess, that's not a pick-up line. It's a warning."

Leaning back against a nearby table, his hands were on either side of his hips, his ankles crossed as though he hadn't a care in the world. Like the rest of the men in the room, he wore black leathers, but his looked as though he'd been born to wear them. They clung to his legs like a jealous lover, hugging powerful calves and thighs before wrapping around slim hips. She swallowed and yanked her gaze away from his crotch. Unbidden, the line about a gun in his pocket came to mind, and amusement started to twist her lips. Amusement that faded as she dared a glance up at his face again.

Dark angel didn't cover it. He had a face worthy to grace any of the classical sculptures — masculine and virile. Mercurial, silver eyes filled with enough heat to power a steel mill stared right back at her. Long, black hair framed those perfect features, falling in loose waves around his shoulders that would make any woman green with envy.

Perfect! She held in the urge to squeal. Finally, a man who didn't look like he'd been made from the cute-boy cookie-cutter-mold. Hell, whatever mold they'd used to make him probably broke at birth.

14

She pursed her lips, adding a little sway in her hips as she put her hands on them. She had more than her share of curves, but she was damn hot. An expensive gym membership hadn't reduced the body she'd been gifted with at birth, but it had given her figure a little boost and the stamina…she could give any man the ride of his life, and she knew it.

"A warning? Damn, and here I was hoping it was a promise." She flicked her hair over her shoulder, turning as if to leave. "Too bad. I guess I'll just have to go and find some fun elsewhere."

Fun? She must be losing her mind. Where the hell had that come from? She'd been looking for a place to relax without having to worry about what her family might say. Possibly drink herself into stupidity and forget her upcoming nuptials. Fun hadn't been in the cards. Until now. She didn't complete the turn, a hard hand on her arm spinning her around. Off balance, she yelped and grabbed the nearest thing, which turned out to be a pair of hard, muscled upper arms as she was hauled against tall, dark, and sexy's body.

"If it's a fun time you're after, Princess, then consider it a threat, a warning, and a promise all rolled into one." He smiled, the quirk at the corner of his full lips taking his face from impossibly handsome to panty-wetting-*fuck-me-now*-ness. "I just hope you can keep up."

Her mind dropped straight to the gutter and made a home there. Keep up? He'd have a hard time getting her off him once she got to touch all those lovely muscles. She was definitely going into no man's land. She shouldn't be talking to that dangerous shifter much less baiting him, but she couldn't help herself. He was hot. Oh, so hot, and the way her body reacted to his proximity wasn't something she was used to. Her temperature had shot out of orbit. Liquid fire melted her to the core.

She wanted him, which was damn inconvenient. It wasn't like she'd decided to go out searching for a man or a one night stand. But now that he stood there, in all his muscled and tattooed glory, there was no way she'd pass up the chance of a wild and crazy night with a biker. Tomorrow she could go back to reality. Right now, she wanted to forget all about everything but getting her hands on him. The sooner, the better.

"Is this going to be all talk? I'm growing kind of bored."

* * *

Bored.

Razor had to blink as his brain processed her reply. Bored? The girl was crazy. She had to be to come in here dressed the way she was. The black dress clinging to her curvy body was obviously expensive, and he recognized the fact that her shoes and bag were designer. A legacy from his *beloved* family. A princess indeed and she'd walked right into the gutter with her nose held high.

"Boring you, am I?" His lips quirked wryly. Good thing she wasn't a mind-reader. She'd run screaming at some of the darker thoughts swirling around his brain. But that wasn't his immediate problem.

The interest from the men around them pushed against his skin like the hot wind on the subway. Chatter had died down to a minimum now, and the tension was palpable in the air. His heart sunk. Shit. There was no way she was getting out of here, no matter what she thought about the matter. The Devil Riders were the roughest and most dangerous motorcycle club in the state. Hell, probably the whole damn country…and that reputation hadn't been built without good cause.

Unlike other MCs, not one of the Devils were human—unless Peach, the half-

Fae watching from the back of the bar, counted. Since the guy was homicidal at the best of times, Razor seriously doubted the human race wanted to claim him as their own.

Right now, she'd walked into *Hell and High Water* – the Devil's bar – which meant she was fair game. He flicked a glance up and confirmed that they were the center of attention. Every man, even the ones with laps occupied by Kes and Fliss, the club whores, had their attention on him and the princess. Fuck, even Scales was watching from the back, the dragon-shifter's eyes the bright gold of his beast. Adrenalin surged through Razor hard and fast. Even though his patches included one that said 'President', if Scales wanted to claim the girl, even Razor was going to be hard-pressed to stop him.

No. Mine. Ours! His beast roared from within, the creature pacing. The outburst surprised him. Unlike some of the other shifters cast out from their packs on the whim of an alpha, Razor *was* alpha. Through and through. His control of his beast was complete. Mostly. Except for when a soft and curvy princess was wrapped in his arms.

Her hands smoothed over his upper arms, the interest in her eyes flaring into her scent, and he breathed deeply. Shit, under the expensive perfume that crawled up his nose just to piss him off was another scent. One far earthier and primal than the stuff she'd sprayed on herself.

"You're a shifter?" He growled, just remembering to inject enough human into his voice to avoid a full-on snarl.

Her grip on his arms tightened just enough to show his question surprised her. She really had no clue what she'd walked into. She scanned the room again with renewed interest. Then met his gaze, her eyes bright with her animal's glow. Despite the danger, she took a step closer. "And if I am?" She lowered her voice and inched even closer. "Are you going to call the dog pound on me?"

"No," he growled, letting his beast flare in his eyes for a second. "But I might call a fucking vet if you can't smell the danger you just walked into, Princess."

She licked her lips and grinned. "Maybe I like danger." Her perfectly arched brows slowly lifted. "Or maybe the big bad biker is really a little scared."

That did it. A warning growl rumbled from the back of his throat. Shit, he was losing his grip here and fast. That hadn't happened since the night he'd left home for the last time. "I don't think you get it, Darlin'. This isn't the sort of danger you play with, and then go home to your ivory castle in the Hamptons."

He yanked her closer, rolling his hips to make his point. His leathers weren't that fitted, but more than tight enough for her to feel the hard bar of his cock pressed up close and personal.

"This is the sort of danger that see's you flat on your back, a cock impaled so deep inside you you'll be spitting cum for a week, and a shifters mark on your neck." He was deliberately crude, hoping to scare her off. He prayed he did because she had to walk out of here. Now. Before she caused a fucking riot.

Her lips formed a perfect O and her eyes widened. A breath later, she inhaled. "Where do I sign up? Or should I speak to one of the other gentlemen here?" She made a move to step away. "I want some fun. You either provide it, or I'll find someone who will."

TWO

F *ind. Someone. Who. Will.*

"Over my dead body," he growled, grabbing a handful of the dark curls at the nape of her neck and lowering his lips until they just brushed hers. "You want to play. You got it. But you're playing with me, no one else. And what I take, I keep. You got me?"

She blinked. A flash of insecurity darted through her eyes so fast if he hadn't been watching her closely, he would've missed it. "You don't know what you're talking about. A night of fun is one thing. No need to involve turning things into some kind of happily *never* after. I'm not after any commitment," she said in an almost inaudible husky whisper. "I want a good time. So what say you teach me if the *save a bike and ride a biker* thing is worth trying."

She fit perfectly in his arms, curves pressed up against the hard planes of his body, her breasts mashed against his chest, and damned if he could think of more than parting those luscious thighs and getting himself balls deep inside her. And if she kept talking, that was going to happen on a table in full view of the entire bar.

"I'll teach you everything you need to know about riding, Princess." He teased a kiss against her lips, the caress so brief she didn't register it until he'd lifted his head. She pouted a soft, sexy sound of frustration in the back of her throat. "But don't knock back the happily never after until you've had me. I guarantee you'll be back for more."

"Sometimes we don't have that choice." She glanced away for a second before meeting his stare. Her gaze slipped down to his lips. "I don't need lessons riding, but you might need lessons walking again when all is said and done." She pushed closer and brushed her mouth over his, catching him off guard by nipping his bottom lip before quickly leaning back. "I don't want promises. I want tonight." She cleared her throat. "One night."

Her quick move surprised him, the little nip shooting a line of fire right down to his cock. He growled and tightened his grip in her hair. He nodded. "One night." *For now.*

He eased his fingers open, one by one, his instincts fighting him all the way, and then took her hand and turned, only to find himself eye to eye with Scales. The big dragon blocked the path, eyes maxed out and lust rolling from his skin as he tried to peer around Razor at the woman behind him.

"Seems she walked in of her own volition. Ain't fair for you to keep the good stuff to yerself," he grunted. "We takin' her out back, show her how to please a coupla' devils?"

Fuck. This was so not what Razor needed.

Scales had been a pain in the ass recently, up in his and Cuff's — the club VP — face all the time. It was a situation Razor knew he had to deal with, but not one he wanted to have to sort out right now. And certainly not with Scales. No one wanted the dragon riled up and ready to go, not without a target to point him at.

The best form of defense was a good offense.

Dumping the controls between himself and his beast, he called power to flood his body and crowd under his skin. Without checking in the mirror behind the bar, he knew his eyes had changed, bright blue swallowing their normal silver. There were many questions the club had asked about them, and about his past. None of which he was inclined to answer, especially not here and now. Not with a woman from a different world behind him looking for some fun.

A whisper went around the bar as all attention fell on the two men. Razor was an anomaly when it came to shifters and fighting. He never fought with the power of his beast backing him. Ever. The baddest of bad-asses amongst the Devils, he'd never needed to, so the fact he was maxed out now didn't escape notice.

"Back the fuck off, Scales," he growled, his voice lower and deeper than human. "This one's mine, and that's how it's stayin'. You got a problem with that?"

Scales blinked, glancing between Razor and the woman peering around his arm. Razor yanked her back behind him, ready to shove her toward Cuffs should Scales lose it. If he did, then the shit was going to hit the fan in a big way, and the club would have to fork out to get the bar refit. Again.

The dragon's attitude folded in on itself, and the amber receded from his eyes to reveal their normal, hazel color. He grinned, further reinforcing the fact that he was one nugget short of a happy meal, even for a crazy-ass dragon.

"Nah, no problem." He backed off, his hands up in surrender as he cleared the path to the back of the bar. "Didn't know you had it in ya, Prez. Glad to see you do."

"Yeah…" Razor stepped forward and pulled his princess with him. He didn't take his eyes off the dragon, just in case, until he had her in front of him. Then and only then, did he turn his back, showing the entire club that he didn't fear anyone or anything. Not even a gnarly pain in the ass dragon.

"Keep walking, Princess," he ordered in a low voice, releasing the power under his skin and letting it flow away. His gaze dropped to her curvy ass and the sexy sway of her hips. His lips curved as a different type of heat replaced the buzz of the change in his veins. "Through the door, turn left, and up the stairs."

* * *

Don't jump him. Don't jump him. Christ, he

smelled good. His scent—pure male mixed with animal—woke even the tiniest of her hormones and propelled her to move. Where the hell was the damn room? It felt like forever before she finally reached a plain, wooden door at the end of the hall and pushed it open. The door swung in with a soft swoosh. The heat from his body enveloped her in a cloud of need. He was so close, and all she could think of was getting him naked as soon as possible. A knot formed in the back of her throat.

Stepping over that threshold meant she wouldn't back out now. Not that she could. But this was real. Her brand-new hopes for a night of wild sex were about to come true. Tomorrow, she'd deal with Chip and her father.

She had to curl her fingers into her palms so she wouldn't fling herself at the big sexy biker at her back like some desperate nympho.

For a moment, there was silence behind her. He was either building anticipation or waiting to see if she'd back out. She paused to check out the room ahead. Silently, she took a handful of steps and stopped at the center of the room, still not facing the door.

Though she wanted to turn, face him, run over and rub her face on his chest, she chose to continue examining his quarters. There wasn't a speck of dust anywhere. The dresser had nothing on it. Not a single decorative accent. Not even a photo. The question on whether or not he had family slipped by her mind, and she quickly dismissed it. Too personal. And it was…clean. She frowned. It was really clean. Cleaner than her room. Hell, probably cleaner than her entire house. And they had maids.

"The guy downstairs, he called you Prez. Is that your name? I mean, is that what you prefer to be called?"

"Nope. It's more a title. Most call me Razor." His voice sounded from the doorway, and her imagination filled in him leaning there, his arms crossed over that sexy, broad chest. He didn't elaborate further.

The double-bed took up most of the room, covered in pristine blue sheets without as much as a wrinkle. If she didn't know better, she'd swear he ironed the sheets. What kind of biker did that? She eyed the bed. It was big and nice.

How many women he'd taken to that bed? A slight throbbing took hold of her chest and grew wings. What the fuck was wrong with her? She wanted this. Him. The last thing she needed was to start getting attached to the man. Asking questions she might not like the answers to. At any other time, she would have loved to see how long a relationship with him would've lasted. Things weren't that simple any more. Her life was no longer hers.

"This room is nice. Really...clean."

"Seems to surprise you."

"Most men aren't known for being tidy."

Scuffling sounded from the door, then the sounds morphed into footsteps, and he finally entered the room. A swoosh was the only indicator he'd shut the door, the lock softly clicking into place. She was alone with him. In his bedroom.

Harsh breaths pounded in her chest. Excitement buzzed in her veins in a drugging high.

Her mind begged her to turn. When she did, she wasn't disappointed. She'd never wanted to knock a man out and drag his ass home to tie him to her bed as badly as she did at that moment. It was laughable. He was easily twice her size. Even with her curves, he had a lot of muscles and height on her. Damn, but she would so enjoy licking him from head to toe. She'd probably never grow bored.

Worn, black leather covered his legs. The pants weren't tight, but she could see he was hard. Big and hard. All for her. A slow sizzle floated over her skin. Her muscles ached from squeezing her thighs together. Tearing her gaze from his cock, she glanced up to his vest — also leather, but not the pretty kind Chip would wear. Not the latest brand with a designer label stitched to the cuff. This was rugged, filled with patches that must mean something in his group.

Her gaze rose to his face. He was nothing like Chip. His hair was long around his shoulders, and he had a look so deep she swore he was peeking into her soul. Chip wouldn't let his hair grow more than his usual three point five inches before he got a haircut. Definitely not like Chip. Then there was that mouth. Dear Lord of orgasms, she hoped that mouth was as good at other things as it was at growling. This man turned her on without doing more than gazing at her from a mere seven feet away.

It was now or never. If Gigi found her, Evva would be in deep shit. She'd lose her one chance with Razor, return to her home to marry Chip, and forget all about independence. She'd probably never see Razor again. Already the daughter of a powerful alpha, once the packs united she'd be slapped with some guards and never be left alone again. It sucked big time, but it was what was coming for her. So she did what she knew best.

She poked the wolf with a stick, and hoped he'd come back growling.

She propped her hand on one hip and grinned, staring pointedly at his crotch. "So what's a girl got to do around here to get you naked?"

He crossed the distance between them, long legs not needing more than a few steps until he was toe to toe with her. The heat of his skin beat at her, helped by so much of his chest exposed under the sleeveless vest he wore. Crawled over her skin like a siren's caress, and made her want to get closer. So close she didn't know where he ended and she began.

His gaze held hers, the silver direct and piercing, as though he could see down into her soul. Could see all her deepest, darkest secrets…the thoughts and feelings she dare not admit to. His eyes darkened, heat flaring in the silver, the expression on his face nearly bringing her to her knees with need.

Reaching out a hand, he snagged her around the waist. "Princess, you only have to ask." His fingers spread out over the back of her hips and drew her to him, fit her snuggly up against him.

Her lips parted on a gasp as she felt his cock, thick and long, pressing against her belly. Her hands smoothed up his chest, dipping under the leather of his vest to reach his shoulders. He rolled them to help her, the leather vest falling from shoulders the size of a small barn to catch on his biceps.

It took her all of a nanosecond to realize she was in charge. Her gaze darted from his chest up to his eyes. Drawing on her instinct to seduce, she leaned forward. In a soft whisper of a kiss, she fluttered her lips over his chest, his muscles contracting at the light touch.

"I was right." She couldn't help the need to taste him.

"Right?"

She grinned inwardly at the roughness in his voice. "I can lick you from head to toe and not grow bored." She licked his nipple.

He jerked, a curse dropping from his lips that fell away into a growl of pleasure. The leather slithered down his arms, dropping to the floor unheeded. She smiled and did it again, adding a nip for good measure. That got his hand driving into the hair at the back of her neck, and he yanked her head back. The blue was back in his eyes, and she smothered a whimper at the evidence he was near the edge of his control.

"No." His growl was deeper, not totally human. "We do this *my* way."

Her heartbeat tripped in her chest. She'd never been so turned on by a man taking charge. She didn't just like it, which was unusual, she was ready to get on her knees and do his bidding. "As long as you don't stop."

He slid his free hand down over her ass, gripping the plump curve then lifting his hand. She jumped as it came back down again, in a sharp, light smack.

"Princess, I don't plan on stopping until you're too hoarse to scream my name anymore."

He kissed her finally, his lips crashing down over hers. It wasn't a kiss from the romance novels she loved to read, or even the erotic novels she only read late at night in her room. It wasn't polished and sexy, designed to appeal to her heart. It was raw and primal, intended to seduce all her feminine instincts. She gasped, the sound cut off as he used the opportunity to slide his tongue past her lips.

The slow sizzle he'd started inside her down at the bar with those possessive looks had developed into explosions bringing her blood from simmering to full boil. It wasn't just his lips and the way he owned her with his mouth and tongue. No. There was more. An elemental, primal connection she didn't want

32

to acknowledge.

He'd spanked her. Actually had the nerve to slap her ass, and instead of being outraged, she wanted to beg him to do it again. One thing was for sure, she was about to get much more than just a night of hot sex.

He urged her back toward the bed, and she didn't stop him. Hell, her higher brain functions had taken a hike out into the wide blue yonder, leaving her defenseless. He broke the kiss, turning her around in one swift move. She staggered on her heels, but he was already there, one arm around her waist supporting her at the same time he yanked the zipper at her spine down.

She moaned as the cooler air of the room hit her exposed skin, suddenly glad she'd worn *the lingerie.* Black satin and lace from one of her favorite boutiques made her feel wanton just touching it…knowing *he* was looking at it? Her panties were in meltdown.

He divested her of the dress with a speed that spoke of long practice. Only his hissed exhale and pause when he'd thrown it aside told her that the sight affected him. Then he moved, pressed his hips against hers, and the thick bar of his cock against her ass told her all she needed to know.

"You're fucking gorgeous, Princess," he

growled by her ear, big hands sliding around to cup her tits over her push-up bra. Her generous cleavage practically overflowed the cups. His breathing hitched. She took that to mean he liked her breasts.

He cupped the girls, his hands not gentle, but not rough either. Just enough to arouse. He found the lace at the edge of the cups, then ventured within. She gasped, biting her lip as his fingers found her nipples, stroking them to attention under the fabric.

"And this is pretty, but it needs off. Now." He reached between the cups and flicked the clasp. It gave, the cups falling away and tumbling her tits into his hands.

She lolled her head back into his chest. His hands on her body felt good. Right. Like they belonged there. She wanted, no, needed more. Her own breathing filled her ears, and need controlled her every move. "One of us is overdressed. And it's not me."

He nipped her ear, the pain small but sharp, shooting a line of fire right down to her clit. It throbbed, as eager for his attention as her nipples. "My way, my rules. Problem with that?"

She wanted to ask too many questions. It was her nature. Instead, she shook her head and followed her instincts. "No. What do you have in mind?"

"What I have in mind? You'll have to wait and see."

He moved, the loss of his body heat against her back making her shiver. His hand landed on her ass again, warming her with an entirely different kind of fire. She jumped, but the sound that emerged wasn't one of pain, but pure desire. Before she could recover from the spank, he tweaked her nipple, making her jump and gasp again. She wanted this, wanted him.

"Seems the princess likes a little bit of pain."

He was back, his breath washing over the side of her neck and stirring the small hairs at her hairline. Another slap and she was ready to squirm and beg. His rough palm stroked over her ass, then his fingers curled under her panties, dragging them down inch by slow inch. For each inch, he played with her nipple. Stroking. Pulling. Tweaking.

The underwear fell around her ankles, and he stepped away. She pouted and made to turn, but his growl warned her to stay where she was.

"On the bed, hands on the headboard. And don't move unless you're told to."

PACK PRINCESS

THREE

She bit her lip to keep from saying the sarcastic reply that came to mind. She was this close to coming without him even doing anything and the last thing she wanted was for him change his mind.

She jumped to do his bidding, all the while wondering what the hell was wrong with her. She wasn't the type of woman to be follow orders. Everyone knew that. She liked bossing people around too much.

Yet... she didn't cower from his aggressive touch, or the kiss that destroyed her brain cells. She pushed the envelope searching for more. He brought out something she didn't think existed in her. Now she wanted to see how far he'd go. She was beyond ready for more.

She felt his eyes on her as she dropped the opened bra off her shoulders and crawled up the bed, adding a little extra wiggle in her hips as she did so. A flush hit her cheeks at presenting her bare ass to him, but he was going to see much more very soon.

Reaching the top, she turned over. Propped on the pillow, she had the urge to cross her legs. She'd never had a shy bone in her body, but today, everything felt new. She lifted her hands behind her head and curled her fingers on the cool metal bars. For a second, she thought of shaking to see if they'd rattle, but decided against it. Her stomach quivered with anticipation. His eyes roamed her body, burning her with the intensity of his gaze.

Her entire being felt branded from those looks alone. She ignored the shiver of insecurity and bent her legs, spreading her thighs open. "Is this good enough?"

His expression tightened, his gaze sliding from her eyes, down the length of her body to fix between her thighs. Heat crawled over her cheeks, but she held her position. Even if her hands did tighten on the bars enough that she felt the metal begin to give. Go wolfy-strength. Normally, she had it under control, but naked in a room with this guy? She felt more out of control than she ever had.

"Perfect." His voice was nowhere near human now, the low, rough growl born straight from his wolf. She bit her lip and watched his hands drop to his belt. Still watching her, he undid the buckle and snaps, then shoved the leather down over his hips.

His cock sprang free, the thick, long, flushed length arcing up toward his stomach. She bit back a whimper. If there was ever a man who was gifted, he was it.

"Are you gonna stand there until I beg?" Because she was damn near full blown on her knees worshipping. The smile, the body, and holy fuck, the cock. She licked her lips, wishing he'd come closer.

He got rid of the leathers, toeing his feet out of the boots. Two steps brought him to the end of the bed. He stopped, just standing there in all his naked glory, glancing down at her. His eyes were human dark, with a ring of blue that told her she wasn't safe. Not safe at all.

"It had crossed my mind." A smile crossed his lips, little more than a quirk, but it hit her right where it counted. Her clit throbbed, as though linked to that little move. "Perhaps I want to see how far my princess is prepared to go to get what she needs."

He moved a hand, wrapping a big fist around his cock and pumping slowly. Watching her all the time. "How far you'll go to get the cock you need. Because you want it, don't you, Princess? I can smell it on you."

How far? For a body like that? She'd already done something she never did, give up control. "I have a question."

He arched an eyebrow, hand never stopping its motion.

"Are you anywhere near as good as you sound? Because if you are, then I'll do whatever you want, as long as you deliver."

And that smile told her he planned on giving up lots of orgasms. She didn't want to miss out on those. She was pretty sure that it was orgasms that were a girl's best friend. Fuck diamonds.

His smile crawled over his lips. "Princess, I'm better."

That did it then. If she got caught, she'd have to go home without her wild night. There was no way in hell she was going home without a taste of *him*. "Well then what the hell are you waiting for? I'm here. I'm naked, and so are you. Move your ass."

"Ever heard of anticipation, Princess?" He finally let go of his cock and put a knee on the bed. The mattress dipped under his weight. "Or are you always this bossy?"

He crawled toward her, somehow making what was normally an awkward movement as sexy as sin. Her breath caught in the back of her throat as he reached her, fingers stroking up the inside of her calf, then her thigh as he moved closer. She shivered, feeling like a meal laid out, ready for the predator before her to feast upon.

"Such a pretty sight," his voice dropped lower as he settled between her legs, pushing her thighs further apart, impossibly further. Crap, how hadn't she noticed that his shoulders were so damn big?

His breath washed over her exposed pussy, her clit throbbing so hard with need that she wanted to scream at him to get on with it. But he paused, and met her gaze. "Just to be sure, it's Razor, okay?"

She blinked, her ability to focus removed by his presence between her thighs. "Huh? What? What's Razor?"

He smiled. "The name you'll be screaming." Then he lowered his head and swept his tongue over her.

Christ. That tongue. He was pure magic. Her muscles locked up tight at the first swoop.

Slow sizzles shot down her spine, straight to her clit—to the same spot he licked.

"Sorry," she panted. "I should have taken your word for it."

He was much more than better. There was no questioning it. He had a tongue she wanted to take home and keep forever. Along with the rest of his body.

Electric pulses rushed through her veins like shots of adrenaline. Whimpers raced up her throat, bursting free with each lick.

He growled in response, readjusting his position. Big hands slid around, cupping her ass before he tilted her hips to the angle he wanted. Then they hooked around her thighs, his shoulders holding them wide open for him, as he parted her pussy lips with gentle fingers.

His tongue returned to feast on her clit. Lapping at it, circling it, teasing and tormenting it. He used the flat of his tongue in long cat-like strokes, and then surprised her with faster, harder licks. She whimpered and moaned, writhing against him, but he didn't stop. Instead, he teased her more, driving her need and arousal higher and higher with his clever tongue.

She squeezed the bars in her hand harder,

metal groaning from her strength. Air thundered in and out of her lungs. Tension coiled in her core, heating every pore. "Oh, God," she choked.

Her leg muscles shook. Every swipe of his tongue urged her closer to bliss. She wanted it so bad. Could taste it so close. Just a little more and she'd be there, riding the wave. "Don't stop!"

Her internal temperature skyrocketed. Perspiration broke over her skin. All her thoughts centered on him. His wicked tongue, and oh, the things he was doing with it. Her stomach quivered with each moan. "Please, for all that's holy, don't you dare stop or I might die."

He wrapped his lips around her clit and sucked, chuckling at the same time. The tiny vibration was pure, unadulterated, perfect torture and the bastard had to know it. She couldn't get words out, not a one as he suckled on her clit, then slid his tongue down to tease the entrance to her body.

She panted, not caring about anything other than him carrying on. He moved, and she barely registered it when he nibbled on her clit again. Blunt, human teeth grazed the tiny bundle of nerves and shattered what was left of her cognitive abilities. If that didn't, then the strong finger he slid deep into her pussy sure did.

Tension seared her muscles and held them in a chokehold, until it cracked. Pleasure unraveled inside her, filling her to near bursting. She might have screamed, or moaned, she couldn't really tell. Heart beats pounded in her ears. She couldn't make anything out but the harsh sounds of her own breathing. Her pussy gripped at his finger, sucking him deep, needing to be filled by more than his digit.

She blinked up at the ceiling, struggling to breathe. That had to be a record. She'd either been sex deprived for too long, or he really was better than good. Her knees shook, and she fought to calm the rapid racing of her heart. Should she mention the broken off metal bars now or later?

"Wow!"

She shrugged to get her heart and breathing under control, the aftershocks still running through her body. Crap, that had to have been the best...seriously the best...climax of her life. She lifted her head to watch him, but he was already moving.

He crawled up over her body, and suddenly she realized just how big he was. Wrapping an arm under her shoulder, he pinned her in place with a big hand at the back of her neck as his gaze bore down into hers.

"What did I tell you, Princess?"

"That I should call you God?"

Amusement flashed between the dark desire in his eyes, and his lips curved again — just that kink at the corner she wanted to kiss, and kiss, and never stop kissing.

"Okay, you get away with that one." He stroked her hair back from her face with a gentleness she hadn't expected. It snuck under her guard and wrapped around her heart that such a big, rough biker could be so gentle.

He shifted, pushing her thighs further apart and lowered himself to the cradle of her hips. She fought back a whimper, biting her lip as he slid a hand between them and set his cock against the entrance to her body.

He stopped, and stared deep into her eyes. "Just checking, Princess. You're not in your heat phase, are you?"

"No, I'm good," she panted. "Got a few weeks before that. Now, get to the good part, and stop the torture already."

He nodded, a tiny expression in his eyes that pulled at the corner of her mind, but then he pushed and nothing else mattered. He was big, her body resisting for a few seconds before he slipped inside half an inch, and they both gasped. She closed her eyes, feeling the burn as he pushed deeper, forcing her tight sheath to accept him. Crap, he was way bigger than any other man she'd ever been with. Though she'd only been with a few since none had been strong enough to handle her personality or her aggressiveness.

He didn't give her a pause or a break, working himself into her with short, wonderful little see-saw movements. His body moved above hers, the muscles of his shoulders and torso working. She whimpered, running her hands over them, entranced by the display. So much power and strength, all bent to one purpose. Pleasure.

She raked her nails over his arms and bit them deep into his muscles. He groaned, and her breath caught in her chest. The pure possessive look he gave her shattered through the wall guarding her emotions. It didn't matter how many times she repeated it was only a single night of sex. Her heart had other ideas. She pushed those thoughts back, focusing on the here and now. On the perfect torture of his body invading hers. A slow, sensual blaze sparked in her core, expanded through her limbs, and combusted in her blood.

His hips met hers, and he paused for a

moment to let her adjust. She whimpered, unable to stop the soft sound in the back of her throat. She felt full, stretched, and it was glorious. His gaze caught hers for a moment, a question in the silver-blue depths. Whatever he saw in hers must have answered because he started to move.

On his first retreat, almost all the way out of her body, she gasped and pouted, missing the fullness. But then he slid straight back in again, a long, slick ride of pure pleasure.

"Fuck!" She hissed. That felt so good. Better than good.

A. Ma. Zing.

He chuckled and did it again, pulling back only to slide back into her. Faster and stronger until he was yanking his hips back and hammering into her in a way she'd never realized she yearned for.

"God, that feels...incredible," she moaned.

His moves were wild with speed. Hard. Fast. Each one fiercer than the last, pressing her deeper into the bed. She bit down on her lip to try and control her urge to praise him. She'd sound like an idiot if she started to thank god for his cock.

"Yeah?" He dropped his head to whisper

his lips against her neck. "You like that, Princess? Like being fucked hard and fast?

"Like it?" She moved her head to the side to allow him better access. "Try stopping and see what happens."

He lifted her shoulders, gripping her hair to pull her head back at the same time he bit her. Not hard, nowhere near hard enough to break the skin with his human teeth, but the zing of pleasure-pain made her cry out, as did the extra roll to his hips when he thrust into her again.

"Not planning on stopping," he growled, upping the pace and intensity of his movements. "Nowhere near stopping. Not until you're screaming and writhing." His voice deepened. "I want to see your face when you come all over my cock."

He'd see her coming soon if he kept up the pace and the sexy as hell naughty talk. Her muscles tightened to near bursting. Fur rolled under her skin. The beast inside her wanted a piece of him too.

Sorry girl, this is all me.

"No," he snarled, perhaps sensing her beast so close and reacting to it. "No hiding, not from me."

The blue ring around his eyes was wider as he looked down at her, letting her have a glimpse of his beast. Her own whimpered, wanting to roll over and submit. Freaking traitor. Well, it would be if she didn't want to do exactly the same thing.

A shudder worked through his body. She felt it run through him all the way down to his cock but it didn't stop him. Still, he powered into her, adding a twist of his hips at the end of every stroke that trapped her clit between them. Pressing on it, grinding it between them. She gasped, her eyes rolling back in her head, but still he kept up the talking.

"That's it, take every inch of it, Princess." He gave another roll and grind. "You like being fucked by a rough, dirty biker, don't you? Like being taken like a little slut instead of the princess you are."

"I thought…." She gasped, breathless. "All men liked a princess in the street and a slut in the sheets?"

"Careful, princess. Talk like that and I might want to keep you here. Naked and chained for me to fuck whenever I want." He nipped her neck again, and the bolt of pleasure zoomed right to her clit. His tempo increased again, but not smoothly. His breaths puffed by her neck and his heartbeat thundered over hers.

Christ, that sounded good. Really fucking good and exactly what she would've wanted from her mate.

"I'd fuck you good. Make you scream every night," he promised, letting go of her nape to sit back on his heels. His hand on the back of her hips tilted them up for him to thrust in again, and she cried out at the change in position. His thumb found her clit, circling and stroking it in time with his thrusts. "Such a pretty pussy…I could eat you for every meal. And just so you know, I'm partial to breakfast in bed as well."

The combination of his words and actions turned her mind and body to mush. Electric shudders raced down her spine to her clit. Tension built in her, rolled into a thick knot that held her immobile. His body pounded into hers. Deeper. Harder. Stronger. So fucking perfectly it felt as if he'd been made for her. Her lungs compressed, sucking for air.

"God, Razor," she gasped the moment her body gave. It snapped hard like a rubber band and shattered into a billion tiny fragments. Then the rush came. A giant wave of pleasure blasted from her groin and shot outward toward her limbs, dissolving muscles in its wake. She rode it, clinging to him for dear life while trying to remember how to breathe.

Her body worked on automatic as he moved over her. His breathing ragged, interspersed with deep groans, but she didn't care. Not when every rock of his hips, every deep thrust, fed her another wave of ecstasy so complete that she could have died right here and been a happy woman. With her track record, she was going straight to hell, but it didn't matter, she'd already seen her glimpse of heaven.

"That's it...fuck, you're perfect, princess. I'm gonna co—" Razor gasped, then slammed into her one last time. Throwing his head back, he roared his release. His cock, buried deep inside her, jerked and pulsed, and for a second, she wished she was in her heat phase. That his seed could find fertile ground.

FOUR

His princess was, in a word, amazing.

Razor lay propped up against the pillows and watched her as she bustled around the room wearing his T-shirt. It hit her just above the knees, hiding her luscious curves from view. That made no difference. He knew what she looked like. In fact, every detail of her delicious body was imprinted on his mind forever, courtesy of one, white-hot night between the sheets.

Content to just lie there, the sheet loosely spread across his lap, he watched as she brushed her hair and piled it on top of her head with clips. The yawn was sly, hitting him blindsides, but it wasn't surprising. He hadn't slept more than half an hour all night, sleep pushed aside in favor of making his princess scream again. And again.

Even now, just watching her do normal things, like brushing her hair, his cock stirred under the sheets. Sheets that held the scent of her and sex; a scent he realized he was rapidly becoming addicted to.

"So Princess, you never did tell me your name."

She stopped, the brush in mid-air held tight in her grasp. She turned to meet his gaze, her face no longer holding that carefree smile. "Evva, but I don't think it matters at this point."

He caught the flash of guilt at the back of her eyes. Was that guilt because she'd had a night of wild, hot sex with a bad-boy biker? Had that been what she'd been after when she'd walked into the bar last night? His wolf snarled, and he had to agree. Being used for sex when they wanted so much more from her didn't sit right.

"Why doesn't it matter?" he asked, careful to mask his expression. Good thing he'd become a master at concealing his feelings. Kind of a given in the pack he'd grown up in. Appearances had been everything, and nothing but the best had been expected from the heir. No wonder he'd run, first joining the army, and then heading out on the road with the Devils.

He added a smile, shoving a hand through his loose hair and watched her as it fell down around his face. He wasn't stupid. He knew how to make the most of his looks to get what he wanted. "Maybe I'd like to know to put a name to fond memories…"

She sucked her bottom lip between her teeth, nibbling on it, indecision clear in her face. "Memories…" Her gaze swooped down to his mouth and continued to the area the sheet lay around his hips. "Memories can be dangerous." She cleared her throat, her gaze rising up to meet his. Desire filled the depth of her eyes. "But sometimes, so incredibly worth it."

His body, already half-hard, reacted immediately and predictably, but he wasn't ruled by his lusts. His heart, that organ that he'd buried for so long, ached at the look in her eyes.

Loneliness. Pain. Longing.

He recognized the first two from his mirror each morning, but the third was new to him. Reaching out, he snagged a hand in her hair and pulled her toward him to press a kiss to her lips. They parted instantly under his, and the sweet kiss he'd intended became something hot and torrid within seconds.

Breaking away, he met her gaze. "Princess, if you're in some kind of trouble, you can crash here. We'll take care of you."

As soon as he said the words, he felt like an idiot. What sort of trouble would a princess from the better part of town possibly be in that would make her take sanctuary in the gutter with the likes of him?

She blinked, surprise evident in her eyes. Her lips lifted in a soft smile. "That might just be the sweetest thing anyone has ever said to me." She raised a hand and slid her fingers through his hair, her smile dulling. "Thanks for the offer, but I won't hide from my problems."

Admiration rolled through him. She planned to meet her problems head on. A good trait to have in a woman. *And a mate*, a little voice whispered in the back of his head. He ignored it in favor of kissing her again. Softly. Slowly. Committing the shape and feel of her lips to memory.

"The offer's always there," he said when they came up for air. What made him unwrap his leather bracelet, he had no idea, but he did it anyway. "Here. Take this." The leather was too long for her wrist, so he wrapped it around twice then snapped it shut. Turning it, he showed her the small metal wolf's head dangling near the clasp. "If you ever need help, give this to any Devil, they'll know what to do."

She rubbed the leather on her wrist with care, almost as if afraid to break the strong material with her touch. "This is..." She glanced at him, confusion clear in her gaze. "This is lovely. Are you sure I can have it?" At his nod, amusement replaced the confusion in her eyes. "So, will flashing this like the bat signal make you appear?"

He smiled, touched by her reaction to the gift. She no doubt had boxes full of flashy, expensive jewelry, yet she seemed ready to tear up over a crudely worked leather bracelet.

"Sorry, Princess. I don't do a rubber suit for anyone. Leather's my thing."

It was getting too sentimental, so he kissed her, reaching down to slap her ass at the same time. "Shower. If you want dropping off somewhere that is."

She squeaked and hopped away. "I'm starting to think you have an obsession with slapping my ass." She wiggled her way to the bathroom, turning to him with a sexy grin.

"Want to help conserve water?"

* * *

Evva's chest compressed with sadness. She was home. What she really wanted was to throw herself at Razor's back, cling to him and beg him to take her far away from the upcoming nuptials. She wouldn't be getting that wish. Couldn't have that wish, no matter how much she might yearn for it.

Though early, she knew the staff would be watching from the moment they came into view of the large house, so she tapped his shoulder and got him to pull over behind the trees near the main gate. They were sheltered from view. Just. It would have to do.

Sliding from the bike as gracefully as she could, she inhaled, pushed back the knot in her throat, and faced him. Hopefully, he wouldn't notice how difficult the whole morning-after chat was now.

Her gaze swept over his rough features, his piercing eyes and the lips that could bring any woman to her knees. She fingered the bracelet, her heart cracking. A slow sting started in her chest, growing until the throbbing made it nearly impossible to stand there without bursting into tears. This big biker with his sweet words, tender treatment, and hot sex had done what no other man ever had. He'd made her fall in less than the time it took her to pick out a new pair of Jimmy Choos. And now, she had to go inside, forget all about him, and marry Chip.

"Thanks." It was all she could get out.

He nodded, a rough grunt his only answer. His gaze moved past her, lingered on the big wrought-iron gates. Once, she'd imagined them to be gates to a fairy-tale castle, protecting her, the princess, within. Now, she saw them for what they were — a prison. Her life, her dreams of true love and marrying her prince charming were just that. Fairy tales. Real life didn't work that way.

"You're a Castillo?" He glanced back at her, his silver eyes unreadable.

It didn't surprise her that he knew of her family. He probably knew Chip's family too. It's how it worked in the shifter circle. Everyone knew the powerhouses, who to steer clear from. She just happened to belong to one.

"I am."

She held stiff, waiting for some sort of comment about her whole princess of the pack status. The ache in her chest increased. This was probably the first time in her life she wished she were just some random girl who could say to hell with everyone and hit the road with Razor. She wouldn't, though. She'd been raised to make her decisions based on the good of the pack. She might be spoiled, but being an alpha, ready to take command if needed, was in her blood.

He nodded, his expression unchanging. She tried to work out if it was a good or bad expression, but he was giving her nothing to work with. She bit back a sigh, he'd make a fantastic poker player.

"Good family," he commented, still sitting astride his bike. She cast it a glance. Big and powerful, it looked dangerous to her, but he handled it like it was nothing. "Heard there was going to be a big Castillo wedding soon. That yours?"

Shit. Even he'd heard of the wedding from hell.

"That'd be me." She shifted, uncomfortable discussing her upcoming wedding with the man she'd be screaming for in bed — and the shower, could never forget the shower — mere hours before. "I get to play bride for Chip."

He lifted an eyebrow, surprise flowing over his features. "Chip?"

"Sorry. The Rasmussen pack first born. Dale something or other." She ground out. She really didn't want to have this conversation. Not with him.

His face returned to the blank expression, but the expression in his eyes made her freeze, her heart pounding. "Their first-born, huh?"

She sighed. "It's supposed to be good for both families. Unite. Create a stronger front. Have super alpha babies. Make one solid pack." She waved a hand dismissively and tossed a strand of hair over her shoulder. "Or some shit like that."

"Politics." He spat the word, disgust evident in his voice. "Can't fucking stand politics. Easier on the road."

He dropped his head back and blew out a sigh. She took a second to just look at him. To ogle the strong body, heavy with muscles, and the way his hair rippled in the breeze. For a moment, she allowed herself to think what life with him would be like.

She'd probably hate him within the month. Maybe. Her heart clenched. She knew she wouldn't. Her mate was standing right in front of her, and she had to walk away from him.

"Like I said, I don't run from my problems.

So this is something I'll see through," She struggled to say the words. "For the good of the pack." She inhaled, her chest and eyes burning with the need drop the facade and cry. "This is who I am." She didn't mince her words. "You're lucky. You don't have to make decisions for people who depend on you." She envied him that. To be able to do whatever he wanted without worrying about anyone else. "Politics suck, but I want what's best for my family, so I'll do whatever I have to do."

Including watching him walk away with her heart.

He nodded, a strange expression on his face for a moment. Before she was even sure she'd seen it, let alone work out what it was, it was gone.

Reaching for her hand, he lifted it to his lips. "Princess, you have to be the strongest person I've ever met."

He smiled, not the small sexy quirk of his lips, but a true, honest smile. The effect was devastating, rendering his appearance from simple drop-dead gorgeous to lethal. Especially when the expression turned tender, and he kissed the back of her hand. She mourned the loss of his touch when he let go.

"Good luck, Evva Castillo." He started the

bike and put it in gear, ready to go. "May your marriage bring you everything you wish for."

And with that, he was gone.

* * *

Razor made it around the corner before he snarled and pulled the bike over with a vicious wrench of the handlebars. The car behind him swerved at his sudden braking and honked. He didn't care, flipping the driver off before cutting the engine and leaning over the handlebars.

"Fuck!"

He'd let her walk away. The woman his wolf told him was his mate, and he'd let her walk away. And for what? So she could fulfill her duty to her pack. *Like he hadn't.*

Shoving a hand through his loose hair, he ignored the fact that it shook. Or that his nails had lengthened to claws as if further evidence of his loss of control was needed.

He glanced back the way he'd come. The trees by the front gates were still visible. His wolf paced and snarled within, demanding that he turn the damn bike around, storm through those gates and go claim his mate.

His lips quirked. If he did that now, his

little mate would probably give him the roasting of his life and leave his ears ringing for weeks. No, he had to do this right. He sat back comfortably, plans turning over in his mind.

She was due to marry the Rasmussen first born, was she?

Reaching into his inner pocket, he pulled his cell free and hit speed dial.

"Cuffs. Get the brothers together. We're going shopping."

* * *

Knock knock.

"What?" she snapped, pacing the confines of the bridal suite at the church.

"You okay in there, sweetheart?" her father asked, his voice hesitant for the first time in her life.

"I'm fine! Don't come in. I need a moment." Or a century. Whatever kept her from the fiasco about to take place. Her dress caught at the hem on something. She growled, ready to yank the expensive material, not really worried about tearing the beautiful gown.

Another knock sounded not a minute later.

"I said I need a minute! Doesn't anyone listen around here?" She made a swift U-turn and returned to pacing. The clickity-clack of her heels sounded louder than the thumping of her frantic heartbeats.

"We just wanted to let you know everything is in place," her cousin Lainie mumbled from the other side of the door.

She'd fully embraced being a Bridezilla. Not so much because she cared that the event went off without a hitch, but because she'd prefer something did go wrong so it wouldn't take place.

"The organist?" she demanded. The hand on her bouquet dug deep into the white satin covering the rose stems.

"She's ready and waiting on you."

"Groom?" She held her breath, hoping against hope that Lainie would say he changed his mind.

"Er, he's here. I think."

Of course he was. Dammit. Chip wouldn't refuse to do something his father ordered. Spineless jerk. She'd chew him up and spit him out within a week.

"I'm sure he's waiting like everyone else is." Gigi's normally patient voice held a note of frustration. "Like we all are."

He could damn well wait for her a few moments. Not like she was going to be going anywhere else after this.

"Evva, I'm coming in."

"I said I need time." She glanced around the room in a panic, now wishing for a window or some way to escape.

The door swung open, and Gigi entered. Frustration was visible on her features, matching the tone of her voice. "What's going on in here?" She shut the door, leaving a wide-eyed Lainie outside the room.

"I…" She gulped and glanced away from Gigi, her gaze travelling all over the room only to stop at the leather bracelet she placed next to her "something blue" garter on the sofa chair.

Razor.

Anguish clasped around her heart, holding tight. She swallowed hard and met Gigi's worried frown. "I don't know if I can do this."

Gigi watched her for a moment before glancing at the leather bracelet herself. "This isn't like you, Evva. You might bitch and complain," she said with a grin. "But you always do what you have to. What's really wrong?"

"If I marry Chip…" She inhaled, choking back tears. Her heart ached, the pain excruciating. If she married Chip, then there was no chance of her *Happily Never After* with Razor. "I'll never be happy."

Gigi marched closer, wrapping her arms around her in a fierce, sisterly hug. "Honey, don't think that way. You don't know that for sure."

She nodded, the tears rushing down her eyes and messing up the makeup artist's hard work. "I do know that."

"How?" Gigi pushed back, her gaze bored into Evva's intently. "What aren't you telling me?"

She blinked repeatedly, trying to stop the flow of tears. This was pathetic. She was uber-bitch pack princess. She never cried. Ever. Except now, she couldn't seem to stop. "I met someone."

Gigi's eyes widened the same moment she gasped. "When?"

"The night we went out." She turned away from Gigi, moving to the sofa and holding Razor's bracelet in one hand. It made her feel better to have it with her. She didn't feel so alone.

"When you left us in the bar and disappeared?" Gigi's tone wasn't accusing, more probing.

She nodded, glancing down at her lap. "I met my mate," she pushed the words through her tear clogged throat. "But worse than that, I fell in love."

"Oh, Evva." Gigi dropped down, squatting in front of her. "Maybe if we talk to your dad, if we explain things…"

She shook her head, not caring about the intricate hairdo with the tiara holding her curls up. "No. I've spoken to him. This is what needs to happen." She sniffled, wiping the tears with the back of her hand until Gigi moved away and handed her some tissues.

"I'm so sorry," Gigi patted her shoulder in comfort.

She wiped the moisture from her eyes. It sucked, but she already knew this was coming. She couldn't find it in her to care about the ruined makeup. Or what others might think when they saw she'd been crying. All she wanted was to get the whole thing over with already.

Standing, she took a deep breath, wrapping the bracelet around her wrist and locked it in place. She might never get Razor, but she'd carry him around with her forever.

"I'm ready. Let's do this."

It was all systems go from that point. Gigi took over like a human...or wolf...dynamo, the makeup artist was brought back in, and within minutes, Evva was ready to go, the image of the blushing bride.

She and her father stood at the door to the church, the strains of the bridal march filtering to them. The music sounded so far away, and when she let herself, she floated free. It was easier this way, like she was watching someone else get married.

Her father led her down the aisle, but she kept her eyes down all the way, only looking up to spot Chip standing before the altar. Waiting for her. He was all smiles. He should be, *daddy's little boy gone done good*. This marriage would make their combined pack the most powerful across the eastern seaboard.

She reached the altar, unable to focus on anything but the flowers on the damn thing. The pastor frowned, but at a nudge from her father, started the service. Squeezing her bouquet to death, she tuned it out. Only half-listened to the words being said. Her mind took her back to the night with Razor.

"Before we proceed, if anyone here knows any reason why these two should not be married, speak now or forever hold your peace..."

She held her breath at the words. Her heart paused painfully in her chest. This was it. This was the last point that something could stop the wedding.

"Yes. I do."

SIX

Evva's gasp was echoed by the congregation as all eyes turned to the back of the church. A familiar, broad-shouldered figured filled the doorway.

Razor.

Her heart turned over in her chest as she lifted her hand to cover her mouth, in case she cried out for him. This was her wild dream, her hope. That he'd find a way to come and rescue her from the travesty of a loveless marriage.

As much as she wanted it though, yearned for it and dreamed of it, she knew it could never be. She frowned. This wasn't quite the way she'd dreamed it.

Instead of the leathers she'd envisioned him arriving in, he wore a tuxedo, and his hair was pulled back into a neat ponytail.

"Oh my," a feminine voice muttered to her left. "He can ride to my rescue any time."

Evva fought back the snarl in her throat. Razor wasn't hers to be jealous over. So why was he here?

The pastor cleared his throat, looking over his glasses at the intruder. "And your reason would be?"

Razor swept a glance over the guests, focusing on Chip's side of the church. "The contract between the Rasmussen and Castillo pack state that the respective first-borns will wed at a mutually agreeable time. However, the groom is *not* the Rasmussen first-born."

Her gaze jerked to her left, to a visibly pale ready-to-pass-out Chip. He wasn't first born? What the hell was going on?

Her father wasn't slow on the uptake either. Stepping forward, he glared at Chip and his father. "What the hell is going on, Rasmussen?" He gestured toward Razor. "Who the hell is this?"

"Let me answer that, since the only time my father is telling the truth is when he's not speaking." Razor's long stride ate up the aisle as he walked toward them. Finally, he was there, just a few steps away, and her heart felt like it would burst out of her chest.

"I'm Casey Rasmussen, first born of the Rasmussen pack." He didn't spare his father or any of his family a single glance as he spoke, but Evva caught Chip's flinch at the words. "When I disagreed with my father on the direction the pack should take after I left the service, we had a parting of ways."

"It doesn't matter!" Chip and Razor's father broke in. "Dale is the pack heir. *My* heir. The marriage will go ahead."

"Ah, no." Evva's father held up his hand. "The contract clearly states that the union is between the first-born children, *nothing* was said about heirs."

Razor — wait — he'd said his name was Casey. Didn't matter. He'd always be Razor to her. He said he was the Rasmussen first born. That meant...

"I'm willing to go ahead with the wedding," she interrupted the arguing, her gaze locked on Razor. "With the Rasmussen first born. And *only* the first-born, as stated in the contract."

"B-but—" Chip's father tried to break in, but she shot him a hard look.

"Unless, of course, you wish to be found in default?" she asked, which meant that the other pack would lose a shitload of property and land-rights to the Castillos.

The shock on the elder Rasmussen's face was pure gold. Evva stood her ground to glare him down, aware of her father flanking her on one side and Razor on the other. They'd have her back. Supporting her as she made her first stand for her pack, her life, and her own happiness.

"No...no," Rasmussen inclined his head, signaling for Chip to back away. Good. He needed to, because she was all sorts of ready to rip his throat out if he dared to argue.

Her father grabbed her arm, tugging softly to get her attention.

She glanced at him. The usual self-assured smile he'd given her for the past few days was replaced with dipping brows and eyes filled with doubt.

"Dad?" She turned to him fully. Worry hit her that this showdown had changed his mind about her marrying a Rasmussen.

He pulled her a few steps away, his gaze travelling back and forth between her and Razor.

"Are you sure about this?" Concern

deepened the lines on his face.

"We have a contract," she answered, not wanting to go into the whole conversation about meeting Razor days back and their night of wild sex.

"I know, sweetheart, but I don't know this Casey person. I can't guarantee he'll treat you the way Dale would have."

She followed her father's gaze to Razor. He stood there. Watching her. Waiting.

"He won't treat me like Chip would have." She smiled, heart filling with anticipation. "That's why I want to do this. I want to marry him."

"I don't understand," he said, confused. He stared at her for a moment, but must have seen some of her feelings for Razor in her eyes. Understanding smoothed the concern on his face. He pressed a kiss to the top of her head and sighed. "No, I do understand."

The fear she'd held on to about marrying the Rasmussen first-born disappeared. Now she wanted to rush over and say the words to make them man and wife.

A quick glance at her father got her a nod, and she turned, reaching Razor's side in a matter of steps.

"Ready to be mine, Princess?" He smiled,

that little quirk of his lips that she loved, and held his hand out.

She grinned, placed her fingers in his, and turned to the pastor. "Marry us. Now."

* * *

"Fuck's sake, Razor...you didn't tell me you were some big-pack kid."

Razor turned to find Cuffs balancing two beers and a bowl of peanuts. Deftly, he recovered the bowl before the contents could end up over one of the other guests. Cuffs could take down anyone in a fight and with a throwing knife, he was beyond beating. But balance when carrying things wasn't his strong point.

"Sit down before you end up wearing that," Razor ordered, putting the peanuts down on a nearby table before liberating the drink from his friend's hand. "And I'm not some big-pack kid. Not anymore."

"You sure about that, bro?" Cuffs lifted an eyebrow, glancing around the room.

The word 'swanky' didn't do the reception justice. The whole place, decorated in creams and golds, screamed money, and not just any money — old family money. Old *pack* money. And that was even more apparent in the guests. Hell, there were more designer labels in evidence than a London Fashion Show, and the amount of high-class jewelry on display would put any couture jewelers to shame.

Razor shrugged, wrinkling his nose as the tux shifted over his shoulders. He hadn't worn a damn penguin suit since he was what...sixteen or something? The rest of the club appeared just as uncomfortable stuffed into their rented tuxes.

Apart from Scales, who was ripping it up on the dance floor. Literally. His jacket was gone, and he'd just torn the arms off his shirt, throwing them aside to beckon to one of the gaggle of women across the other side of the room. Razor sighed. There was one deposit they weren't getting back. That wasn't the worst of it. Scales was as short-sighted as fuck without his prescription shades on, so he'd come onto anything female, no matter if she was married or not.

"Get someone to go and rein Scales in before he hits on the wrong girl and causes a pack war, will you?" he grumbled, his gaze following the dragon's to the other side of the room.

The giggling women surrounded a vision in white. His princess. His bride. His wolf stopped pacing within, it's attention focused on the woman who had stolen their attention that night in the bar and his heart by morning.

Cuffs snorted in his beer when he spotted Scales, levering himself up. "On it, boss."

Razor nodded, sitting there nursing his beer and watching his bride. She seemed happy, her high-pitched laughter as she chatted with her friends reaching him all the way over here. His wolf wuffled happily, the creature's contentment wrapping itself around Razor's heart.

Riding away from her that morning had been the hardest thing he'd ever done. He'd really thought he could do it. Walk away from her like he had every other one-night stand. Somehow though, his princess had gotten herself under his defenses and wound herself around his heart. Somewhere between trying to make her run in the bar and the scorching sex they'd had in the shower that morning, he'd fallen hard and fast.

Finding out that she was a Castillo, due to be married to his little brother Dale, had been the final piece of the puzzle. In that instant, he knew what he had to do. Go home. He'd left after war had changed him, given him a strength of mind his father couldn't handle, and no threat, no promise of guilt trip had brought him back to his pack.

Only Evva and the fact that she was to wed the Rasmussen first-born could do that.

There had been just one problem; no one had seen fit to invite him to his own damn wedding. So he'd invited himself.

The sound of a throat clearing beside him made him turn around. His expression set. Speak of the devil and he shall appear. His father

"What do you want, old man?" he growled, grip tightening around his beer. "And make it snappy, before you piss me off. I'd hate to ruin Evva's day by getting blood on the wedding decorations."

Kurt Rasmussen shifted his weight from one foot to the other. "Look, Casey…"

"It's Razor now."

"Erm…Razor," Kurt corrected, the scent of desperation rolling from him in waves. "We need to talk. I need to know what your intentions are—"

Razor's eyebrow winged up. "Intentions? You mean other than to find my bride and claim her?"

Kurt shook his head, color rising high above the collar of his monkey suit. His gaze flicked from Razor to something behind him. Turning, Razor spotted his brother Dale, lurking in the wings. As soon as he met Dale's eyes, the younger wolf looked away. Wouldn't hold his gaze.

They were scared. Shit scared because he was back. A slow smile worked its way over Razor's lips. "You think I want to claim the pack."

"A-hh well," Kurt stuttered, then paused. When he spoke again, his voice held that note of superiority that had always pissed Razor off. "You've been gone a long time. Dale's done so mu—"

He surged to his feet, dwarfing his father. The older wolf skittered back in alarm, and then stopped as if he remembered that people could see him.

"Listen, old man. I don't give a flying rat's ass what Dale's done or not done. I don't want your fucking pack, or anything to do with you or it. But let me tell you something for nothing." He put his empty beer down on the table and advanced on his father.

"My wife is the alpha of the Castillo pack, so if I hear *anything* about dodgy dealings, or you try and fuck her over, you'll have me to deal with. Do I make myself clear?"

* * *

The reception hall was amazing. Straight out of a fairy tale. There were flowers everywhere. No expense had been spared. The moment they'd entered, family members had rushed up to her and crowded around, to the point she'd been separated from Razor. The women in her family had a lot to say about her groom.

"Oh, my God, Evva!" Lainie gasped. "He's hot and sorta scary."

Evva choked on the champagne she'd been given, the drink cooling some of her heat. "He's not so bad."

"Not so bad?" Lainie's head cocked to the side, studying Razor and his biker friends. They'd lined the back walls of the church, ready to step up for their president if needed. "Who's that other guy there?"

Lainie pointed at the one Razor had called Scales at the bar. "I'm not sure, but I think you probably don't want to get on his bad side."

Her cousin continued to watch them with interest. "He doesn't look very dangerous."

"Trust me, honey, he's—"

"Was he the one?" Gigi brushed up beside her, interrupting her conversation with Lainie.

"Yeah," she grinned, glancing over to her

man chatting with his friends. "Not sure how this happened, but I'm not going to fight it."

"Hmm. Looked more to me like you were ready to argue if it didn't happen," Gigi giggled, her gaze stuck on the men. "So who are those guys surrounding him?"

"His biker friends," she answered, waiting for him to turn her way so she could nod toward the door. She wanted to have a few words with him. Wasn't going to happen as long as he was way over there, and she was way over here.

"That guy he's talking to, he's got that whole rough and rugged sexiness going with a side of wow."

She heard the interest clear in Gigi's voice. She followed Gigi's gaze. Ah, interesting. Gigi had her sights set on one of the guys from the bar. The guy Evva had first spoken to when she waltzed into the bar the night her life changed. He was eyeing Gigi like she was going to be his next meal.

"I think his name is Cuffs. He was actually really polite when I showed up at the bar," she giggled. "Tried to get me out of there before I caused trouble."

"Poor guy. Guess he realized within thirty seconds how right he was." Gigi sipped from her drink, her gaze stuck on the big wolf.

"I need to talk to him," Evva grumbled.

"Cuffs?" Gigi frowned.

"No. My husband." Wow. It was so strange to say that. But he was her husband, and she had quite a few questions for him.

"Oh," Gigi finally broke off from her visual attachment to Cuffs and glanced at her. "I can help you there. Go stand by the entrance, and I'll guide him your way."

"What are you going to do?" she asked, ready to do what Gigi suggested.

"Tell him you're ready to start your wedding night, and if he doesn't hurry you'll go on without him."

She laughed and tried to appear composed as she half-ran half-strolled to the door. She bit her tongue at every pause to say hello to someone and smile at a new congratulatory remark.

Her breath tripped in her chest when she watched Gigi say something to Razor, motioning toward the door. He tipped back the champagne, swallowing the entire contents in the flute in a single swig, his gaze locked on her. Then he marched straight for her. People moved out of his way, the look in his eyes that of a predator ready for a chase. She gulped. What the hell had Gigi really said to him?

He reached her within seconds, the blue ring around his silver eyes again. Heat and darkness swirled in those mercurial depths.

"So...a little birdie tells me that you're planning on starting the celebrations without me," he said, his voice silky smooth and oh, so dangerous.

"I don't think that would be in my best interest." She swallowed hard. Damn, he was so sexy in that tux. Maybe she could get him to strip out of it. Slowly. Wait, what the hell was she doing thinking sex? She had questions that needed answers.

"We need to talk." She eyed the people over his shoulder. His friends watched them. One had humor written all over his face and dollar bills were being passed back and forth. "Are they betting at our reception?"

The corner of his lips quirked. "There seems to be quite a book going, yes. Mostly on how long it'll take us to disappear. Although Scales has an outside bet on me not waiting until we're out of the door before I strip you naked and make you mine, and Peach over there is betting on you slapping me. In fact, I think he's offered money to anyone to suggest it to you."

Clearly having him for a husband meant she'd never be bored if this was any indication. She shook her head. Men. "I don't think I could smack you for getting me out of here when that's exactly what I'm wanting. Except for the naked part. Let's wait till we're alone for that."

She had to tamp down the urge to get closer to him. Ask the questions. Then hot sex.

"Why didn't you tell me who you were when you brought me home? We discussed my wedding. But you didn't say anything."

"I like to hold my cards close to my chest." He shrugged, the one shouldered movement nonchalant, but the heat in his eyes anything but. "If I'd told you who I was, you'd have realized my family were lying about Dale. Somehow, I doubt you and your father would have gone through with the wedding if you'd known."

He grinned, taking a step closer to snag her around the waist and pull her up hard against him. "And I was *very* invested in this wedding going ahead."

She blinked, now very interested in his words. She knew her reasons. Love. She'd fallen for the big sexy as sin biker and didn't want to let him go. Even if it was by signing a contract for marriage. "Why did you want this wedding to happen?"

He stood for a moment, his expression unreadable. Just as it had been before he'd ridden away from her the other morning. Her heart stuttered, contracting painfully for a second. Perhaps this wasn't the fairytale she'd hoped it would be. Perhaps he didn't feel the same way.

Then he smiled. A full, genuine, drop-dead gorgeous smile that opened up his expression, and she could see all the way down to his soul. "Because I fell in love with the pack princess who walked into my bar."

SEVEN

"You...love me."

She knew she'd heard the words, but it took a second to register. Happiness soared in her heart, thumping hard at the walls in her chest. Tears clogged her throat, and she flung herself into his arms. She didn't need to ask how that was possible. Hell, she'd fallen for him just as fast. She could tell he'd been uncomfortable in the tux, but he'd shown up the picture-perfect groom for them. For her.

He wrapped his arms around her, strong and protective as he lifted her off her feet.

"Of course I do, Princess," he whispered against her neck, not seeming at all bothered that she'd flung herself at him in front of all their guests.

In his arms, she could easily believe it was just the two of them. In their own little world. He put her down, but kept tight hold of her to lean back and stared deeply into her eyes.

"From the instant you walked into the bar that night, I knew you weren't leaving with anyone but me. By the morning, I didn't want you to leave at all. When you did, you took my heart with you." His lips lifted in a small smile, his deep voice a balm that wound around her soul as he bared his. "Taking you home was the hardest thing I've ever done. I seriously thought about just riding off and taking you with me."

"Even after you clearly rejected this life," she said with awe. "You came back for me." She grinned. "Of course, you did. I'm adorable!"

He blinked, surprise flowing over his features, and then chuckled, shaking his head. "Why do I get the feeling I may regret that decision?"

Then his expression changed, his hand spreading out over the back of her waist. The sudden heat in his eyes was enough to send shivers rolling over her skin. "How about we get out of here and I'll show you exactly why I came back?"

She laughed and planted a kiss on his chin. "There's an idea I can fully embrace, back and invest in." She glanced over her shoulder at the spectators. "Let's go before they start betting on when we'll conceive our first kid. I'd hate to hear someone say outside this door."

Her words were music to his ears. With a low growl, the beast slipping from his lips, and he didn't care to stop it, he swept her up in his arms. The guests erupted in cheers, lewd comments called across the room, mainly from the club who had stationed themselves near the bar. One comment, called in a deep voice, skirted the line of acceptable but was quickly followed by a meaty smack and a small yelp. Razor hid his grin, knowing that Cuffs was doing his job and keeping the brothers in line.

A gaggle of women in the doorway stopped them, and he cocked an eyebrow at Evva, held tight in his arms. Heat and need pulled at his body, tightening all his muscles and...other parts further south. Their night together felt like a lifetime ago. If he didn't get her out of here soon, he'd explode.

"They want me to throw the bouquet," she whispered, smiling at his obvious impatience.

"Well, throw the damn thing and let's get out of here."

Evva glanced around for a second and then smiled. There was a wickedness to her smile he would have worried about if directed at him. Then she threw the bouquet directly at the woman, Giselle, who'd spoken to him earlier. "Good luck, Gigi!"

He didn't miss the tall figure of his second in command behind her, his eyes bright with interest and a healthy dose of lust. He chuckled. "I have a feeling she's going to need it."

Considering they'd done their duty, he swept out of the door with her still in his arms. Long strides took him away from the reception hall. Even in his previous life, he hadn't visited the Castillo estates, but he'd checked out the general layout on the ride into church this morning. One structure stood out, a barn set back from the main buildings. He headed that way in silence rather than head up to the main house. After so many years of looking after himself without servants underfoot, he didn't want to be bothered with them now. Reaching the door, he shouldered it open and strode within.

She glanced around the barn, her brows rising. "So, um, did you have a particular reason in mind for coming here?" She blinked and smiled. "Not that I mind the horses and all. In fact, I love them, but um..." Her gaze darted down to his mouth. She leaned forward to brush her lips over his. "I'm babbling. Forget the barn." She twined her fingers into his hair. "I don't care where you take me, as long as it's just the two of us."

He grinned, feeling very much like a wolf in sheep's clothing, and pushed open the door to the nearest clean stall. Kicking the door shut behind him, he dropped her feet to the ground and backed her up in the same movement. His lips crashed down over hers for a brief, hard kiss.

"Reason..." He broke away to kiss along her neck, nipping her ear. "It's been too long since I've been inside you, and the house has too many people between us and a bedroom."

"Mmm," she moaned. "Yeah. Too far. Not good." She ran her hands down his shoulders under his jacket and yanked at the shirt tucked in his pants. "Whoever invented dress clothes needs to be killed. Too much stuff in the way."

He sucked in a hard breath as her small hands found skin. His own weren't idle, wrestling with the frothy voluminous skirts of her dress seeking her legs. "Like this dress," he growled, frustration biting deep until he managed to fight his way through the damn stuff. His hand wrapped around her thigh, slid higher. A shiver worked its way through him to wrap around his cock, already hard in his dress pants. Her skin was so soft, so smooth. For an instant, he felt like the brute so many had called him, but her soft gasp of pleasure as he reached the curve of her ass and her hands fumbling with his fly sent the thought skittering out of his head.

"Impatient much?" he teased, amused by her growls of irritation when she couldn't get his fly open. Instead of helping her, he hauled her thigh up, pinning it by his side as he stroked his fingers over her satin covered pussy lips.

"Oh, god!" She gasped, followed by, "Fucking hell! Get these pants off before I shred them."

Amusement escaped in a careful laugh, a sound he hadn't heard himself make in years. Reaching between them, he flicked the fastenings on the fly loose with a practiced gesture. She crowed in triumph, already reaching for him, but he beat her too it. At the same moment, her little hand closed around his newly-freed cock, he slipped his fingers under the satin and sank a finger deep into her tight, wet pussy.

"Please! Don't tease," she whimpered. Her lips swept over his jaw, stopping every other second to suck and nibble. "I've missed you." She gave another lick, then and a bite before she stroked her hand up his length slowly.

"I mean it," she moaned and jerked him in her small hand. "I don't think you realize how much."

She had all his attention, centered on the motion of her small hand. He groaned as she stroked again, in as much agony with this teasing as she was. "I realize, love." He turned his head and claimed her lips, this time in the knowledge that their claiming was to be for a lifetime. Moving her hand, he adjusted position, setting his balance to lift her easily against the wall behind. Pulling her panties to one side, he rubbed the head of his cock between her lips, using the juices of her own arousal to lubricate their joining. Setting the thick head against her entrance, he eased his grip, letting gravity slowly impale her on his cock.

She tore her lips from his, panting. Her gaze met his. "God, that feels amazing." She clung to him, digging her nails into his suit jacket. She moaned and leaned her head back against the wall, showing off the curve if her neck and her erratic pulse.

She wiggled, trying to urge him to speed up. "I'm. Going. To. Die." She puffed each word out between moans. "You're killing me here."

How he managed to arch an eyebrow with the little temptress wriggling like that on his cock, he had no idea, but he did.

"Oh? I think we have to work on your patience issues, Princess," he ground out, lifting her off his length. This time though, he didn't let her slide back down. Instead, he slid a hand up her back to clasp around her nape, driving up into her at the same time he pulled her down onto his cock. She gasped, her head back and her eyes closed. Her expression was pure bliss.

She was speechless, a first for his princess. Triumph surged through him and he did it again, ignoring the earth-shattering pleasure that coursed through his body in favor of driving into her hard and fast. "How's that, Princess? You like getting taken hard by your mate, in your wedding dress?"

"I don't like it." Her pussy flexed around him, legs squeezing around his waist. "I love it. Can't wait for the naked version of this." She inhaled deep. "But there's... Too much talking," she groaned. "Need more fucking."

Hell, *yes*. He could really get behind that

93

idea. His groan echoed hers as he drove into her again, their passion rattling the very wall they leaned against as he took the woman he loved with everything he had in him.

*

Another moan tore from the center of her chest to rush out of her lips. Tension turned her muscles stiff. The feel of each thrust hit so much more than just her body. Every plunge felt like a new branding from the inside. Her pussy clenched tight around his cock.

Oh, lord. But then he'd pull back and drive even harder than before. With so much power. Hard. Deep. So fucking good she swore she'd pass out from pleasure. Oxygen beat at her lungs, fighting its way in. She couldn't speak at that point, her focus solely on his body owning hers.

The soft growl that slipped from his lips, reverberating against her neck where he kissed her rolled through her entire body, reaching her clit, which ached in response. Everything about him found a response in her. A perfect dance, like their souls touched at the same time their bodies became one.

"I love you," she moaned. Couldn't she have done this later? Like maybe after he made her come? Apparently, her emotions and her animal were in agreement, wanted to be known. Not the best timing but what the hell?

She cleared her throat, pressing back the knot growing there. "Not because you fuck like a god, which you do."

She loved the wildness of his features. The blue glow to his eyes was one she'd always be turned on by. Tension twined around her core, building to that giant ball she knew would soon crack.

"I can't even really explain it other than to say my heart hurts when I'm not with you." She swallowed hard, her eyes almost rolling to the back of her head from how fucking delicious he felt pumping into her. "From the first moment our eyes met, something about you slipped deep into me. So deep it reached my soul."

He pulled back and drove into her, adding a twist of his lithe hips that made her eyes cross in absolute pleasure. "The mate bond," he muttered, his voice raspy with a growl. "I felt the same way. As soon as I saw you, I knew you were trouble."

"I'm not trouble." She moaned, tension twined inside, turning her muscles stiffer. "Okay, maybe a little."

Her body's temperature shot through the roof. Hotter than ever. Everything inside her

PACK PRINCESS

woman and animal loved the way he pounded into her. Reckless. Every thrust pushed her, urged her closer to release. Just a little more and she'd be there.

Hell, she wanted it so bad. To feel him deep and hard inside when she came. Then, as if he'd read her mind, he increased in speed. Gliding his teeth by the curve of her neck. Her breath caught in anticipation, waiting for his teeth to pierce her skin. Waiting for the bite that would claim her more thoroughly in their word than the human ceremony they'd been through.

Tension coiled within her, so tight that it felt like she'd shatter apart if he didn't *do* something. The pause between him pulling back and surging into her again took an eternity. He thrust. Bit. Pleasure and pain surged through her body, shards of ecstasy exploding through her veins.

A half-choked scream tore from her throat. Her body quaked with waves of pleasure skating within her and stealing her breath away. He groaned as her body clamped around him, the strong walls of her pussy milking his cock. Pulling his teeth from her neck, he thrust hard within her again. Once, twice, then threw his head back and howled as he came deep within her.

"I..." She tried to calm her racing heart. Not happening. Had he not been holding her, she'd have slid down that wall into a boneless, quivering puddle on the floor. "I should probably ask how you feel about children."

He leaned back to look in her eyes, his chest still heaving from the exertion, and the blue ring of his wolf in his eyes. "They're cute, but I couldn't eat a whole one?" The quirk of his lips gave him away, and he reached up to smooth a loose curl back behind her ear. "I like kids. Why do you ask?"

"Well," she cleared her throat, visualizing a smaller female version of Razor. Just as badass but in a cute pink skirt. "I hope you like them a lot more than that." She watched him lick his lips and almost groaned. Christ that man had a mouth she could kiss forever. "I should probably tell you that I'm in my mating moon. And unless you plan on not doing what we just did again for a while, we might be headed in that direction."

He blinked, utter shock flowing over his hard, beautiful features. She held her breath, expecting the worst. Perhaps he didn't want kids at all?

Then he smiled, and the breath she'd been holding punched free.

"Actually," he said, moving in for another, perfect kiss. "That's just gonna make me want to do it more."

THE END

ABOUT THE AUTHOR

New York Times and USA Today Bestselling Author

Hi! I'm Milly Taiden. I love to write sexy stories featuring fun, sassy heroines with curves and growly alpha males with fur. My books are a great way to satisfy your craving for paranormal romance with action, humor, suspense and happily ever afters.

I live in Florida with my hubby, our boys, and our fur children "Needy Speedy" and "Stormy." Yes, I am aware I'm bossy, and I am seriously addicted to iced caramel lattes.

I love to meet new readers, so come sign up for my newsletter and check out my Facebook page. We always have lots of fun stuff going on there.

SIGN UP FOR MILLY'S NEWSLETTER FOR LATEST NEWS!

http://eepurl.com/pt9q1

Find out more about Milly Taiden here:

Email: millytaiden@gmail.com

Website: http://www.millytaiden.com

Facebook:
http://www.facebook.com/millytaidenpage

Twitter: https://www.twitter.com/millytaiden

If you liked this story, you might also enjoy the following by Milly Taiden:

Sassy Mates / Sassy Ever After Series

Scent of a Mate *Book One*

A Mate's Bite *Book Two*

Unexpectedly Mated *Book Three*

A Sassy Wedding *Short 3.7*

The Mate Challenge *Book Four*

Sassy in Diapers *Short 4.3*

Fighting for Her Mate *Book Five*

A Fang in the Sass *Book 6*

Also, check out the **Sassy Ever After Kindle World on Amazon**

A.L.F.A Series

Elemental Mating *Book One*

Mating Needs *Book Two*

Dangerous Mating *Book Three (Coming Soon)*

Fearless Mating *Book Four (Coming Soon)*

Savage Shifters

Savage Bite *Book One*

Savage Kiss *Book Two*

Savage Hunger *Book Three (Coming soon)*

Drachen Mates

Bound in Flames *Book One*

Bound in Darkness *Book Two*

Bound in Eternity *Book Three*

Bound in Ashes *Book Four*

Federal Paranormal Unit

Wolf Protector *Federal Paranormal Unit Book One*

Dangerous Protector *Federal Paranormal Unit Book Two*

Unwanted Protector *Federal Paranormal Unit Book Three*

Paranormal Dating Agency

Twice the Growl *Book One*

Geek Bearing Gifts *Book Two*

The Purrfect Match *Book Three*

Curves 'Em Right *Book Four*

Tall, Dark and Panther *Book Five*

The Alion King *Book Six*

There's Snow Escape *Book Seven*

Scaling Her Dragon *Book Eight*

In the Roar *Book Nine*

Scrooge Me Hard *Short One*

Bearfoot and Pregnant *Book Ten*

All Kitten Aside *Book Eleven*

Oh My Roared *Book Twelve*

Piece of Tail *Book Thirteen*

Kiss My Asteroid *Book Fourteen*

Scrooge Me Again *Short Two*

Born with a Silver Moon *Book Fifteen*

Sun in the Oven *Book Sixteen (Coming Soon)*

Raging Falls

Miss Taken *Book One*

Miss Matched *Book Two*

Miss Behaved *Book Three*

Miss Behaved *Book Three*

Miss Mated *Book Four (Coming Soon)*

Miss Conceived *Book Five (Coming Soon)*

FUR-ocious Lust - Bears

Fur-Bidden *Book One*

Fur-Gotten *Book Two*

Fur-Given Book *Three*

FUR-ocious Lust - Tigers

Stripe-Tease *Book Four*

Stripe-Search *Book Five*

Stripe-Club *Book Six*

Night and Day Ink

Bitten by Night *Book One*

Seduced by Days *Book Two*

Mated by Night *Book Three*

Taken by Night *Book Four*

Dragon Baby *Book Five*

Shifters Undercover

Bearly in Control *Book One*

Fur Fox's Sake *Book Two*

Black Meadow Pack

Sharp Change *Black Meadows Pack Book One*

Caged Heat *Black Meadows Pack Book Two*

Other Works

Wolf Fever

Fate's Wish

Wynter's Captive

Sinfully Naughty Vol. 1

Don't Drink and Hex

Hex Gone Wild

Hex and Kisses

Alpha Owned

Match Made in Hell

Alpha Geek

HOWLS Romances

The Wolf's Royal Baby

Her Fairytale Wolf *Co-Written*

The Wolf's Dream Mate *Co-Written*

Her Winter Wolves *Co-Written*

Contemporary Works

Lucky Chase

Their Second Chance

Club Duo Boxed Set

A Hero's Pride

A Hero Scarred

A Hero for Sale

Wounded Soldiers Set

If you enjoyed the book, please consider leaving a review, even if it's only a line or two; it would make all the difference and would be very much appreciated.

Thank you!